STRANGERS IN THE PINES

A.J. RIVERS

Strangers in the Pines
Copyright © 2024 by A.J. Rivers

PROLOGUE

O LIVIA KNEW THAT IT WAS A LITTLE TOO LATE FOR A RUN AND YET she went to the park anyway. She needed it. Her body ached for it. When she had a particularly long day she needed to move her body. Stretching, working out, running, walking, something. It was less about her body and more about her mind. Her brain needed a rest. It needed to focus on something other than an interview or her coworkers. By focusing on moving her body, her brain was afforded a reprieve.

She placed her ear buds in her ears and turned on her music. Seether blared in her ears. Metal music was what she ran to. It was so loud that she didn't have a chance to think. It pushed out all thoughts. Her body started moving. The entire trail was long, so she always started off with a walk. something to wake her body up.

She glanced around looking for anyone else out for a walk. She was alone. While she liked it that way, it was still a little worrying to be alone on such a long trail.

Olivia turned her music down so she could hear if anyone was around. After walking a quarter mile, she started running. The path grew darker as the sun disappeared behind the trees. She paid it no mind. The lights along the path turned on at dusk. Low lights, but it was something. For a second, not even a full second, Olivia thought about turning around. She had a treadmill she could have used. She didn't have to run the trail by herself. But she liked being outside. She was the kind of person that walked longer when she had a destination in sight. She didn't have that on a treadmill.

Outside she knew where she was going or where she wanted to end up, and that helped her keep moving. And the scenery was beautiful with its lush, tall trees. Wicked looking trees with twisted bark and big heavy limbs. Beautiful flowers that cradled the path. The sound of birds chirping overhead. It created the perfect oasis. There was a pond deeper in the trail, but she wasn't going that way. She followed the path and then turned right. There was another path, but it wasn't paved like the other. It was a clear path but paved in dirt. She liked the path and took it often. It was longer than the other one and wasn't as straight. She loved circling the different trees and flowers. And the big tree in the middle of the forest. The largest tree in the area, it hovered over all the others with an imposing shadow.

She always wondered why it was so big. It was so deep in the forest that people rarely saw it. She had tried to explain it to people and most of them didn't seem to know what she was talking about. She kept running. Her lungs started to burn. Her legs ached, but she knew she could keep going.

If Olivia had been paying closer attention, if her music wasn't so loud, she would have heard the footsteps behind her. They weren't running, but they followed her every movement as if they already knew where she was headed.

If she had been paying better attention, she would have seen the rock before her feet. But that was what she loved about running. She loved the way it allowed her brain to zone out and focus on moving her body.

She stumbled on the rock, falling to her knees. Her right knee hit the sharp edge. She yelped as the pain rippled through her leg.

"Dammit!"

Her earbuds fell out of her ears and then she heard it. Feet shuffling behind her. Before she even had the chance to look behind her, a cord moved in front of her eyes.

Next thing she knew, she couldn't breathe. The back of her head fell against a hard surface. Her hands pulled at the cord around her neck. She couldn't pull it away. Her fingers dug into the hands pulling the cord tighter and tighter, but the surface was too smooth. Olivia fought. Kicking, scratching, doing everything she could, but nothing worked. Her vision blurred; her lungs burned for more air. Then nothing.

Olivia woke with a jolt. Cold water cascaded down her face. She struggled against the rope pinning her to the large tree she had been heading toward.

"What are you doing?" Her head ached. Her throat was raw. Pain radiated throughout her entire body. Her head flooded with thoughts and worries. Her heart vibrating in her chest.

She looked up. Her breath caught in her throat. Several hooded figures stood before her. Olivia struggled against the ropes even harder. Fear crept up her body. Tears stung her eyes.

"Please don't hurt me." Olivia pleaded for her life, but nothing changed. The hooded figures just looked up at her, their faces partially covered. She couldn't see the expressions on their faces. They didn't seem to care. No one said anything or moved.

"Please let me go! I won't tell anyone, I swear. Just let me go." She repeated the words over and over until her throat was raw and she tasted blood. Still, no one said anything. It was like she wasn't even there. Like they were looking through her and not at her. "Please, please don't kill me." Her voice was weaker now, barely above a whisper. "I'll give you whatever you want!"

One hooded figure stepped forward. "This is your punishment. We've sent you several letters asking you to publish them. To put the word out about us, and you refused. We tried and tried to get you to listen, and you refused. So now as you plead for your life, we will refuse to hear you or heed your cries." The figure turned and looked back at the group. "This is a lesson you must learn, and hopefully others will see this and learn from it. We didn't want to hurt you, but you've left us no choice."

Olivia screamed. Each hooded figure took out a knife. Olivia screamed again. Each figure took turns stabbing her. The leader was the first. The blade slid in between her ribs. Carefully they tried to avoid her heart. They didn't want her to die before it was all over. When the knife was removed, Olivia tried to scream again, but nothing came out. She wheezed as she tried to breathe.

The next stab wound was in her thigh, then her arm, her hand and so on

3

"One more thing we have to do." They took turns carving a symbol in her chest just above her heart. They all stepped back and watched. Olivia wheezed as blood soaked the tree and the ground below her.

As they left, Olivia's soft wheezing continued in their wake.

CHAPTER ONE

Jamie Washington

J AMIE WAS SPRAWLED ON THE FLOOR NEAR THE STAIRS, HER FINgers slick with blood, quickly drying and cracking every time her fingers jerked. The slight twitches happened ever so often. Her hands moving slightly as if she was still stabbing, still slashing.

She might have been in her dream. She had dreamed of killing her mother so many times that doing so in real life might not have been enough for her. She had stabbed her mother so many times, and so fervently, that she had tired herself out. Murder made one sleepy. So sleepy she couldn't pull herself up the stairs and into her bed. Her gentle snoring rippled through the house breaking up the silence.

When Jamie slept this deeply after a bout of vigorous activity, she always dreamed of her sister. Not the last time she saw her bloody and broken. She thought of her when she was younger. When Marie couldn't escape. Marie never liked being home.

Once Marie turned eighteen, their mother found it even more difficult to control her, but she could always guilt her into coming back. Until the last time, when she left for good. Marie didn't seem like she had a lot of friends. Or none she brought home with her. It was like she was ashamed of them. Ashamed of Jamie. But that didn't deter her. In fact, it only made her work harder at getting Marie to like her.

It never seemed to work though. It seemed like the harder she tried to get Marie to like her the more Marie pulled away from her. Detested her. But even with Marie's feelings toward her, she still kept her secrets, and still looked the other way when Jamie did something she shouldn't have.

She was thankful for that but wished it would have brought them closer.

Jamie dreamed of Marie now, even after she killed their mother. She didn't want to, but Marie crept into her thoughts and psyche no matter how hard she tried not to let her in. Especially now. Jamie was pissed that Marie and Everly lied to her about who her mother was.

Marie was her birth mother. Jamie didn't know what to think. She couldn't understand why after all these years they never tried to tell her the truth. How would her life had been different if she had known.

It explained so much. She couldn't figure out why she hadn't seen it. Marie used to hate looking at her. It tapered off as she got older, that look of contempt. But when she was younger Marie couldn't look her in the eye.

Her disdain for Jamie had been obvious. She was the product of rape, and to have that constant reminder would have been excruciating. That she understood. What if they had told her when she was younger or sent her away? Why couldn't Everly have just sent her away? If she had, how different everything would have been. Maybe she would have turned out differently. Maybe she wouldn't have been a lonely child with no friends. Maybe wouldn't have predilections for hurting people. If she had grown up in an environment where she was loved, genuinely loved, and not just tolerated, would that have made a difference?

Marie was nice to her in front of people, but Jamie had always known better.

Marie had a way of being nice, even when she didn't like you. Most people couldn't tell. They'd look at her smile and bright eyes and calm demeanor and think she was their best friend.

But Jamie *could* tell. She could always tell. In tune with the changing of her moods, better than her own. Marie had a tell. A look that was so quick, if you were looking at her and paying attention, you'd still miss it.

But Jamie didn't miss it. She had seen it a million times. Every time she looked at her. Until Marie learned to cover it. A mask reserved for Jamie and a few others. Yet Jamie could still see the disdain in her eyes.

But she was nice now. She loved Jamie now. She would never leave her. She would always be there for her no matter what.

It was a shame she had to die first, but Jamie decided to let that go. If it took Marie dying for her to finally love her then so be it. It almost made Jamie happy that she was dead, even if it *was* an accident, it all worked out in the end. She would have Marie and Dani, and they could be one big happy family. The kind of family Jamie had always wanted. It would be just the three of them forever.

That was the last thing Jamie thought before her body gave in to sleep. Her dreams always started out pleasantly, but then took a swift turn into something darker. She dreamed of them when Jamie was a child, and her mother had talked Marie into coming back. Marie was visibly upset by it, but she could never resist her mother's sob stories. Or she could have but chose not to. Jamie was never sure which was the right answer. Marie kept to herself and rarely told them what she was thinking. At least not Jamie. Her mother would often talk to Marie and start crying and then next thing Jamie knew Marie was back at the house. But it was clear that she didn't want to be there.

She didn't seem to like them anymore. She seemed to hate her surroundings like Jamie hated being around people. She looked like she wanted to jump out of her skin. And yet she still came back. Jamie often wondered if it was to be close to her. But that wasn't it. It had to be something else. Her dream morphed from a happier time in her life, to the night a wild storm caused the power to go out a little after midnight. Jamie had woken with a start due to the tree limbs lashing against her window. She had jumped out of her bed thinking something was trying to get in. When she looked outside, she saw rain whipping against the trees. Pounding on her window. The street was dark and quiet.

Jamie had sat on the edge of her bed for a long moment, listening to the wind and rain and something else. Voices, harsh and low. She stuck her head outside her bedroom door. Unlike other kids her age, Jamie wasn't afraid of the dark, instead, she welcomed it. She knew every inch of the house. She could walk it in the dark and no one would notice. She knew where the floorboards creaked, and which door needed oil on its hinges. She was careful not to make any sound. Jamie learned early on that when people didn't think you were listening, they were more likely to tell you things. The voices came from the last door down the hall—her mother's room. Jamie ducked into the bathroom. The door was already open and if someone came out of the room, she could say she was just going to the bathroom. She leaned against the sink and closed her eyes.

She knew the voices, Everly and Marie, but she didn't know what they were talking about.

"I don't know why you hate it here so much. Your father left us this house."

"He wasn't my father! And he didn't leave us this house, he left it to you and Jamie. I have nothing to do with it," Marie replied.

"He loved you. He loved all of us. He would have wanted us to live here like a real family."

"Maybe. Or maybe what he would have wanted was to live."

Everly shushed Marie harshly. "Keep your voice down."

Marie: "Oh, I'm sorry. You don't want Jamie to know what you made me do," Marie retorted.

"I didn't make you do anything that you didn't already want to do. As I recall I didn't have to try too hard to talk you into it. You liked it."

"How dare you!" Marie's voice was strained and hoarse. Jamie wondered how long they had been talking like this. "I never would have thought about doing it if it weren't what you wanted. You could have done it yourself, but you put it on me. You can never do your own dirty work."

"He was dying, it was what he wanted, and that is all that matters," replied Everly. "And may I remind you, don't act like this was the first time. You've done it before, and you will do it again. It's your nature. You're just like your father, a bad seed..."

Jamie didn't want to hear anymore, so she went back to bed and closed the door. She didn't understand any of it, nor did she want to. She crawled back into bed and listened to the rain until she fell asleep, and another dream took hold.

This time, it twisted into another memory, shortly before her mother had married her father. It was to be their last summer in their old rundown house. Jamie was too young to understand what was going on that summer, or why Marie seemed so agitated. Jamie couldn't wait to live with her father in his big house. Marie acted like it was the last thing she ever wanted to do.

Jamie and Marie sat on the front porch of their rundown home watching traffic pass by. It was the only house on the street that had chipped paint and an unkempt yard. The only one with a hole in the screen door and a broken front step.

Jamie knew the state of their home had made Marie self-conscious, which was why she couldn't understand why she wasn't looking forward to moving. Jamie didn't care how it looked. It was a roof over her head and Jamie didn't care what it looked like on the outside. She was never one that cared for what people thought. She had been without a roof over her head, Marie had not. When their mother sent Jamie—and only Jamie—to stay with some relatives for a week during the summer, she was not treated like a member of the family. Instead, she was treated like a dog. She wasn't allowed to eat with them. Her aunt would lock the back door, leaving her outside, even in the rain. They didn't like her. She never understood why.

As she and Marie sat on the porch, Marie started rocking back and forth. Seven-year-old Jamie knew what that meant. It was Marie's tell. She had something on her mind, usually it was something about her. Marie was nineteen then. Yet there was something so childlike about her. Something that reminded Jamie of the other kids her age.

"I know what you did," she whispered.

Jamie blinked. Her jaw twitched, but she kept her eyes on the road. On the cars zooming by.

"I know what you did to Luis next door," she whispered a little louder. "It wasn't right."

"It felt right." Jamie turned to look at her sister. "I know what you did to his sister, and if you can do it then why can't I?"

Jamie woke on the hardwood floor of the house she had been renting. Her body slick with sweat. Her head swimming with thoughts too loud and jumpy to pick out. She felt hot and nervous. Her body pulsed with anxiety, every nerve on fire.

The house was dark and quiet. "Why am I on the floor?" She struggled at first, but eventually, she was able to pull herself upright. The muscles in her stomach screamed with every movement. Her arms felt like stones attached to her body. It took her three tries, and once she got to her feet, she rocked back on her heels, unable to steady herself. She leaned back against the wall. Her chest hurt with every breath. Her fingers fumbled for the light switch. When she found it and flipped it on, the light was brighter than she thought it should be. She raised her hand to shield her eyes. That was when she saw it. Dried blood coated her fingertips, cracked as she made a fist.

She checked her body for wounds wondering if that was the reason for the pain she felt, but there was nothing. The blood wasn't hers. She stumbled left and then she saw her. Her mother's body was in the doorway of the kitchen.

Jamie could tell she was dead. Her body was so still and drenched in blood. Her chest did not move. In her head, there was a gaping bloody hole where her eye should have been. Her stomach lurched, but she swallowed hard to stop the acidic bile from bursting past her lips.

The events of the night came flooding back, first in little snippets. Then the images took shape to show her the full picture. Bile coated the back of her throat. She slumped to the ground. The sight of her mother's lifeless body was a remarkable sight. She wasn't sorry that she had killed her, or that she was dead, for that matter. She should have felt something, though. Anything. This was the woman who had raised her. She didn't do a decent job, but still, she was there in some capacity. Yet Jamie felt nothing. Not even a twinge in her heart. No tears threatened to fall.

Her eyes rested on a round ball next to her fingers. It wasn't until she lifted it that she noticed that it was an eye. Everly's eye. It didn't look damaged, though the connective tissue was gone. Probably still stuck in the socket. She rolled it through her fingers, feeling the sticky wetness that coated the eye. She wanted to crush it between her fingertips, but she knew it would have caused a sensory overload and made her sick. Instead, she set it on the cool floor and rolled it back toward the body. It should stay there for when she started to clean this up. She didn't want to forget anything.

Jamie's lips curled into a smile. Now that Everly was dead she could go after Dani as she wanted. Her mother was a hindrance. Always calling her and wanting her to change her mind. Always pressuring her as if she knew more about what Marie wanted than Jamie did. Now it was just her. Everly could never talk her out of anything, this they both knew. But Jamie was tired of hearing her persistent pleas for Jamie to just go home. She couldn't persuade her, but she could nag her to death.

Her stomach soured as she continued to stare at the body. Everly was a bloody mess. The state of the body explained why Jamie was so tired and her arms were so heavy. The hairs on the back of her neck stood straight up when a realization settled over her.

"Dammit."

Now she had to get rid of the body.

CHAPTER TWO

Riley Quinn

NEEDED THIS WALK, I THOUGHT AS I HEADED BACK TOWARD MY
house. Sometimes I walked around the lake to get some exercise or to
clear my head. I could have gone to the beach, but I didn't really feel
like driving all the way there and then driving back. Walking around the
lake was easier and Luna seemed to enjoy it. She bounced around me
chasing a butterfly.

"You have way too much energy so early in the morning, Lu."

She wasn't listening to me. She was caught up in her butterfly friend
that flew around her head as if it understood the game she was playing.
As I neared my house a car pulled into the driveway behind my car. It
wasn't one I recognized. I watched as a man, tall with broad shoulders
and a hat pulled low, crept up to my front door and knocked.

He knocked several times before turning around and walking back
to his car.

"Can I help you?"

His shoulders nearly touched his ears as he spun around. I neared the car and stopped. Luna stopped playing with her butterfly friend and sat by my side. I patted her head gently.

"I didn't see you there. Thought no one was home."

"I noticed. Who are you?"

"Are you Riley Quinn?"

"Detective Riley Quinn," I stressed the word 'detective' just in case he felt like trying something. My gun was in the house, but there was plenty to work with outside.

A smile tugged at the corner of his lips. "Right. Well," he threw his hands up, "I didn't come to hurt you or start any kind of shit. I just thought I should warn you."

My arms folded across my chest instantly. "Warn me about what?"

"You keep looking into our cases."

"Some of your cases are shady." I knew he was from Oceanway as soon as he said it. Their cases were the only ones that I was looking into and had been warned to stay away.

"I understand that," he said quietly. "But you need to stop. They know you're searching through their cases. You're only going to get yourself hurt if you continue."

"Hurt by whom? How do they know?"

He pressed his lips together as if he was trying to stop himself from answering the question.

"I hear them talking. If you continue, you *will* get hurt." He opened his car door and got it before I could ask another question. The car was unmarked, and the license plate was taped over. I should have called it in. Taken him into custody and pressed him on what he knew and who was after me. But after taking down Officer Blaese, I wasn't exactly popular with the uniformed officers in Pine Brooke. I would have to talk to Zelina about this, but there were few others that I knew I could trust.

I glanced down at Luna who was watching the car driveway. "You need to become a guard dog real quick."

She looked up at me sheepishly. Luna was not the guard dog type and much rather chase birds and, butterflies than attack intruders. I patted her head and leaned into my thigh. "I know it's not going to happen. I know."

I spent my first day off in a long time sleeping. I had a million things in my head that I could do, or rather should do. I've neglected so many things that I didn't feel like doing them. When I woke up in the morning, I sat on the edge of my bed, mentally scrolling through everything I had to do in my mind. But my body wouldn't move.

It was like I had so much to do I didn't do any of it, because that was the better option. I finally got out of bed and got dressed. Luna and I needed to eat actual food this week, so I needed to go to the grocery store.

"You're awake?"

I tried not to be offended by the exaggerated level of surprise in Zelina's voice at the store. "So are you, which I think is more surprising."

"I respect that. Pick up for the week?"

"Yeah, Luna and I need food. Then I'm going home and going back to sleep."

"Not doing anything with your day off? Why work so hard if you can't enjoy it?"

"So Luna can have the life she deserves." I picked up a loaf of bread and placed it in my basket.

"Luna's a dog, right?"

I glared at her. "Luna is a crucial part of my family, and she deserves the world." I struggled to keep the laughter out of my voice.

Her lips curved into a smile. "You are so stupid." She glanced down at her basket filled with microwave dinners and things she could just toss in her air fryer.

"Not a vegetable in sight."

"I got jalapeno poppers. Jalapenos are a vegetable."

"It's a pepper. That doesn't count."

She rolled her eyes. "Fine. I'll go down the freezer aisle and see what vegetables I don't mind eating. But then I'm done."

"Happy hunting." Cops really had horrible diets. Fast food, takeout, and anything you could just pop in the microwave. It was understandable. After a long day, the last thing I wanted to do was cook a full meal. The sooner I ate the sooner I could crawl into bed so anything microwaveable was ideal.

I finished my shopping and headed toward checkout. Zelina was about to leave when she saw me. She held up two bags of frozen microwaveable broccoli, one with a cheese sauce. I gave her a thumbs up. It was a start.

After checking out I went outside and placed the bags in the trunk. I just bought food, but I was hungry now.

"Riley?"

I spun around and saw my sister. "Hey, Ag!"

She waddled over to me and gave me a hug. "Thought you were enjoying a nice day of sleeping."

"I was, but needed food and figured I might as well go ahead and pick up groceries for the week. What are you doing?"

She gave a half-shrug before rubbing her protruding belly. "Just walking around. Doctor Elwood said I needed to move around more even though sometimes it hurt. Baby is hitting all of my internal organs feels like."

I rubbed her round belly. "You hungry?"

"I could always eat."

We walked to the diner. Well, I walked, Agatha waddled slowly behind me. When she slid into the booth relief flooded her face.

"You look so tired."

"That's because I am. I haven't been sleeping well since I entered the third trimester. I lay on one side, it hurts. I lay on the other, it's extremely uncomfortable and I feel a lot of pressure in my back. If I lay on my back, I can't breathe."

"Have you tried sleeping in a chair or something? Doesn't Ricky have a recliner in the living room?"

"As much as I wanted him to throw it out, I'm happy it's still there. About the only place that's still comfortable. But now he can't sit in his chair which has him annoyed and sighing around the house."

I giggled. "Well, tell him he shouldn't have gotten you pregnant."

Aggie grinned. "Not like he was there by himself."

"If he had been you wouldn't be pregnant right now." This comment elicited a smile and a burst of laughter.

"I'm going to tell him you said that."

Dana, long time waitress, and one-time fiancé of my brother's, stopped at our table. "Hey, girls. I'll be with you two in a moment, just let me take Mr. Thorton his coffee."

I looked behind me. Mr. Thorton sat at a booth by himself reading a book. He glanced up and waved at us with a large grin on his face. Mr. Thorton was my ninth-grade English teacher. He instilled a love of books in me that I didn't think possible. Mr. Thorton had a way of teaching that made learning fun. He always told us reading is fun when you find a genre you love.

One assignment was just that. For the course of a year, we had to read a different book in several genres. He gave us a list, and then we had to stand up in front of the class and talk about which one was our favorite.

There were a lot of romance readers for various reasons. Some horror, and fantasy, but I loved thrillers and horror. My two picks were 5 and *And Then There Were None*. I still had those books even now. I waved back before turning away.

"I loved his class in high school," said Aggie.

"Me too. Was about the only one I liked."

"Alright ladies, what can I get you?" Dana took out her notepad and pen. She and my brother ended things a long time ago. They got engaged shortly after high school. Two years of college and he decided the relationship wasn't what he wanted. He believed she didn't have any ambition. He was an asshole the way he ended things.

Dana had plans of going to college, but her mother got sick, and then died, and then her father got sick. Someone had to take care of him and she was the only one there. My brother just couldn't understand that. Even with the breakup, we still treated her like family and if he didn't like it, he'd have to take it up with our mother.

"I want a bacon club with—what's the soup of the day?"

"We have a creamy lemon chicken soup and a sausage and potato soup."

"I'll take the lemon soup."

"And Aggie?"

"I'll do the same, but with sausage and potato soup."

"Should have known you two are ordering practically the same thing," she laughed "Be back in a few."

"So how are things?" I asked Aggie. My sister generally kept to herself. She had her life and her family on the other side of town and that was her life. I respected that. But because she kept to herself sometimes, I felt like I missed so much.

She talked to Mom every day and she was always there when I needed her, but I still felt like there was a distance between us that I couldn't figure out how to close.

"Same ole stuff. Kids are doing good. Getting into stuff and annoying each other. But more importantly, how are you ... and Logan?"

"What do you mean?"

She grinned. "You know what I mean. Mom and I talked a lot about Logan when he came over for dinner. He said a lot."

"No, he didn't." I rolled my eyes and leaned back. He didn't say anything because there's nothing to say. We haven't done anything. "Stop trying to start something."

"I wish you would start something. And he's a *doctor*."

"Who is still processing his wife's death. You want me to just jump on him."

"Might help him move on." She sipped her soda slowly. "I'm just saying he's hot and available."

"Not emotionally."

Her shoulders sank. "No, you are just making excuses. It's clear that he likes you. I saw you giggling next to each other during the movie."

"I don't giggle. There was no giggling."

"Please! You were cackling!"

A smile pulled at my lips. I refused it. "Shut up."

She laughed. "Whatever you say. But we know. I'm just saying we know."

"You know nothing."

Dana returned with our food and we dug into our soups.

"We know more than you think, and we know it's been a loooooong while."

"The fact that you dragged out the word 'long' is upsetting and uncalled for. And it hasn't been that long," I whispered. Truth be told, I couldn't remember the last time I went on a date, but I kept that to myself. She didn't need to know everything.

And again, there was nothing to know. No matter how many times I said it, my mother and my sister would not believe me.

Was Logan Elwood hot? Of course, but that didn't mean there was anything going on. He was still in love with his wife and dealing with raising his young daughter. He just needed a friend, and that was what I gave him.

Friendship. Nothing else.

It was clear to me my sister didn't believe me in the way she rolled her eyes at my comment. But truly, I wasn't in the mood to date. I just didn't have the desire or the energy, especially not in our small town. I didn't know all the men in town, but the ones I did know I wasn't interested in.

"You ready for the baby?"

She sighed and rubbed her belly. "I don't know. We have a lot of the stuff already from our other two, but we still need to get the crib."

"What you two need is a new house. You're running out of room, or one of you needs to move out."

She laughed. "Good point. I told him he needs to get a vasectomy since it's considered minor surgery. I don't think he'll go through with it though."

"You should put a few conditions on it. I bet he'd do it then."

She laughed. We talked about the cases I had been working on, about our brothers and our parents. Our parents were getting older and we—or rather I—was getting worried about them. They could still take care of themselves, but my father had some heart problems and my mother was famous for spreading herself too thin. I was worried about them, being in the house by themselves. My sister wasn't though.

"You know Dad. When they need help, they'll let us know. That's how they've always been. Sure they're both stubborn and might be reluctant to hand over the reins, but... I don't think they're there yet. I think we have a little while longer before we get to that point. They're still active, which helps."

My lips twisted slightly. It reminded me of a conversation I had with Logan about dementia and Alzheimer's.

"I don't think you have anything to worry about right now," he'd said. "Both of your parents are in good health. Your father needs to work on his blood pressure and stress."

"We've been telling him about that for years," I replied.

"But other than that, they're good. Your parents read the papers and stay active outside of the house. All of that helps with staving off dementia unless there is some family history of early-onset."

"I don't think so." At least I'd not heard of any.

"Stop worrying."

Logan saying that had made me feel better, but I was a planner, and I wanted to know that we had a plan. If our family history were anything to go off of, if and when it happened it would be on me to sort things out. My sister had her children, and that would be an excuse to not take part in helping take care of our parents. One brother lived out of town and my other brother... well, it would be up to me.

I needed to make sure plans were in place. I'd let Aggie slide with that because she was pregnant, and her mind was on other things. But after the baby was born and they had time to adjust, I intended to bring it up again.

CHAPTER THREE

Logan Elwood

"I JUST FIND THIS SO INTERESTING." BERT SAT AT THE TABLE STAR-ing at the files he brought with him. "I mean the fact that no one was ever caught in connection to the fire boggles the mind. Even all these years later."

"Are they even sure it wasn't an electrical fire? Someone trying to cook in their room and had too many things plugged in at once?" That had been my first thought, because I remembered when I was in college how they told us not to cook in our rooms, but no one listened. We had microwaves which were safe, but some had hot-plates and that caused a few problems. Didn't burn down the dorm, but they left a couple of the rooms pretty charred.

Bert slid a sheet of paper across the table. I stared at it for a long moment. It was a report from the Fire Marshal who was sure that the fire that burned down St. Mary's School for Girls was an arson, not an electrical fire. "This *is* curious. Are we both thinking that Jamie had something to do with it?"

While we were married, Marie tried to get me to think the best of people. It was something she did so effortlessly it amazed me. "You never know what someone is going through or has experienced. Never go out of your way to judge them so harshly." At the time she said it, she was talking about her sister, but it was something she applied to everyone. I could never do it, not with Jamie. I could see her burning the school down because she wanted to go home. Even as a child.

"I know I am; I don't know about you. It seems the most logical explanation. I don't believe in coincidences." Bert paused, then continued. "On top of that, there is something about her that I don't trust. Given everything we've seen from her, I wouldn't put it past her."

I slid the sheet of paper back across the table. I knew what he meant. I had always thought that. It was something I had noticed from the minute I met her. Something not quite right. That feeling only solidified over the years. Jamie could be nice, but mostly only to Marie. She always had a dark energy about her. Like a dark cloud hovered over her and followed wherever she went.

"I understand that. I just… I find it amazing that Marie never mentioned any of this." I couldn't understand it. We talked about everything. I told her all about my past and my mother and Isaac. I told her everything. I thought that was our relationship. I never thought she would keep anything from me. Nothing this big. I tried not to feel hurt by it. It was over and done with now and Marie was gone.

But it made me wonder what else had she been hiding. What other secrets had she kept for her sister? For herself? The thought made me shudder.

"It's her sister. You tell her everything about your brother?"

"Of course I did. I thought that was how we were with each other. We told each other everything. At least I thought we did."

"Maybe she thought she was protecting her, but now you need to protect Dani." Bert placed the folders in his briefcase, but he left one on the table. "Families are strange, I know you know that. I'm sure she had her reasons."

He exhaled silently. Bert looked like he had aged a few years since I first met him. The mediation had surprised him. I had told him about Jamie's temper and what she was like when she didn't get her way. But hearing about it and seeing it first-hand were two different things. Even her own lawyer looked surprised by it. This was our first dinner together alone since the mediation and Bert looked worried.

He was right, I needed to protect Dani. That was my only goal at the moment. The only thing I cared about. I wouldn't be able to stand it if Jamie were able to get visitation—or any kind of rights—to my daughter. She was her aunt, it wasn't a requirement that she have a place in Dani's life, even though she seemed to think so. "So what do we do now?"

"Well, I'm still going to have my private investigator to continue searching for any dirt that we can use against Jamie. If this goes to court, I feel confident that the judge will see this for what it is. A bunch of bullshit. She has no right to Dani, and with the reports from the social worker, I don't think this will be taken seriously. There is no reason for her to have custody of Dani."

"Thank you, Bert. For all the work you're doing."

"Well, it's all the work you're paying me for, so technically I'm just doing my job." He grinned. A soft chuckle bubbled up my throat. If Bert wasn't worried about me losing custody, then something else was bothering him.

He was right. I was paying him, and he was doing his job, but it was the way he was doing it. Paying attention to every detail. Following leads that I would have never thought of. I would have hired a private investigator. I thought about it but settled on not doing it because it seemed too invasive. And I was sure they wouldn't have found anything, but it appeared I was wrong.

We finished our dinner, and Bert noted something else.

"Something else I found interesting is that only Jamie and one other person made it out unscathed. They didn't have a scratch on them. No smoke in their lungs. Neither were they covered in soot."

"How could that happen? Unless they were outside when the fire started? Was the other person a student too?" Questions were coming out of me of their own accord.

Bert flipped through the file. "No, she was a nurse there. My investigator tried to speak with her, but she refused to even see him. I don't think she wants to remember the fire or dredge things back up. Which I understand."

"Yeah, it must have been horrifying witnessing the place burn down. I wouldn't want to think about it either. I wouldn't want to talk about it with anyone."

"It would be nice if she didn't feel that way, but such is life. He's looking for more leads. Jamie lived quite a life… all over the place, before she got married."

"Yeah. She moved a lot, but only to cities that were close enough to Marie. She always had to be close enough to drive right over whenever she wanted to. It was annoying."

"I bet."

"Can you give me the number and address for the nurse? I want to see if she'll talk to me."

He handed me a slip of paper with the information. "I guess it's worth a shot."

I paid for dinner and we both got up to leave. Bert started to walk to his car, but then he froze. His back angled toward me. For a second, I thought something was wrong. Maybe he forgot something inside the restaurant. Before I could open my mouth, he turned around slowly. His brows pulled together slowly. Bert opened his mouth to say something and then paused for a long moment. I inched toward him. Something was clearly on his mind. Judging by the look on his face I wasn't going to like it.

"I feel obligated to warn you." He took a deep breath. "I don't think you'll lose custody of Dani, but after the mediation... the way Jamie acted... she's dangerous. I don't know for sure if she started the fire when she was a kid, but if she did, I can't imagine what she would do now. Don't let Dani out of your sight. I honestly don't think you've seen the last of her."

His warning sent a shiver down my spine. He said what I had been thinking since the mediation. The way she blew up at us, at her own mother, it was scary and worrisome. She looked like she wanted to hurt all of us. Kill us in that room and walk away. I was surprised she hadn't done just that and then walked away. I knew I hadn't seen the last of her. If I could find enough evidence to have her arrested for the fire, I would never have to see her again. That's what I wanted. That's would protect Dani and everyone else in my life.

I thanked him for his warning. We said our goodbyes, and I went home eager to see Dani and the rest of my quirky little family. It was nice having Isaac at the house. I knew he wanted to get his own place eventually, but I was thankful for his presence in the house. Dani loved her uncle and I... well, he lightened up the place. He brought laughter and fun back into our lives. We all needed it, even Bonnie. Her husband had died a few months before I contacted her about being my nanny. She was referred to me by another doctor who thought she could use the distraction, and I could use the help. Having a full house was nicer than I thought it would be.

I walked through the door, the smell of bread hitting me as soon as I opened the door. "Did he make bread?"

"Who is this he you are referring to?"

"You know what?" I closed the door behind me and locked it. "Please don't start with me." I followed the laughter into the living room.

"Yeah, I made bread for our grilled cheese sandwiches," Isaac called out from the kitchen.

"You made bread so you could make a sandwich?" I collapsed onto the sofa.

"And it was good. There's still some bread in there if you're hungry."

I shook my head. For dinner, I'd had a steak, roasted garlic risotto, and steamed broccoli. I was stuffed.

"What did he say?" Bonnie stared at me while her hands were busy knitting or crocheting something. I always confused the two, and it was clear she was tired of correcting me, so I kept my comments to myself.

"He said his private eye was still looking into her. He found a survivor from the fire, but she refused to speak with them. Turns out she and Jamie walked away unscathed. No soot or smoke in their lungs. Makes me think that they were both outside when the fire happened, and didn't go inside to help anyone."

"Huh? You gonna call her?"

"Yeah, I will. Just need to work up what to say and how to say it. But I'm curious as to how she got out of the fire without a scratch on her and why she didn't help any of the kids get out."

"That's curious," said Bonnie. "Maybe she had just gotten back when she saw the blaze or something. I hope you talk to her. I want to know about that myself."

"Me too," added Isaac.

"I'll keep you two abreast of the situation as it unfolds."

Isaac chuckled.

"How did things go here? Dani sleeping?"

"She went to bed a couple of hours ago," said Bonnie. "She wanted to tell you about her day, so I'll let her tell you in the morning."

"Good or bad?"

Isaac grinned. "It was good. Don't want to spoil the surprise."

It annoyed me, him knowing something I didn't. The grin on his face made it worse. "Well, since I have to wait… how was your day? Anything weird happen?" I glanced at Bonnie.

"I didn't see her. No one was outside the house and waiting for us. I checked for cars following us as I walked her to school. Nothing. Maybe she's licking her wounds or maybe her mother was able to talk her down finally. No news is good news, I say."

"I think she's biding her time," said Sac. I don't think Jamie is one to give up or get talked out of something she wants."

I was inclined to agree with him. She was biding her time. Like a snake hiding in the bushes ready to strike.

Isaac and Bonnie went to bed. I stayed in the living room for a bit, before heading to my office. I was tired, but I didn't want to go to bed.

My phone started ringing as soon as I turned on my computer.

"Hello?"

"Hey, stranger."

Riley's chipper voice was a welcomed surprise. I felt like I hadn't seen her or spoken to her in a long time. Seemed like weeks even though it had only been a few days. Just the sound of her voice made my muscles relax. The tension in my back eased with every spoken word.

"Hey yourself. How are you? And why are you calling me so late? Did you hurt yourself?"

"Logan, take a breath. I just wanted to see how mediation went. You never gave me an update." Her voice sounded lighthearted, but there was a trace of something there.

A laugh bubbled up my throat, a low rumble in my chest.

"That bad, huh?"

I told her what I could remember, which at that moment, wasn't a lot. Just the highlights. She was so quiet on the phone, for a second I thought she had hung up or walked away.

"Wow! Well, it would seem you have one less thing to worry about."

"What do you mean? I think she's going through with her petition."

"I mean, you have witnesses to her unhinged behavior. No judge in their right mind is going to grant her custody of anyone. Dani isn't going anywhere."

"You think?"

"Yeah. You don't have anything to worry about."

Riley sounded certain, and I was more apt to trust her because she was a police officer. She had probably dealt with a few custody cases throughout her career. And I wanted to trust what she said. I wanted to cling to her certainty like the only light in a sea of darkness. But I still had a bad feeling about this. Something was going to happen, and I couldn't let go of that fear. It was like a weight on my chest slowly crushing me. Suffocating me. I exhaled slowly.

"Stop worrying, Logan. I think it will all be okay. It's not like Jamie is so unhinged she'd murder all of you and take Dani."

My chest tightened. "Why would you say that?"

"Sorry. I was trying to be reassuring. Guess I failed."

"Miserably. But I appreciate the effort."

We spent the rest of the night, an hour or so, talking about her last case and how she was doing. She asked me about Dani and how she was adjusting to everything going on. I thought she was adjusting well, but I knew it was mostly due to Bonnie and Isaac. They made the atmosphere in the house change drastically. It wasn't dark or gloomy anymore. It was lively; filled with laughter, good food and joy. Something we were all missing.

It was a relief to have it back. I hoped we would have it for a long time.

CHAPTER FOUR

Riley Quinn

LAST NIGHT ZELINA CAME BY UNEXPECTEDLY TO TALK AND EAT. I was making dinner, and it was easy to add more for her.

"So. What are you doing here?" I set her plate in front of her.

"We haven't hung out in a while. Not in between cases anyway."

She was right. We used to hang out outside of work all the time, but lately we had been so busy it seemed like we only had time to sleep. "Aww… you missed spending quality time with me." I grinned.

"You found a way to make that weird," she said. "You know, as partners we need to stay in sync."

I sat down next to her. "You mean I need to know your business and you need to know mine so we can continue getting along. You have to know what's going on in my head."

She laughed. "I'm not sure that's what I meant. I just wanted to touch base with you. We've been going, going, and going. This is the first time I feel like I can take a break, and breathe, in weeks."

"I know right. It's been case after case after case. A lot of murders in this town as of late."

The meal I made was simple, mostly because I didn't feel like doing anything elaborate when it was only me eating it. Beef and broccoli with a side of protein mac and cheese. I needed to introduce more protein into my diet along with vegetables, per Logan.

I was a runner in high school, but once I moved to the city that habit tapered off quickly. And it hasn't come back. I did like walking along the lake so that was still exercise. It was good even though I used cottage cheese and cheddar cheese for the sauce. Better than I expected.

"You just came over because you didn't feel like cooking or heating something in the microwave."

Zelina laughed. "You caught me. I guess that's the reason. That and I have a big decision to make, and I need to talk it out with someone who's not related to me. And I need an honest opinion."

I sat up straight. My fork dangled from my fingers and hit my plate. "Now I'm intrigued. What's going on?"

Z sighed. "A cousin is having a hard time with her daughter and wants me to take her in for the rest of the school year."

I stared at her. I never pictured Zelina having children or adopting any. She liked her free lifestyle too much. She could be the fun aunt though. "Umm... that would change your life as you know it." I was sure she had thought about that, but I still felt like it needed to be said.

She nodded. "I know. I know. But my cousin sounds like she is at her wits' end. The girl is fifteen and she is a handful and has been since her father died. They think that because I'm a cop I might be able to get her to act right."

"Okay," I said slowly. "And how would you do that? You aren't some scared straight program where they can drop their kids off when they can no longer deal with them. You have your own life. Also, their children aren't your responsibility. If they can't manage them then they need to figure it out. It's not on you."

"I know. I know. I just feel so bad for them, and I think I could help. I don't have children or any dependents. I have the money to take her in if need be. I just ... I know my life is going to change and I'm just not sure what—"

"You're not sure if you are ready for that." I didn't let her finish. I knew.

"She only has a couple years left of high school. It's not like she'll be here for a long time, and maybe I can get her to think about college. Right now, it doesn't look like she's given any thought to her future. Which is another problem."

"Okay. So what *is* her problem?" I pushed my plate away. "Like what is she doing that has them so upset?"

Z took a deep breath. "Well, naturally, there's the boyfriend no one likes. Her mother caught her and the boy having sex in her room while the rest of the family was at church. She's been drinking, smoking weed, skipping school. Last straw was her tattoo. Her mother told her she couldn't get one, and she did it anyway."

"So she's being a spoiled brat."

"I guess. My cousin has three other kids, all under ten, and she can't keep up with Marissa anymore. She's frustrated, and every time she tries to focus on one child, another one falls through the cracks."

I leaned back. "I see. Well, I can't tell you what to do. It's your family and I know you want to be there for them, which is understandable, but you should set some guidelines if you're going to take her in. They can't make this a habit. You're not an orphanage. They can't just drop their kids off at your house for you to parent. If she stays with you, you have to be able to discipline her."

"Yeah, I know. I've already told her all that. Not to make it a habit and that I need to be able to discipline her. And she needs to understand that this is not a vacation."

"Sounds to me like you already made your decision."

"I don't know. I have until the summer to make my decision. I haven't seen Marissa in a while. She was such a cute kid and super smart. I think she wanted to be a doctor at some point."

"But then her father died." I remember Zelina talking about it.

"Car accident. He was hit by a drunk driver. The kids are struggling with the loss, and so is my cousin. I want to be able to help her. I know how difficult it is to pick yourself up after a loss and if I can do anything to help her, I want to. But taking in an unruly teenager... might be a bit much."

I respected Z for even thinking about it. I wasn't sure I could do it. Children were never a priority for me. I still wasn't sure whether I wanted any or not. Taking in someone else's child, a handful at that, wasn't something I thought I could do. But Z was far more patient than me. She wasn't sure she wanted children either, but I always thought she would make a great mother. Maybe this would be practice for her.

"I think she also stole her mother's car. My grandmother would have strangled me if I did even half the shit she did. My cousin needs to discipline her, but I think her husband was in charge of that and she hasn't gotten the hang of it."

"Well if you need any help with that let me know. I'll loan you my mother."

Z laughed. "I might have to take you up on that. If I let my temper get the best of me, I'll be the one in jail."

Yeah, Zelina had a bit of a temper. If Marissa knew what was good for her, she would do whatever Z told her to do. We sat and talked for a long time about what she would have to do to get her house ready for a teenager. Z seemed annoyed by the prospect, but I sensed a little happy too. No matter what she said, she liked helping her family. She loved them and wanted to do her best by them, like her grandmother would have done.

Her grandmother took her in when she had nowhere else to go. She was thankful for that to this day. I knew she wanted to do the same for someone else. That being said I hoped she wasn't biting off more than she could chew. By the time she left, I knew she would do it even though she said she was still thinking about it. She had made up her mind before she said anything to me. After she left, I crawled into bed with Luna and watched TV until I fell asleep.

"Seriously? But it's my day off!" My voice was heavy with sleep and my eyes were still closed when I answered the phone. I didn't have any plans for the day, but they didn't need to know that. I tried to add a little annoyance to my voice,, but mostly at myself and my own excitement at having a new case. I was excited and I felt bad about being excited. I loved my job, even if I complained. "Fine. I'll be in." I hung up and jumped to my feet.

I knew I shouldn't have been as excited as I was. My having a case meant that something bad had happened, and that was nothing to be excited about. But I didn't like sitting on my hands or taking time off. I liked staying busy and my job kept me busy. I was better when I had a lot to do, when my mind didn't have time to wander. It always wandered to the same point when it was quiet. But when I had other things to focus on, it never crossed my mind.

I slipped on my work clothes. Luna whined at my feet. "I know. I know, but you don't like me being here anyway. You have the whole house to yourself and the yard. I know, you're going to have fun." She nuzzled her nose against my leg and then she ran to the door. "I know, I'll let you out in a minute." I grabbed my keys and wallet and shoved them into my back pocket. "Okay." I opened the door. "You can go have fun." I grabbed my phone off the counter and locked the door behind me.

Zelina was already at the station when I walked in, as usual. She was always there first. She lived closer to the station. She could walk if she wanted to. "Did they tell you what was going on?"

"Just said I had a case." I walked past the woman standing at the front desk. I set my things on my desk and sat down.

"Detective Quinn, Captain said this is your case." He gestured to the woman. "She was sent here to file a report."

I got up an extended a hand for her to shake. "Hello." I placed a chair by my desk and gestured for her to have a seat. "What kind of report are you looking to file?"

"A missing persons report." The woman looked uncomfortable. Uncertainty etched into her face. She shifted in her seat and then placed her purse in her lap.

"Family?"

"Friend," she said. "A really good friend, but also a coworker. My boss said I should come down and file a report."

"Okay." I took out a folder and the report. "Let's start with your name?"

"Donna."

"Okay. Who are you filing a report on?"

"Olivia Tucker. She collaborates with me at Channel Seven News."

"The anchor?" asked Zelina with her eyebrows raised. She moved from behind her desk, inching closer to the woman.

"Yes, that's her. She was supposed to come in early this morning like always. She usually gets to the station around half past four. She's the first one there and the last one to leave. Her not coming in is... it just doesn't happen. And if she were to take a sick day or something she would call in."

"Alright. We need you to start from the beginning. What happened this morning?" asked Zelina.

Donna took a deep breath. "Well, when she didn't get to the station by five, I called her. And called her and called her. Then I told my boss, who also called her several times. She never answered. We had to scramble to get the morning show ready. At the station we had everyone running around trying to get fillers in. We looked like chickens with our heads cut off. Once the morning show was done, I called her again. My boss Mr. Wilt called into the station and told me to come down and file a report. He's worried, but I thought you had to wait twenty-four hours."

"People think that, but it's not true," I said. "If someone you know has gone missing and this behavior is really unlike them or if you have a reason to suspect foul play, you come down and tell us. The sooner we get the report filed the sooner we can start looking. And that increases our chances of finding them. Never wait twenty-four hours."

Donna smiled. "But that's just it, we don't know when she went missing. I would say at least a day, but I'm not sure. I spoke to her Friday after work. She was excited for the weekend. I told her I would talk to her Sunday night, but I called pretty late, and she goes to bed early to prepare for the morning show."

"Makes sense. So she didn't answer when you called last night?" asked Zelina.

She shook her head. "It was after ten when I remembered to call her. I at least wanted her to see I didn't forget. She didn't answer her phone. The thing is… it wasn't turned off, which is usually what she does when she goes to bed for the night."

"She turns her phone off before she goes to bed at night?" I asked. I never did that. I might turn the volume down, but I didn't turn it off.

Donna nodded. "It just ensures she can get some sleep without her phone ringing off the hook. Everyone knows to leave a message. But last night when I called her the phone didn't go straight to voicemail. Instead, it just kept ringing and ringing. I thought it was strange, but I don't know… maybe she forgot to turn it off and just had it in another room."

"Okay." I finished filling out the report. "We need her address, a photo of her, and the make and model of her car." I slid the paper over to Donna so she could fill out the details. I looked at Zelina, who nodded before walking back to her desk. We had been partners for so long most of the time she knew what I was thinking before I even finished the thought.

She picked up her phone and I knew who she was calling before she said anything. I didn't want to tell Donna; she seemed shaken up. Rightfully so. Her friend was missing, and she was worried about her. And we needed crime scene techs to meet us at Olivia's house.

Olivia was a great news anchor. I watched her almost every morning while I got ready for work. She was personable and had a great voice.

She also seemed concerned about the town and was always trying to get the word out about different causes and activities that might benefit someone. What had happened to her?

CHAPTER FIVE

Jamie Washington

JAMIE STOOD NEAR THE BACK DOOR, FRESHLY SHOWERED, WRAPPED in a robe. Everly resided in the downstairs bathtub, basting in ice water. She thought that might control the smell. It was hell getting her into the tub. Jamie thought it was almost impossible. She never had to drag a body down a hall and into a bathtub before. Everly was heavier than she looked. She debated chopping her up and then moving her but decided against it. It would have made a bigger mess, which would have been more blood, tissue, and sinew, all of which she would have to clean up.

It was difficult getting the blood off the hardwood floors, the walls, and the ceiling. She didn't want to add to it. Against her better judgement, the only way to get her down the hall without pulling a muscle was to roll her over onto a rug and pull her down the hall. Rolling her over was hard. Everly's forehead had hit the hardwood with a thump so loud, Jamie had jumped. It sounded like someone had knocked on the door. After checking and seeing there was no one there and then resting against the door, waiting for her heart to calm down, she resumed her work.

The sun was setting by the time she finally got the body in the tub. Jamie was exhausted and covered in blood, her fingers sticky, and caked with dried blood. She collapsed near the stairs and stared up at the ceiling. There was still so much that she had to do to get the house presentable. It wasn't as if she was expecting guests or anything, but this wasn't her house. She was renting. If the owner wanted to stop by, she would be in serious trouble—she might have to kill another person and stick them in the tub next to her mother.

That would have caused a whole other set of problems.

She stared at the ceiling dotted with blood splatter. *How was she going to get up there?* Who would come in and look up, anyway? She knew the odds were slim, but she didn't want to chance it. She'd have to find a ladder and get some cleaning supplies, and some ice. A million things ran through her mind while she lay there. She mentally made of list of all the things she would have to buy. Hopefully she could get them from different places so it wouldn't be too obvious what she was doing. So many people watched *CSI* that someone might put it together. Bu Everly's body would only last so long before it started stinking.

Everly lying dead in her bathtub was bad enough... she didn't need her stinking up the place. She thought about buying an industrial-sized bucket of cleaning product from the local hardware store, but that would also be suspicious if anyone looked too hard at what she was doing before she ran out of town.

She didn't care about anyone finding her mother once she was gone, but she didn't want to give anyone the excuse to search the house yet.

She had a little time. Jamie doubted anyone would ever come looking for her mother. The only person that would look was Marie, and she was dead. Jamie would never have looked for her. She wouldn't care if she were missing or kidnapped. It didn't matter to her in the slightest. But Marie... even though they didn't always get along, she wouldn't have been able to rest until she knew where her mother was.

Other than her, no one else cared for Everly. She made a lot of friends, but she could never keep them. She used them for what she wanted and then once they figured it out, they were gone. The cycle had repeated constantly since they were children. The girls learned early on not to get used to anyone their mother brought into their lives. They were there one minute and gone the next.

Everly could never keep a boyfriend, or husband, so she doubted she had one now. She hadn't mentioned anyone, nor would she—not to Jamie, anyway.

She stared out into the backyard. "Where to stick you?" Her forefinger tapped the glass. Maybe she could bury her in the backyard. That was one way to get rid of her. Bury her so deep no one would ever find her. Or deep enough that it would take them a while. It was either that or stick her in a wall or something.

She thought about it, long and hard. Where was she going to put her dead mother?

The thing that bothered her the most was the smell. There was nothing like the smell of a dead body rotting. It was worse in the sun.

"If I did put her in the wall…" She tapped her chin. It dawned on her that she didn't know how to open a wall and then close it back. If her search history were ever investigated, having that in her search history would look suspicious. If people weren't already asking questions, they would start.

But… she did know how to dig a hole. Maybe not a person-sized hole, but a hole, nonetheless.

She'd just have to make it a little bigger and a little wider. She could do that.

Jamie stepped away from the back door. Before she could go outside and survey the backyard, she needed to get dressed.

It was cool outside. Cooler than it looked from the window. A soft breeze shook the flowers in the back flowerbeds. They were beautiful, but they'd have to go. She needed that flowerbed. It was just big enough for her purposes. She'd try to replant them when she was done. She needed to make sure that she took a picture of their placement so she could put them back exactly like the owner had them. She hoped the plants wouldn't die with her mother's body underneath them.

Perhaps they would use her decomposing body as nourishment.

"Hi, neighbor!"

The sudden voice nearly made her jump out of her skin. She spun around, eyes wide, nails digging into her palms.

"Sorry. Didn't mean to scare you there."

Jamie's neighbors stared at her with large smiles on their faces. It made her uneasy. What were they looking at?

"Hi."

He was a heavyset older man with dark hair and wild eyes. She was petite with golden brown hair and bright blue eyes. Jamie smiled at them, at least she tried to. She knew people lived next door, but she had never seen them. They looked nice enough.

"Again, sorry to scare you. We weren't sure anyone lived next door. It's been empty for a while and we didn't see you move in."

"Didn't have much stuff to move in." In fact, she had nothing to move in except the bag she brought with her to town. She bought some groceries every week, but other than that, the place was fully furnished, so she hadn't needed to spend the money.

"Ahh, starting over. I get that. Sometimes you just need pack up your stuff and start over in another town." He looked back at the woman Jamie assumed was his wife. "We're about to have dinner. How about you come over and get a hot meal in you? Tammy is the best cook in Pine Brooke."

Jamie weighed the invitation. She didn't know these people, nor did she like them. They looked shifty and odd, and she wasn't sure why they would invite her over for dinner.

They didn't know her. She could have been a crazy ax murderer. They could have been ax murderers. They could have been serial killers who led unsuspecting victims into their home with promises of a good meal. She wondered how many people fell for that.

"Umm..."

"We aren't murderers. We promise." He held up his left hand with a chuckle. "We just want to welcome you to our little town. Hope you stay awhile. We need more young people in this town. They all seem to move away."

"The city can be distracting. It does kind of call to you when you're young. I know it calls to me sometimes, but it's just not a good place to be." Jamie didn't like the city because of the people—it had nothing to do with crime rates. She didn't care about the crime rates. She never stayed in a part of town that had a lot of crime.

"I get that. I was in the city too at one point. But now I just want to live a nice quiet life. Come on. Come to dinner. We can tell you all of the town gossip." He grinned.

She didn't want to be around them or have to feign interest in them and what they were saying. But she could use a hot meal that wasn't microwaveable or riddled with sodium. She felt her ankles swelling at the thought of eating another microwaveable meal.

"It has been a while since I had a home cooked meal."

Tammy smiled. Jamie always knew the right words to get a gullible person on her side. It came naturally to her. Like breathing. She could talk anyone into anything. She could make a person believe that she was a kind woman who would never hurt anyone. And she wouldn't if she didn't have to.

"Well, you're in luck."

She allowed the couple to guide her into their home, which smelled like food. A lot of food. It was all mingled together. Meat. Garlic. Onions. Something sweet. Something spicy. Barbeque, maybe.

It was clean, which surprised her. From the looks of them, she thought she was walking into a pigsty. Or a home cluttered with angel figurines and porcelain dolls. But it was far better than she imagined. She might actually eat the food there.

The hardwood floors looked freshly polished. The living room was clean and free of clutter. On the walls were a bunch of pictures of the couple and others. Family and grandkids. Everyone smiling, A picture perfect family. She could see the love in the pictures. It practically leaped off the frames. None of her family pictures looked like that.

She stood near the door looking up at the pictures trying to remember if they had any family pictures. She couldn't remember taking any. She turned to her right and saw the dining room table. On the table were ribs, baked beans, macaroni and cheese, cornbread, okra and tomatoes, greens, and a pitcher of a dark liquid.

"You two aren't from California."

"Oh, no. We're from Louisiana, originally, but we've been here for well over twenty years. We leave for a bit, but we always come back. Sometimes we miss good ol' Southern cooking so I splurge a bit. Hope you're not allergic to anything."

Jamie grinned. "Nothing I know of."

He pulled her chair out for her and Jamie sat down. He sat at the head of the table while Tammy sat on his left. "My name is Bruce, by the way."

"Nice to meet you, Bruce and Tammy. It smells so good in here."

"Well thank you, sweetie."

At first, Jamie thought it strange, their welcoming attitudes. They were so nice, but then again, they were from the South. Southern hospitality and all that. Now it made sense.

Tammy fixed her plate, giving her a little bit of everything. "Just to see if you like it. If you want seconds, you are more than welcome."

Jamie stared at her plate eying the okra and tomatoes. "I thought okra was supposed to be slimy. Like snot."

Tammy grinned. "It depends on how you cook it. In Africa, some people like the slimy texture so they cook it differently. In the States we don't like that so much. I know I don't. It you fry the okra first, either in vegetable oil or bacon fat and then drain the oil, it won't be slimy."

Jamie didn't need the cooking lesson, but she still found it interesting. Tammy and her husband liked to talk, as most southerners did. At least that was what she assumed. She didn't know many Southerners… or any really.

They talked among themselves mostly. Jamie chimed in when she was asked a question or had something to say.

"I saw you looking at the flower beds out back. You plan to get some gardening in?"

Jamie's heart stuttered in her chest. "Umm… I think so. The flowers are really pretty."

"Well if you do it's best to do it at night. It gets so hot around here, if you do it during the day you might pass out from a heat stroke."

"Oh, I'll keep that in mind."

Jamie ate two plates. She had ribs, what felt like a pound of mac and cheese, biscuits, and some greens.

"This was amazing. I haven't eaten anything this good in a long while." That wasn't a lie. It really was the best plate of food she had ever had.

"I'm so glad you liked it. Let me pack you up a plate for later." Tammy jumped to her feet.

Jamie was going to say she didn't have to, but… she might be hungry later and it seemed to make Tammy happy.

Jamie thanked her for the food and went on her way. She eyed the flowerbed on her way inside. It would be the perfect place for her mother to rest. The house was cold. Much colder than her neighbor's home. She forgot she turned down the thermostat to make sure her mother didn't start decomposing and stinking up the place. She placed the food in the fridge and collapsed on the sofa.

Her phone rang in her pocket. "Hello, honey." She was in a good mood. Maybe it was the food. Or maybe it was because she knew that soon she'd never have to see or hear him again.

Chris's voice was cheerful as always. She rolled her eyes. "Hi! We miss you desperately."

"I miss you too. How's everything?"

"Umm… we're okay here. Kids are at their friend's house."

"You let them go to a friend's house? Why?"

"I know. I know it's not something that you would do, but they wanted to hang out with their friends. I felt like it would be good for them to get out of the house."

Jamie took several deep breaths to calm herself down. She had rules for her children. People would say she was strict, but Jamie didn't see it that way.

She was protecting them. She had their best interest at heart. But then it dawned on her, it didn't matter.

It didn't matter anymore. At the end of the day, they could do whatever they wanted. Once she left Pine Brooke, she would never see them again.

CHAPTER SIX

Logan Elwood

FOR THE THIRD TIME, I CALLED THE NUMBER BERT HAD GIVEN ME for the nurse at St. Mary's. She didn't answer. I even tried different times of the day just in case she was working or something. Nothing. It was like she knew why I was calling and avoiding me.

I didn't see how. No one knew I was calling. I had told Isaac and Bonnie that I was going to call, but never said when. Maybe she was just ignoring the phone all together. I tried calling Everly too, but she didn't answer, and I figured she was avoiding me too. She probably washed her hands of the situation and went back home. I wouldn't blame her. I wouldn't blame her if she never came back. Who would want to be caught up in this shit? Everly knew better than anyone that she couldn't change her daughter's mind once she was set on something. We all knew that.

I've known that since I met her. I stared at the folder for a long moment while I sat at my desk. I was supposed to be looking through files and checking on patients. While I had made a dent in the stack, I couldn't focus on it. The fire plagued my every thought.

I turned on my computer and stared at the screen. My fingers started typing before my brain had time to catch up. I wasn't sure what I was looking for. Not at first. after deleting and retyping several times, I settled on a phrase that might get me what I was looking for.

Catholic school fire, thirty dead.

It was the first thing that popped up. I clicked on a news article. Above the article, there was an image of the school, black and white of course, but I could still see the crumbled building in the background. I could make out the charred remains of the school and a body. At least I thought it was a body, but I wasn't sure. The photo was focused on an officer and a fireman talking. Around them was chaos. People caught running around the scene.

After a quick scan, and then a more in depth read, I learned that police believed a student might have had something to do with the fire.

"St. Mary's, home to many troubled youths over the years, may have been targeted by current or previous students. The entire student body and what's left of the faculty are being questioned at this time.

I wondered for a brief moment if Jamie was questioned. "Of course she was."

If she was one of two people who got out of the fire without a scratch on her, they must have found that suspicious. I did and I wasn't a police officer. I couldn't figure out why no one was arrested. Surely someone must have seen something. How could someone start a fire in a building filled with people and not get caught? No witnesses. Evidence was probably burnt up in the fire. But the students and faculty that were left must have seen something. I envisioned the night the fire claimed the school.

I picture how crazy it must have been with smoke everywhere and people screaming. Maybe it just got lost in the chaos and smoke as people tried to escape. It was also possible that someone had seen who started the fire and died before they could tell anyone.

I had to shake it all out of my head when my next client came in, though.

Mr. Drake Winters was in his early thirties and a bit of hypochondriac. He came in often. The previous doctor told me about him and his frequent visits to the doctor's office. I wanted to take his concerns seriously. These days people his age were being diagnosed with cancer all the time. I didn't want to tell him was overreacting and then later find out he had cause for concern. The most important thing I could do simply listen to him.

"How are you today, Mr. Winters?"

Drake Winters was thirty-two with dark brown hair and light brown eyes. He had a long, jagged scar along his jawline from a bike accident when he was a kid. The same accident resulted in a compound fracture in his right wrist. He walked into the room clutching a folder he kept his medical files in.

"I'm okay, I guess. Still having the same problems though." He sat in the chair across from my desk and set the folder on the edge. "Still have the muscle twitches and pain in my left calf and my chest."

"I see." I opened my file on him and glanced at his test results. "Well, looks like all your tests came back normal. No cause for concern there. Your heart is in great condition, and you don't have any blood clots in your leg. Your kidneys are in good working order. Now, your blood pressure is a little high. Higher than I would like, but other than that, everything looks good."

Drake's shoulders dropped. He had been coming in for the same problem since my first week. I ran several tests to put his mind at ease and they all came back negative. I felt bad. I didn't know what else to tell him. "Is there anything else you've left out? Anything that could help me with a diagnosis?"

"I don't think so."

"Any medications that are not in your file?" I flipped through his file and saw that he was taking vitamins and nothing else.

"Um..." Drake adjusted in his seat. It looked like I struck a nerve.

"You have to be honest with me if you want me to be able to help you. I can't get to the bottom of everything if you're holding something back."

He exhaled loudly. "I'm on some antidepressants."

I leaned back. "Okay. How long have you been taking them?"

"A few years." Drake looked visibly uncomfortable. In some places, especially small towns, mental health drugs and therapy were still taboo. It was clear he didn't want anyone to know about it, but as his doctor, I needed to know everything. His entire body looked tense.

"I just didn't want you to judge me. People always do when they hear I'm on medication." His voice was low, barely above a whisper.

I leaned forward. "What people?"

"My parents, a few friends. My last doctor. My mom said I had no reason to be depressed. Other people have real problems, and they aren't depressed. My father said I didn't have ADHD, that I was just lazy and lacked discipline."

"Are you on medication for both?"

He nodded.

"What are you taking?"

He took a deep breath. "Zoloft and Wellbutrin."

"I see." I leaned back and stared at him for a long moment. "Well, those two medications can cause side effects. The involuntary movements in your limbs that you've been having. Jerky movements in your legs, muscle twitches, tremors, muscle pain, joint pain, and chest pain. Your high blood pressure can also cause chest pain. Have you tried other medications?"

"Nothing else worked."

"Right. Okay, now we at least have a starting point. I'm going to prescribe amlodipine besylate at a low dose, for your blood pressure, but I want you to monitor it. They have wrist cuffs you can use to check it at home I'm also going to schedule you for a CTA with contrast. It's basically a cat scan of your heart. I think the chest pain might be from your blood pressure, but I want to make sure nothing else is going on. For the muscle and joint pain you can buy creams for that and see if they work. As far as the involuntary movements...you need to speak with your psychiatrist. It could be TD. I'm sure you've seen those commercials on TV."

Drake lifted his chin slightly.

"If it is, there's medication they can prescribe for you. But I believe that's only if it is making your life difficult. If it's getting in the way of your work or making you self-conscious. Is it really bothering you?"

"Not when I'm at home by myself, but when I go out, I feel like everyone is watching me. Like everyone can see it."

"That has to be frustrating. Let them know that, and they should be able to give you something."

"I didn't think it was a side effect of the medication. I was starting to think I had MS or something."

I gave him a smile. "I understand that. I bet you spent a lot of time on Google searching for symptoms of cancer and all that."

He laughed. "Yeah, probably shouldn't have done that."

"Please don't," I said. "And … look. No more off-book medications, okay? I have to know what you're taking in your body, or it could lead to some serious complications. We don't want that. If you can promise me complete honesty, I promise you I won't judge you one bit."

He looked up, a glimmer of hope in his eyes. "Really?"

"Really. My job is to make you better. Which means we've got to work together as a team. Deal?"

I reached out a hand. Drake looked down at it for a long moment, then finally took my hand and gave it a firm shake. "Deal."

I smiled. "Great. Now, I'm going to send this prescription to your pharmacy, and you should be able to pick it up later today. Take it in the morning with a glass of water. Also get that blood pressure cuff. They have them at the drugstore."

"How often do I take it?"

"In the morning and in the evening before bed. Write the numbers down and when I see you for your next visit bring the log with you."

"Okay."

Drake jumped to his feet. He looked relieved. He had been coming to this office since before I got here with the same symptoms, but he never told the doctor that he was taking other medication. If he had, this could have been dealt with long before now.

That was the thing about secrets.

CHAPTER SEVEN

Riley Quinn

OLIVIA TUCKER LIVED IN A NICE NEIGHBORHOOD WITH WHITE picket fences, manicured lawns and what looked like the same house, copied and pasted several times, but in a variety of different colors. As soon as her friend finished filing the report, Z and I called the techs and headed over to her home. Part of me was sure that it was nothing. Maybe she went to bed late and overslept. Maybe she didn't feel like going in and needed a break. Another part of me, a quieter part, knew something wasn't right. In all the time I had watched the news, Olivia was never not there. She looked like she took her job seriously and avoided calling in sick. She reminded me of me, in that regard.

There had to be a reason, and it had to be a big one. We stepped into the house before techs arrived. The front door wasn't locked. I knocked several times while Z looked around the house. She checked the back door, but there was no sign of forced entry or broken windows. The house should have been sealed up tight. I knew of no young woman who lived alone and left her front door unlocked. Granted we lived in a small town, but still, it was dangerous, and Olivia, being a news anchor, would have known that. After slipping on a pair of gloves we entered the home. I stood in the foyer calling her name. There was no answer. Zelina and I exchanged a look.

We watched as the crime scene techs entered the home. I figured we should give them some space and time to look around. The house was empty. Her home looked like it had been newly renovated. Everything was top of the line. The dark gray hardwood floors, stark white crown molding. A wrought iron staircase that led to the second floor. It was an open floor plan. I stood in the foyer and could see all the way to the back door. Near the front door was a dining room and on the other side of that was the large kitchen with white cabinets, stone countertops, and the biggest fridge I had ever seen in a home. Her decorating style was minimalist. No clutter. No pictures of her family or friends lined the walls. Nothing out of place. She liked the color white and wood tones.

Upstairs, I walked into her bedroom and was amazed. The bed was made up, and there was nothing on the floor: no shoes or clothes. There was no clutter on her dresser, nightstand or in her bathroom. Her makeup was neatly placed in their acrylic containers. No dirty towels or clothes on the floor. I touched the inside of her shower; the marble wall was bone dry and so was the loofah and the soap. I spun around and stared out the doorway. Either she was a neat freak, or she hadn't been home in a couple of days. That was concerning. By the time I made it back downstairs the crime scene techs had arrived.

"I want every surface dusted for prints," I announced on my way out the door. There was no sign of foul play or of a fight. No sign she ran out of the house in a hurry. It was just a clean house. There was no sign she had been there at all. Maybe she went somewhere else after work, didn't tell anyone, and she got tied up. It happened. It happened to Zelina on more than one occasion. I had to call her and remind her she was an hour late to work. I often covered for her with the captain, but something told me this was different. Olivia wasn't answering her phone. That was the part that worried me.

Her car wasn't in the driveway, though that could have been for a variety of reasons—most of them nonthreatening. Maybe she left on her own accord. Went for a drive to clear her head or took some time off. Or maybe she was forced to drive to another location. It didn't feel like an abduction, though. Granted, it was too early to tell, but when I walked into her home it felt… right. It didn't feel like something bad happened there. Z said it was just my gut acting up. But I trusted my gut. If she was taken, if something bad did happen to her, it didn't happen in her home.

While the techs were examining the home, we decided to talk to the neighbors. Donna hadn't spoken to Olivia since Friday, but they might have seen her since then. We needed to nail down a timeline of her last known whereabouts. Until we had that, we didn't know where to start.

We strolled over to the white house with an olive-green door. I knocked. A long moment later a woman with dark brown hair and hazel eyes opened the door. Her eyebrows drew together when she saw us.

"Hello?"

I held up my badge. "I'm Detective Quinn and this is my partner. We need to ask you a few questions about your neighbor."

The woman craned her neck out the front door and looked at the house next door. "Something happen to Liv?"

"We're still trying to figure that out," said Zelina. "Can we ask you a couple of questions?"

"Of course." The woman's eyebrows relaxed for a moment before knitting together as she took a step back and gestured for us to enter the home. It smelled of freshly brewed coffee and something sweet. Pancakes, maybe, or cake.

"Umm … we're in the kitchen right now. Follow me." She led us down a long hallway that opened up into the kitchen. A man stood at the stove while two teenagers sat at the table scrolling through their phones.

"I'm Dorothy Clemmons and this is my husband, Ron. And our girls, Nia, and Lauren."

Only when their mother started talking did the girls actually look up. I smiled and waved.

"Is everything okay, Mom?" The concern in Lauren's voice was palpable. She set her phone on the table and her sister did the same. Both girls straightened in their seats as if they knew something was wrong and were intent on paying attention.

"I'm sure everything is fine. What do you need to know about Liv?"

Mr. Clemmons spun around for a brief moment, and then turned back around and turned off the stove. He moved the pan he was working on to another burner. "Is she okay?"

Their kitchen resembled Olivia's in some ways, and in others it was completely different. The layout was about the same. But the Clemmons kitchen had color. Instead of white cabinets, theirs were turquoise. it was beautiful and eye-catching against the white marble countertops. They had a gas stove instead of electric and an equally large fridge. The backsplash was a mixture of white, turquoise, and gray that helped tie in the cabinets, countertops and appliances.

Around the kitchen and the dining room were pops of blue that caught the eye immediately.

I took a deep breath. "We aren't sure at the moment. A missing person's report has been filed. Since your family lives right next door, we thought you could tell us the last time she was home so we can create a timeline."

Dorothy gasped. Ron rushed over to his wife and wrapped an arm around her shoulder. "I can't believe it."

"She's missing?" Lauren's voice cracked.

Nia stared at her sister for a long moment. "She was home Friday, but not for a long time. She comes home, changes her clothes after work and then goes for a run. She says it relaxes her."

"She finds running relaxing?" asked Zelina.

"That's what I said." Dorothy shook her head. "I find a hot bath and a glass of wine relaxing after work, but hey that's just me."

I understood, though. I found walking after work relaxing. It always eased the tension in my shoulders and helped me clear my head. Having to report on news stories every day was probably taxing. "Did you see her come back?"

Mr. and Mrs. Clemmons looked at their girls. "I don't think she came back," answered Lauren.

"I don't remember seeing her car Saturday. I'm not saying it wasn't there. She could have come back and then left after she changed her clothes, but I don't remember seeing the car."

Lauren looked at her mother. "Mom, the cameras."

"Oh!" It was like a light bulb went off above Dorothy's head. "She's right, we have a Ring camera, and we have security cameras around the property. Can't be too careful. Would you like to look at the footage? One of the cameras is pointed in that direction."

I smiled. "We would love that." I wasn't expecting to get footage of Olivia's house during the time she might have gone missing. With the influx of home security cameras in recent years, it seemed like everyone back in the city had them. But Pine Brooke hadn't really gotten the message yet. Some people had them, but most people didn't. My mother didn't want one even though I insisted and offered to pay for it.

"How could our neighbors trust us? They would think that we didn't trust them, and I would hate that," she always told me. "Not to mention who would hurt us? It's not that kind of town."

The next time I talked to her I would be sure to mention that this town has had and caught two known serial killers. It is that kind of town, and precautions should be taken."

"We got it after Tory Craster was caught and turned out to be a serial killer." Dorothy led us down a hallway with three doors. "I just couldn't believe it." She opened the first door to reveal an office. "Ron worked with Tory on a couple of jobs when the girls were a little younger. We had him over for dinner several times." She sat at the desk and turned on her computer.

"We've been hearing a lot of stories like that," said Zelina. "Everyone loved him."

"It's true what they say, you never really know someone." She clicked through a series of folders. "Okay, this is from the camera that's pointed toward her home." She moved out of the way and pressed play on the footage from Friday evening. In the video, Olivia came home, spent ten minutes in the house, and then got back in her car and left. We fast forward through the footage. Her car never pulled back into her driveway. We watched it all the way through until we got to Monday and saw our car pull up to her house.

She never returned home. When she left, she was wearing work-out clothes and had her headphones around her neck. She was ready to run. There was no bag or anything that she could have stuck a change of clothes in. She didn't even have her purse with her.

She was set to run and come back home. So where did she go?

"My daughter was right, she never came back," said Dorothy. "I would say maybe she went to her boyfriend's, but I don't think she has one. Very focused, that one. It's all work, all the time."

"Really?" asked Zelina. "She wouldn't be going out on a Friday night? She's young."

Dorothy shook her head. "She always says she doesn't have time for it. She knows what she wants to do and where she wants to be in the next five or so years. Anything that would distract her from that is not allowed in her life. She's very... resolute in that way."

"Can we get a copy of this footage?" I asked inching toward the door.

"Of course. I'll get Ron to make it for you. He knows how to do stuff like that. I just know how to play it back."

"Thank you."

We followed her back into the kitchen. She asked her husband to make a copy of the video for us and he rushed out of the kitchen to do so.

"Did she come back?" asked Lauren. Neither girl had their phone in their hand. They looked worried.

"No," said her mother.

Lauren's shoulders dropped. Nia leaned against her shoulder. "Maybe she fell," said Lauren.

"Fell where?" I inched toward the table.

"During her run. I can show you." She jumped to her feet. "I used to run with her in the evening. I was preparing for a track meet, and she helped me. I know the route she takes."

"Is it the same route every time?" I asked. She tilted her head.

"Yeah, she loves it. She always says she likes the quiet." She glanced at her mother. "I could show them. I want to help if I can."

I smiled. It would be better if we had someone to show us the possible route she might have taken. It would cut our search time in half, but there were two problems with that suggestion. First, we didn't know if she was still on that path. Maybe someone coaxed her away from it. Maybe she fell and landed away from the path. But it would give us a starting point.

The second problem, the one that I was most worried about: what if someone had done something to her and left her on the trail. Lauren would see her body, and I didn't want that for her.

CHAPTER EIGHT

Riley Quinn

I HATED HAVING TO BRING LAUREN AND HER PARENTS TO HELP US walk the path. She sat in the back seat with her hands tucked in her lap and her eyes cast down at the floor. Her shoulders were nearly touching her ears. I hoped she wouldn't see anything. I hoped that Olivia was just hurt, and we could get her to a hospital. My stomach soured at the thought.

If we weren't searching for a missing person, it would have been a beautiful day. It was hot, but not scorching, with a light breeze that promised a cooler night once the sun went down.

We pulled into the parking lot of the park. This park had several paths and trails a person could take. Some of them merged and some went in the opposite direction. There were two parking lots, one near the northside entrance and one in the south. The first one was empty.

I didn't know if that was a good sign or a bad one. It was one I didn't like either way. I watched Lauren as she stared out the window. Her body so tense it seemed to fold in on itself. She didn't want to be there, and I didn't want her there. I hoped she didn't see anything that would scar her for life.

"Detective Quinn? We think we might have found the car you're looking for." The voice sounded familiar on the radio.

"Where?"

He said the location. Lauren inhaled sharply behind me. I glanced at her in the mirror, her hands were balled into fist in her lap.

"That's near the south entrance," I muttered. We drove toward that parking lot and saw three police cars and a dark blue sedan. Zelina parked, and I jumped out. "I'm going to look at the car and if everything's okay, I'll come back and get you."

Lauren inclined her head, but didn't utter a word. She was quiet the whole time. Never made a sound. The girl was clearly worried about something. She and Olivia seemed to be pretty close, as they went running together every evening. That had to be it. The quicker we got through this the sooner she could go home. I walked over to the officer who had his pad out and was staring at the license plate.

"It's the same number and the same description as the report."

"Have you looked inside?"

"No ma'am. We were waiting for you."

"Thanks." I slipped on the pair of gloves I kept in my back pocket.

"Who's the kid?"

"She's the neighbor of our missing person. They used to run this trail during the evenings. She's going to show us the path she took." I opened the driver's side door, while Zelina looked in the back seat and popped the trunk. No signs of a struggle. No blood. No purse. Nothing.

"Anything in the trunk?"

Zelina shook her head. "It's clean." She slammed the lid of the trunk. "So, if something did happen to her it wasn't near her car." The car might have been used to transport her body to somewhere in the forest, but there was no blood in the trunk. I stared at the trees that framed the park, tall with thick leaves and wild branches. Maybe she did come here for a run on her own. I did another search through the car.

Her phone and keys weren't in the car either. She probably used her phone to play her running playlist so that would be with her. "Okay." I walked back to the car and opened the door for Lauren. "You can come out now."

"Is she in the car?"

I shook my head. "Nope." I closed the door behind her. "Does she take her phone with her on her runs?"

She smiled weakly. "She has this playlist filled with like hardcore metal and hip hop. She says it gets her in the zone and makes her run faster."

"Hardcore metal, huh? Never would have thought that. She doesn't really seem like the type"

Lauren smiled. "Yeah, she's always showing me cool bands and stuff. When we come out together we put the playlist on at the same time in our separate headphones, so it's like we're listening to it together."

"You come out here to run a lot?"

"Not so much lately, but yeah. It's relaxing. I overthink a lot, and it's hard for me to turn my brain off all the time. Running gives me something else to focus on. It helped drown out all the other thoughts, and all I have to do is focus on moving my legs."

"I get that." We stopped at the entrance. Three trails went in different directions at the entrance. The officers stood behind us as we waited for Lauren to choose the trail. She pointed to the trail on the left.

"She starts with this one most of the time."

Slowly the group started walking. Zelina and I wore gloves. We instructed Lauren that if she saw something that might have belonged to Olivia to let us know, but not to touch it herself.

"Does she follow the same trail all the way through?" asked Zelina.

"No. This one splits off, and she takes the right one. Then it splits again. There also might be deer and tortoises. I saw one once."

We followed the first trail, slowly. Our heads were on a swivel, looking for signs of a struggle or blood or something of hers that might have fallen. We found nothing. We followed the trail until it split and then it split again and again and again. Lauren stayed with me and Z, while her parents hung back with the officers a little behind us.

Olivia was not on the trail or around it. While we walked the trail, the officers branched out on either side and combed the wooded areas that surrounded the trail.

We reached the end of the trail and turned around.

"Sorry I wasn't any help."

I squeezed her shoulder. "You did help us. Now we know she was here, and we found her car so we can dust it for prints and see if anyone else drove it. You were a great help."

Her shoulders dropped a little.

"I think I found her!" The voice on the radio sounded panicked.

Lauren froze. I squeezed her shoulder again. "Let's get you back to the car."

"I'll take her," said an officer. "Her parents are already heading back to the car."

"Better yet can you drive them home?" I asked. "Take care of them."

"Yes ma'am."

I waited for them to move through the trail and out of sight before I turned around. I didn't want Lauren to break away from him and follow behind us. I didn't want anyone following behind us. News—especially tragic news in a small town—traveled fast. I wouldn't have been surprised if people around town already knew about Olivia's disappearance. It was the one thing I hated about living in a small town... everyone knew everyone's business. The detective part of me didn't mind it though. It was the primary way we learned anything. That being said I'd hate for my business to get around town before I had the chance to tell my friends or family. *Guess it's a good thing I don't have any business outside of work to speak of.*

"Where are you?" Zelina asked into the radio.

"I'm near the end of the trail. Ed is standing by the trail waiting for you."

Ed met us near the end of the trail. His face was soaked with sweat. He opened his mouth to say something. A scream sliced through the science like a knife. The three of us immediately drew our weapons.

"I think it came from where the body is. Follow me." He led us through the trees, jumping over raised roots, fallen branches, and rocks.

The sobbing got louder and louder until I saw her. A dark-haired woman, her hair pulled into a messy bun on top of her head, was being cradled by an officer while she sobbed into his shoulder. He looked up when he saw us. "This is the victim's mother."

I blinked. *How did she get here so fast?* I tore my eyes away from the grief-stricken mother on the ground and turned to my left. All the officers were facing that way.

"I didn't know there was a tree this big back here," whispered Zelina.

When one of the officers moved to the side, I saw what they were staring at. Olivia was tied to the tree. "That's a lot of blood," I murmured. No need to distress her mother further.

I walked over to the tree, while Zelina stepped away to call for the coroner. I glanced behind me. "Get her out of here!" She shouldn't have had to see her daughter like that. Tied to a tree covered in blood. I knew the town gossip moved fast, but she beat us here. How was that possible? We would have to interview her later.

"We'll start setting up the perimeter," said an officer and he stepped away.

Olivia was tied to the tree with rope wrapped around her and the tree several times. "Interesting," I mused. For her to be in that position, her wounds must have been inflicted first and then she died. And then they tied her to the tree.

I examined the tree, careful not to disturb the body too much. The metallic scent hung thick in the air around the body.

"Huh." I lifted part of her left side. "Or maybe she was tied to the tree first." The part of the tree underneath her body looked like it had been stuck with something several times. Each mark corresponded with a wound on her body. "How did they get her on the tree?"

There had to be multiple assailants. Maybe she was drugged first. Or unconscious. Her thick black hair stuck to her neck and the side of her face. I lifted the hair from her neck. There was a thick dark line across her neck. "Maybe that's how."

I looked up and down the tree. There was blood spatter up the trunk and on some of the leaves. She was definitely stabbed while she was on the tree.

I stepped back and looked at her. Her clothes were still on, along with her shoes. She didn't look like she was raped or assaulted. She had no bruises on her face or on her arms. She was just tied to a tree and stabbed.

"What the hell is that about?" I stripped off my gloves. "Was any of her stuff found? Phone? Car keys?"

The officers around us shook their heads. "We haven't found anything. Just her. The keys might be in her pocket, but we didn't want to touch her before the coroner got here."

"Okay. I'll tell him to search her pockets."

"I will."

I spun around. Keith walked through the trees with his bag in his hand. "You got here fast."

"I was told this was a priority so…" he exhaled sharply when he saw the body. "Damn."

"Yeah. I want a tox screen done."

"Looking for anything in particular?"

My head tilted slightly while I stared at the body. "It looks like she was tied to the tree before she was killed, and if that's what happened I want to know how they got her up there. It was either drugs or she choked until she passed out and then put up there."

"Alright. I'll let you know what I found."

"Also prints from the rope and see if you can get any from the tree, if that's possible."

He sighed. "I'll give it a try, but don't hold out hope."

"I usually don't. Thanks."

"Now we need to talk to her mother," Zelina said.

CHAPTER NINE

Logan Elwood

NICOLE AND I WERE AT THE DINER FOR A LATE LUNCH WHEN RILEY and her partner Zelina shuffled in, both looking exhausted.

"Hey," I waved them over to our table.

Despite the heavy look on her face, Riley smiled. "Hey guys. How's it going?"

"Not so bad We spent all day moving things around the office and cleaning out a few rooms that are not being used."

"And haven't been cleaned in decades," added Nicole.

There was so much caked up dust that we had to wear masks to finish cleaning. When I went home, I could still smell the bleach and Pine Sol after I took a shower and washed my hair. It was like it was embedded in my nose, in my skin for days.

Riley laughed. "Well, it's good that you guys are finally cleaning up the place. I think the old doctor only cleaned the rooms he used."

"Yeah, we noticed that," said Nicole. "How about you guys? Are you on a case?"

"Yeah, but we're waiting on some results, so there's nothing we can do, and I'm starving." Riley glanced at the menu. "What's the special for today?"

"Hot honey fried chicken, a side of roasted garlic mashed potatoes, green beans with bacon and caramelized onions, and a buttermilk biscuit," said Nicole. "That's what I ordered."

"I see Isaac is working today."

"You're gonna need a nap if you eat all that," said Nicole. "Which is why I'm gonna get it to go, that way I can eat half now and the rest later."

I shook my head. It did sound good though. "Guess I'll get that too."

Nicole handed the waitress the menus and placed the order. Zelina ordered a plate of fries accompanied by a salad. She looked up at me.

"Trying to eat more vegetables. This one won't shut up about it."

"Potato is a vegetable," said Nicole. My lips curled into a smile.

"Yeah... but I think once you add butter, cream and all the fixings, it loses its vegetable-ness."

The table erupted in laughter.

"Vegetable-ness," repeated Riley, a smile on her lips. Quiet settled over the table again. Riley nudged me with her elbow. "Tell me more about the mediation and your troublesome sister-in-law."

I glanced at Nicole, who rolled her eyes. I explained everything that happened to Riley for the second time. She seemed like the kind of person who liked to hear a story multiple times so they could pick apart the details. Which was what she did.

"You might want to watch out for her," said Riley. Zelina's head bobbed in agreement. "She sounds like trouble."

I bit my bottom lip to stop myself from saying anything further. It was the third time in a week that I heard that.

"You gonna tell them about the fire?" asked Nicole.

I stared at her.

She pointed at Riley and Zelina. "They're cops. They might have a way of looking into it or getting access to files you can't."

"Yeah, dude," said Zelina. "Listen to your nurse."

Riley nudged me with her elbow again and I told them everything that I knew, which I planned on keeping to myself.

"Wow," said Riley when I'd finished the story.

You really think she could have done that?"

"I just can't help but feel like something's off about it," I said. "I need to find out more."

Zelina leaned back and placed her hands flat on the table. "That is crazy. They should not give her custody of anyone, let alone herself."

"She can't have custody of herself?" asked Riley.

Zelina folded her arms across her chest. "I said what I said."

"And I concur," said Nicole.

The tension in my shoulders eased slightly. The sound of their laughter made me feel like everything was going to be okay.

"You think she had something to do with the fire?" asked Riley.

I nodded.

"Be careful about investigating this yourself. If she did start the fire, I doubt she'll be happy to hear you're looking into it. I would help, but we just got a doozy."

"What case?" Nicole leaned forward waiting for one of them to say something.

"We just found the body of a news anchor—"

"Olivia Tucker?" She shook her head. "I noticed she wasn't on the news this week. I went to school with her."

Now it was Riley's time to lean forward and engage Nicole.

"What was she like?"

Nicole chewed on a green bean. "I'd hate to speak ill of the dead."

"We need to find out what happened to her. So, you have our permission to ignore those feelings," said Riley.

Nicole's lips twitched into a smile. "Well, alright then. She wasn't exactly a nice person. I thought she was manipulative and only out for herself. She wanted to get to the top, and she didn't care who she had to step on to get there. Now people get older and change. I don't know if she did, because I didn't have anything to do with her once we graduated."

"Was she in any of your classes?" asked Zelina.

Nicole rolled her eyes. I took that as a yes.

"We had a group project in science once. She did her part, and I did mine. We got a great grade. An A, I believe. Guess who took the full credit?"

"Really?" asked Riley.

"Yeah, she told our science teacher that she did all the research and the only thing I did was part of an experiment. She took full credit and said I didn't help her with anything else. Which caused him to take that into consideration when he did my grade."

"He changed your grade because of what she said?" I asked. That didn't make any sense. Why would he even believe her?

"Yup. She got an A, and I got a C with a warning. 'Next time there is a group project it's important that I participate the whole time and not just for the experiments.'"

I leaned back. "Did you confront her?"

She dropped her head. "She said he must have misunderstood her. But there was nothing she could do about it now."

Riley's mouth hung open. "Wow! Now I see her in a whole new light."

"I'm not saying she deserved to be murdered or whatever… but I can't imagine what shit she got into these last few years."

"Did she have any friends? Was she popular?" In my mind Olivia was one of the popular girls. I watched her on the news almost every morning. When I got to the office, Nicole had it on in the background.

She was pretty. Reminded me a beauty queen. Straight white teeth with a smile that almost looked fake. She was perfect for TV, and she knew it.

"She did. She was with the in crowd. Reminded me of the movie *Mean Girls*. They were popular and had full rule over the school. Everyone knew them, though I don't think people really liked them. You know how everyone just wants to say they hung out with the cool kids. Teenagers want to be cool."

"I wonder where they are now?" I asked. If she still hung out with them, or if they left her in her hometown. Nicole's story about her was interesting, but I had to remind myself that Olivia was a victim. Being mean in high school didn't mean that she deserved whatever bad thing had happened to her.

"I heard most of them moved away. All of them, I think. But then again, most kids in my graduating class left as soon as they graduated. I mean I knew a girl had her stuff packed in the back seat of her car. As soon as she got her diploma she was out. She went one way, and her family went the other."

"Damn. She was ready to get the hell out of here," said Riley.

I related to that. I didn't move out the same day as graduation, but I moved to my college town before the end of the summer. Before the beginning of the summer really.

Sometimes you just had to leave a bad situation. Even if you have to leave on your own. I was so ready to get out of that house and away from my mother I wanted to leave as soon as I graduated, but my mother talked me into staying for a couple of weeks.

We all finished some of our food, and then we went our separate ways. Riley and Zelina were working on Olivia's case and had to get back to it. Nicole and I had patients to see.

CHAPTER TEN

Jamie Washington

JAMIE HATED GETTING HER HANDS DIRTY UNLESS IT WAS NECES-
sary. Getting rid of her mother's dead body made it necessary. She
waited until it was dark before she started digging up the flowerbed. The backyard was quiet. She looked up at the house next door
and noticed that all of the lights were off. It was after midnight, so they
might have gone to bed. She moved quickly.

The flower bed had been dug up. The hardest part was dragging her
mother without being seen. Every noise made her freeze. At least until
she got to the flowerbed, and then she moved quickly. She dumped her
in and then started covering her with dirt. She planted the flowers and
added a few she bought from the store. She also rearranged them, so it
looked like she had a legitimate reason to dig it up.

She didn't want to throw any kind of suspicion her way. Once she was done and everything was to her liking, she brushed the dirt off her legs, grabbed her tools, and went back inside, careful not to drag any dirt into the house.

Jamie took a long shower, washing off all the dirt and mud from her fingertips to her hair. She felt lighter when she got out of the shower. Like she was ready for a fresh start. She drifted into sleep, but didn't dream. All she heard was Marie's voice softly whispering to her.

The next morning, she woke up well after the sun had come up. She slipped on a dress, something comfortable for when her lawyer arrived. She had sent Jamie a request to sort out the next steps. Jamie hadn't seen her since the mediation, which did not end well. She knew she had let her temper get the best of her, but she couldn't help it. She felt consumed by it. There was a raging fire inside her and every word out of Logan's mouth and Everly's stoked it. The bigger it got the more she felt like she was going to explode. Jamie couldn't even imagine what her lawyer thought of her. Hopefully, she would let her explain.

Her lawyer arrived a little after noon. Jamie was happy to see her, but she didn't look so happy. She looked tired. Exhausted. Like she hadn't slept in days. The bags under her eyes would have been considered overstuffed luggage.

"Thank you for meeting with me," she said as soon as she walked through the door. She set her briefcase on the table and opened it. "Here you go. Social workers stopped by his house. As you can see, they observed Dani lived in a loving and stable environment. They see no need to remove the child from her father's care.

Jamie balled up the piece of paper. "You believe me, don't you? I know what I saw."

Her lawyer winced. Jamie knew she didn't believe her. She saw it in her eyes. She didn't want to represent her any longer. "I guess I don't need a lawyer anymore." Jamie struggled to keep her voice light and upbeat. "Thank you for everything that you've done. I really appreciate it."

She returned her smile. "It was my pleasure to help you." She closed her suitcase and left.

Jamie paced the floor. "That cop must have been looking out for him. Bribing the social worker." She moved back and forth between the front door and the opening to the kitchen. Her blood boiling in her veins. The more she thought about it the angrier she became.

She hated them. She hated all of them, and they would pay. She just needed to think of a plan to make sure that happened. Jamie needed custody of Dani like she needed to breathe. No one could take care of her like she could. No one could love her like she did. They were two halves of the same whole. She was her niece.

Wait, that wasn't right. She wasn't her niece; she was her sister. The only sister she had left in the world, and she would protect her. She would have her. Like she had Marie. The sounds of glass breaking and tires screeching shook her from her thoughts. The metallic scent of blood hung in the air.

"How can I fix this?" Jamie didn't want to get another lawyer. She'd have to start the whole process all over again and she didn't want to. She just wanted Dani. But without a lawyer, she couldn't do it the legal way. She would have to go the illegal route. She'd have to do it herself. She couldn't depend on anyone to do it for her. They'd probably turn her in and take the money.

"What should I do?"

"What do you mean? What else can you do, Jamie? You have to get Dani away from him. You need to bring her home."

Marie's voice rang in her ears, burrowed into her bones. She felt it in her chest, reverberating through her body. She knew Marie was right. She had to bring her home. That wasn't in question. She needed to know how she could do it.

"Well if you insist on taking her, you might as well do whatever is necessary to bring her back." Everly's voice bounced off the wall aiming directly at her. She was always talking to her.

"Mother! Don't say that! Do it within reason, Jamie. Don't hurt anyone if you don't have to."

Everly elbowed her way into the conversation. *"She must. It is too late to turn back now. Look at what she's done so far. Everything she's done. The lives she's ruined. Why stop now?"*

"Jamie, if you don't have to hurt anyone don't. Only if it is truly necessary."

"But that's her favorite thing to do. Hurt people. I'm missing an eye, for Heaven's sake. Why deter her from what she's good at?"

Jamie found a corner and slid down until she curled in on herself like a child. They were talking about her like she wasn't in the room. She hated that. They both made some good points though. Her favorite thing was hurting people. She loved it. But hurting anyone else would just make things worse. Did she care about making things worse?

"I'll take her," she announced. The arguing stopped and then she continued. "I will take Dani away from him and I won't kill anyone if I don't have to." Now that it was settled, Jamie thought about hiring someone to kidnap her and then waiting for a little while before joining them somewhere. She'd be the first suspect, and if she wasn't there, it would look suspicious.

She shook her head. That would get too many people involved. Plus she couldn't think of anyone that would be willing to do it. She could do it herself. It would be easier that way. Dani knew her and would come with her willingly. Better her than a stranger.

But before she could act on her plan, she had to learn their schedules. Logan was always at work, as was Isaac. The nanny was usually home. If she chose the right night, the house would be virtually empty. She could knock the nanny out and take Dani.

There was a soft knock on the back door. The sound startled Jamie to her feet. She inched toward the door. "Who is it?"

"It's just your neighbors. Sorry to scare you."

Her shoulders sank immediately, as relief flooded through her muscles. She unlocked the door and opened it. "You scared me."

"I know. I figured it would. Have you eaten?"

"Umm..." Jamie glanced at the clock. It was already past six. Where had the time gone? "No, I haven't."

Jamie blinked and found herself sitting at Tammy and Bruce's table before she could even argue. Before she even realized she had left her own house.

Bruce smiled "Always nice to see you."

"You too." Jamie stared at the spread on the table. Cornbread was the only thing on the table she knew. She suddenly realized she hadn't eaten anything since yesterday when she'd been here. Was it yesterday? How many days had it been?

"Well, we have cornbread, butter beans, okra, and tomatoes, smothered turkey wings, and some jambalaya." She took Jamie's plate and piled the food on.

She wasn't sure she could eat it all, but she would try.

"So how have you guys been?" she finally managed.

Tammy beamed. "Our son and his wife just had our first grandchild. We are grabbing an RV and heading over there as soon as we can."

"Next couple of weeks would be ideal," Bruce added.

"That'll give Rose some time to get out of the incubator."

"Was she okay?"

Tammy glanced at her husband. "Our daughter-in-law got into a car accident, so the baby was born a month earlier than planned. But the doctor says she is doing fine, and her lungs are good."

"That's great." Jamie cleaned her plate twice. She was hungrier than she thought she was. She finished everything with an extra helping of turkey wings and butter beans. Tammy packed her up a plate so she could have it for lunch the next day. Jamie listened to Tammy go on about her children. As she listened, she wondered if this was what a real mother was. Someone who loved you unconditionally. Someone who listened to you? Someone who was proud of you. Whose face lit up every time they talked about you. Her's certainly lit up when she talked about her son and two daughters.

"I can't wait until the other two give me some grandchildren, but they have time. I told my girls to live their lives first before they get swept up in some man and get pregnant."

"That's good advice."

She smiled. "Is that what you did?"

"Yes and no. I lived a lot of life before I got married, but it wasn't a good life, if that makes sense? I don't think it counts."

"Did you learn from it?"

"A lot. I'm still learning from it."

"Well, then that counts. Hardships and mistakes are there to teach us something. You just gotta pay attention."

A smile bloomed on Jamie's lips. Tammy was such a better mother than hers. She was nicer and had kinder eyes. If she had grown up with Tammy instead of Everly she might have turned out differently. Possibilities were endless. But more importantly, she would have been loved. The thought stabbed her in the heart. A tear sprang to her eye. *If only.*

"With you being new in town have you heard any town gossip?" asked Tammy.

"Small-town gossip, in Pine Brooke?" Bruce joked. "I can't imagine that."

Jamie gave a small shrug. She wasn't too concerned about town gossip as she wouldn't be in town long enough to care. Tammy looked eager to tell her something. "I haven't really heard much of anything. I've been focused on getting everything together, I haven't had much time for anything else. Why did something happen?"

That was all Jamie had to say and then the flood gates opened.

"So many things. It's been a long year, and one filled with murder." Tammy shook her head. "I never would have thought the things I've heard in the last few months would have happened here."

"And the year isn't even close to being over yet," Bruce added.

Now Jamie was curious. She didn't pay much attention to the news, so she didn't know what they were talking about. "Like what?"

Tammy took a big gulp of sweet tea while her husband leaned back like he knew it was going to be a long conversation, so it was time to settle in and get comfortable.

"Where to start? In the last few months, we've had two serial killers caught and sent to prison. It's such a small town to have two..." she shook her head again. "I just never would have thought... I wonder how rare it is."

Pine Brooke was a small town, yes, but only when compared to big cities. It wasn't that small when compared to other small towns. Medium-sized town was probably a better description. A medium-sized town with a lake and a beach.

"Two serial killers?" Jamie vaguely remembered hearing something about it, but she wasn't paying attention. She had been focused on Dani, and getting her away from Logan. She had no time for anything else.

Tammy fiddled with her pearl earring and grinned. She had a weird smile on her face like she was proud of the news. Maybe she was. Jamie thought that odd. She also thought that Tammy might have been proud because something was finally happening in her small town. Something newsworthy.

"Other things have happened over the years, but not so close together."

"What else has happened?"

Tammy glanced at her husband. "Well, there have been quite a few cold cases in this town. One that comes to mind—"

"Maybe we shouldn't talk about that one." Her husband knew what she was going to say before she said it. It must have been something that they talked about before. Something she was interested in, but that he was cautious of. This intrigued Jamie even more. He wanted something kept hidden, and she wanted to spill everything.

"Someone should talk about it. There's no reason this shouldn't have been solved. Who kills a police officer and just gets away with it?"

Jamie's back straightened immediately. "Someone killed an officer?"

Tammy took one long look at her husband before turning her attention back to Jamie. "Yes. It was a long time ago. Officer Quinn was a nice man and everyone in the community loved him. I think his granddaughter is a detective now—anyway—he was found in his patrol car a few days after he went missing. Some people thought he ran off or something because when he disappeared, some money from a bust went missing with him. It was a lot of cash, and they figured he took it and ran."

Jamie frowned. "When they found his body, did they find the money?"

"No. They found him in his car, shot in the head. Gun on the seat, but no money. I heard he might have been robbed before he could leave town."

"And since he no longer had the money to live, and couldn't go back because he stole the money and would be found out, he killed himself." The reasoning sounded plausible to Jamie. It was his only way out. Cops didn't do well in prison, so he had to shoot himself.

"That's what people say... but I heard there was no gunpowder residue on his hands and the gun was by his right hand, but he was left-handed." Tammy looked at Jamie, her eyebrows raised.

Jamie blinked. "Oh. If he wasn't right-handed then how did the gun get on the seat?" Jamie didn't know much about suicide, but she knew you couldn't shoot yourself in the head and then throw the gun onto the seat next to you. That didn't make any sense. And if it didn't make any sense to her, then the police should have had their own questions.

"Cover-up." She blurted the words out before she realized.

"Exactly!" Tammy pointed at Jamie and smiled. "Although who and why is beyond me. He was a good man. He wouldn't have stolen anything."

"There's no way he would have left Shirley and April behind. He loved them too much. April was his whole world. He loved that girl. And Shirley was pregnant."

"They used that as an excuse as to why he stole the money. He had another mouth to feed, and he needed the extra cash."

"That doesn't make any sense. If he stole the money to provide for his family, then why was he leaving them behind? Sounds counterintuitive," Jamie said.

Tammy looked at her husband and smiled. "Finally, someone gets it." She slowly sipped her tea. "I know it's been so many years now, but his name has been besmirched and it needs to be cleared. Someone killed him and they need to be brought to justice."

"They're probably dead now."

"So?" Bruce sighed. "I know his granddaughter had a hard time getting on the force. It's been forty years, but small towns have long memories. I'm sure some of them brought it up from time to time. Especially when she was a rookie. It must have been relentless."

"She's a detective now, so I'm sure they've let it go," Bruce said.

Jamie sipped her tea for a moment. "Any theories as to who did it and why?"

Tammy shook her head. "I can't think of anyone who would ever want to hurt him."

Jamie looked at Bruce, who was no longer looking at them, but had his hands on the table. He knew something or he at least had a theory he hadn't told his wife about yet. Jamie weighed her curiosity over her indifference. It didn't matter now, as it happened over forty years ago and it in no way affected her. Deciding she didn't care, she didn't push the issue. "I guess all small towns have their secrets. Is it a closed case or solved and ruled a suicide?"

"There were too many discrepancies to rule it a suicide, but there were no leads on the money or who might have pulled the trigger. It's a cold case that no one is looking into. Probably can't even find the file for it."

"So out of sight out of mind. That's crazy. I wonder what his wife thought."

"She never thought he did it. Never. She knew how he loved her and their daughter. He wouldn't leave her behind, but she also didn't raise a big stink about it either."

"Why?"

"She couldn't prove anything. On top of that, her husband was gone, she had one child and another one on the way and no job. The first few years after he died her life depended on charity from her neighbors. If she made a big deal on how she thought her husband was framed and murdered, people might have been less helpful. She had to rely on her neighbors."

It made sense to Jamie. Women in those days had less options to make money. She didn't want to rock the boat. While Jamie finished drinking her tea, she wondered how Shirley felt about it now.

Jamie thanked them for dinner and took her plate home. She was suddenly so tired. She could barely keep her eyes open as she walked up to her door. After setting her plate in the fridge she collapsed on the sofa. She needed to go to sleep. She had a busy day in the morning.

CHAPTER ELEVEN

Riley Quinn

I WOKE IN A POOL OF MY OWN SWEAT. MY SHIRT WAS DRENCHED AS was my hair. A restful night's sleep seemed impossible after finding Olivia's body, even though the short dinner with Riley was much appreciated.

My mind replayed the interview as I tried to sleep. Her family no longer lived in town. Her parents moved after they retired. They had wanted to travel. Her mother wanted to see the Ozark mountains, so they were headed that way. They had been there for a couple of days when Donna called asking if they had heard from Olivia. Her mother was worried and couldn't get the thought out of her mind, even though Donna said it was probably nothing. She tried calling her daughter several times, but never got an answer. So they started driving back.

"But how did you know your daughter was in the park?" I'd asked once she had calmed down. It had taken a long time for her sobs to subside. Her husband helped calm her.

"Donna called and said she had filed a missing person's report for Liv. She said last time anyone heard from her was before she went for a run Friday night. I just had a feeling. I thought she might have fallen on the trail or gotten hurt some kind of way. I told her she shouldn't run there at night." A sob bubbled up her throat. "I was just walking while he went to the house to check. I know the trail she likes and the big tree. We used to walk it when she was younger. Took pictures near the tree. I started there."

I handed her a tissue to wipe her face. "I'm so sorry you had to see your daughter like that. While we have you, we do need to ask you a few questions. I hate to do this now, but its better just to go ahead and get it out of the way." The couple shared a look. He nodded as he wrapped his arm around her shaking shoulders.

"Had your daughter been threatened or had she been afraid of anyone in the last year or so?"

She shook her head. "Everyone loved Liv. She was a good person. Helpful, bright, and beautiful. She was mostly focused on her work. That got all her attention she didn't have time for anything else."

"Do you know if she was working on something?"

"No," he answered. "She never told us about her news pieces she was working on. Not until they aired, and we would see her on TV. She'd tell us to make sure we were watching, and we knew she was covering some exposé or something."

"I can't think of anyone that would hurt my daughter," her mother said softly, her breath hitching.

I was apt to believe them. *They* couldn't think of anyone that wanted to hurt their daughter. Parents often had a hard time picturing someone hating their child. No matter how old they were, in their parent's eyes they would always be sweet and loving and everyone's friend. This happened in most cases. I suspect it wasn't true though. It was true to them, but for someone out there, she had not been their friend.

It took me forever to fall asleep, but I couldn't stay asleep. The tremble in her mother's voice still rang in my ears. I couldn't shake the sound. The scream that tore through the quiet. How violently her body shook as she sobbed into the officer's shoulder. Finding her body in the woods reminded me of Delilah's case. Both went missing. Both were found dead in the woods. Both mothers were devastated.

I sat up in bed. The sheets underneath me were soaked with sweat. The cold air from the air conditioner mingled with my sweat. A shiver raced down my spine. It was so cold. If I didn't know any better, I would have sworn someone turned it down to sixty.

Luna lazily lifted her head from the dog bed in the corner of the room. She looked at me, decided she wasn't concerned, and laid her head back down.

"Thank you for your concern."

She didn't even lift her head again. It was clear Luna was sick of my shit and felt like I needed to get it together. Going back to sleep would be impossible at the moment. I glanced at my pillow.

"Not going back to bed." I rolled out of bed and went to get dressed. Sometimes when I had a hard day or needed to sport through some things I went to the beach. Sitting at the lake was great, and a much shorter distance, but sometimes it wasn't enough.

At the beach, the sound of the waves crashing against the sand gave me something else to focus on. All I needed to do was focus on the sound. It helped calm me.

The town was quiet at five in the morning. It felt like my car was the only one on the road. I heard the waves as soon as I got out of the car. There were two other cars in the parking lot, one of them looked familiar.

I strolled to the sand, took my shoes off, and squished the sand between my toes. A smile bloomed on my lips. I walked toward the water.

Logan sat toward the end of the beach with the water lapping at his feet. He was alone. I figured he might want to stay that way, and I shouldn't intrude, but I was curious. Why was he out here?

I inched closer to him. "Logan?"

His head jerked backward. "Hey?"

"Are you okay?"

He looked from me to the waves and back again. I sat next to him, my legs folded underneath me.

"I just needed to think in a quiet space."

"I get that. Me too. I couldn't sleep."

"Me either.

There was a somberness to his voice I hadn't heard before. Another shiver tore through me and I found myself shivering. Logan took off his jacket and wrapped it around my shoulders.

"You don't have to do that."

"I insist." He finished adjusting the jacket. "So what's keeping you up?"

. "We had to tell the parents who came from out of town about the body. Talking to the mother just made me think about... all kinds of stuff."

It brought back memories of Delilah's case, but it also made me think about my past. Having to tell my friend's mother that she was dead was the most difficult thing I had ever had to do. I insisted on being the one to tell her because we had been so close, because I had wanted to go out, so she came with me. I shouldn't have done it

Her mother was so angry. She screamed and cried and cursed and blamed me for it.

I never went back. I went to the funeral and steered clear of her family. Her mother wouldn't even look at me and I couldn't blame her. She was right, it was my fault. If I had stayed home like she wanted or gone out by myself none of it would have happened.

I shook the thoughts from my mind. "Why are you out so early?" I asked, trying to change the subject.

"Just turning over some stuff in my mind. Couldn't sleep."

"I get it," I said. "How's Dani?"

"She's good. Nothing to report, really. Been doing good in school, been keeping busy. I just keep thinking about that fire I told you about."

He told me more about what he learned about the fire and Jamie. He sounded—and I might have been wrong—like he was asking for permission to investigate on his own. I understood his need to do it before court proceedings started, but I didn't really approve. Civilians conducting their own investigations almost always did not end well. But he looked so dedicated.

I focused on what he thought he needed to do. "I know if I tell you not to do it, which I want to, you're going to do it anyway. And I respect that decision. That being said, all I can say is be careful. You don't know who did this or how it has stayed covered up for so long. Someone might not want you digging into this, so you need to plan accordingly. Don't go interviewing any suspects by yourself. Take your brother, he looks like he can handle himself."

His lips twitched into a smile. "I can handle myself."

"Probably, but he looks like he's had a lot of practice at it."

"Clever way of saying Sac looks like he's gotten his ass beat a lot. I mean he did, but I didn't think it was that obvious."

It was my turn to smile. "It is. I've seen that look many times."

He laughed. "Me too."

"How is Dani holding up?"

He shrugged. "I don't think she fully understands what's going on. Or how it can affect her. She likes her aunt, but she doesn't understand what she's doing. I tried to explain it to her the best I could. I don't know if she doesn't think it would happen, or if she doesn't mind spending time with her aunt."

"She might not get the full picture. But it's not going to happen, so that's okay. I think you are way too worried about this. No one, no judge in their right mind, would take Dani from you and give her to Jamie. Not with the social workers pleading your case."

"Deep down I think I know that, but… I just have this fear… I can't explain it. It's… it's crippling. I'm terrified she will get taken away from me and more importantly, she will want to go. I think that's what scares me the most. Maybe Jamie could give her a better life."

"I don't think Jamie will ever be happy. And that's not a good environment to grow up in. She would be miserable with Jamie. It might be fun at first, but that would wear off pretty soon. She wouldn't be able to keep up the charade of being a good person or a good mother."

He sighed. "Thanks for that. Really."

"Anytime. And if you ever need help on the case, let me know."

"I might just take you up on that." The waves lap against our feet. ""What's going on with you? You said the case made you think of other things."

I exhaled. I told him about my friend and how she was killed and how her mother reacted.

"Every murder is not your fault. Her murder was not your fault. You didn't kill her. You didn't make the robber kill her. She still could have said no, and told you to go on your own. This isn't on you."

Tears pricked my eyes; I blinked them away. He was right. I knew he was right. But my brain wouldn't let me believe it. He was saying it because he felt sorry for me, and even though I knew that wasn't true, I clung to the thought like a life raft in the middle of the sea.

I had to hang on to the guilt, it was the only reason I was there. I didn't think I would have come back to Pine Brooke if it wasn't for her death. I wouldn't have quit my job or become an officer. Her death made me who I was. Believing her death was my fault made me who I am. Without it, what would I be? Would I even be a cop anymore? Would I quit?

"Is that why you became a cop?"

The sound of his voice pulled me out of my rabbit hole. "Yeah, it was. I didn't want anyone to ever feel the way I felt during that situation."

He smiled sadly. "It's nice to be able to talk about this stuff with you."

I looked at him. "Yeah."
We watched the waves until the sun peeked over the horizon.

CHAPTER TWELVE

Riley Quinn

LEFT LOGAN AT THE BEACH AFTER I CHECKED MY WATCH A DOZEN times. It was almost time for me to head to work and I still needed to take a shower. He had to get back home to Dani.

I didn't want to leave, and even though it had been a while, I didn't think he wanted to either. I enjoyed our little talks when it was just us. I felt my cheeks flush as I got back in the car.

I hurried home and threw on a pair of jeans, a tank top and my shoes. After feeding Luna, who looked at me like she was wondering where I was this morning, I ran out the door and jumped back in my car to head to the station.

My phone vibrated in my back pocket, but I didn't check it. When I got to the station Zelina was already there staring at her computer.

"A little late?" She winked and I had no idea what it meant.

"Is there something wrong with your eye?"

"Don't play stupid. It's very unbecoming."

I sat at my desk. "What are you doing?"

"Looking up sex offenders. Keith says he doesn't believe that she was sexually assaulted. Her clothes were on the right way and showed no signs of being removed and put back on."

"Well, that's something."

"I'm still looking for sex offenders in the area because... I don't know, it just looks weird and feels like something I should be doing."

"Find any prospects?"

"Only two promising ones in the area. One tortured and raped a woman. I was thinking maybe he got interrupted and didn't get the chance to rape her."

"Possible. Maybe someone else was out for a run and he heard their footsteps."

"Exactly."

"Okay. Give their parole officers a call and let's go wake them up." We called the parole officers and then decided to split up. Zelina took one sex offender, and I took the other.

Officer Howie Marks waited by his big black truck. He had to be at least six feet tall. He was bald with a bulletproof vest on. I stared at the vest. Did he know something I didn't?

"I was on my way out of town when you called. Another parolee messing up." He looked back at the house. "What do you think he did?"

"A woman was found in the woods not far from here—"

"Oh, the news anchor. Saw that on the news. It's a sad thing." He looked back at the house. "I don't know if that's his style, but to tell you the truth, I don't put anything past these guys. If he was angry enough and determined not to go to prison, it could make him desperate."

"Yeah, that's what we were thinking." I followed him toward the house. When he knocked it wasn't a normal knock. It sounded like he was trying to take the door off the hinges. Because he was on parole, that made him subject to a search without a warrant. His parole officer could drug test him and search through his things if he thought he was violating parole in some way.

He knocked again. Two patrol cars stopped in front of the house.

I thought it was better to bring backup, just in case something happened. Finally, the door opened. A man stepped in the doorway all tattooed with a long red beard and bright blue eyes.

He scowled. "Why are you here again? I didn't do anything."

"This time," Howie said. His voice was a low rumble. "But I get to come through and make sure you are keeping out of trouble anytime I want. This detective here has a few questions for you and these officers are going to search your place."

Howie didn't wait to be invited in. He just walked forward and everything in front of him got out of his way. The door opened wider, and he stumbled back.

The man looked at me like he was seeing me for the first time. Like he didn't know I was there before.

"Detective? For what? I haven't done anything." His arms folded across his chest. "I swear. I've been good. You know that." He looked at his parole officer waiting for him to agree with him. It never came. Howie was too busy searching the couch cushions. "I've been working my program. It's hard as hell, but I'm really trying this time."

I felt bad for him and part of me believed him. "A woman was murdered in the woods the other night."

The shocked look on his face was startling. "I didn't do that! I never murdered anyone. Howie, come on, you know me."

"I know. But this is just a formality. Covering all of our bases, and you are a rapist. You raped two women. You might be escalating, we don't know."

His shoulders sank.

"I know you are working your program and I'm proud of you." Hearing that he perked up a little. "But we still need to do this, and you need to answer all of her questions."

He leaned against the wall. "Okay. What do you need to know? My whereabouts?"

"Yes. But I need you to come down to the station."

"Now?" He looked behind him as the officers were making a mess of things.

"Tomorrow morning. Come in tomorrow morning, and I'll have a list of questions for you."

"I'll be there. You have my word. Howie, I won't let you down."

We finished searching his home. He sat on a counter in the kitchen, careful not to touch anything and staying out of the way. We finished. There was nothing strange or suspicious in the house. Nothing that belonged to Olivia.

"Okay. I'll see you in the morning."

"Yes ma'am."

We had no evidence nor a reason to hold him other than his past record, and that wasn't going to cut it with a judge. We left and he closed the door behind us. When we got away from the house I spun around. "You really believe him?"

"I don't put anything past anyone. But he raped those girls. I know he did that. He was high on meth, and doesn't remember it. And that's not an excuse. I can't help but think if he stays clean, he might have a chance to course correct."

"I guess believing in people is not a crime, but... I don't know. That's your choice, I guess. Thanks for the help."

"Anytime."

He went his way, and I went mine. I got back in the car and my phone started vibrated again. When Z had something to say, or if she found something, she called. I thought it was her texting me this morning, but I was already on my way, so I didn't check it.

I fished the phone out of my pocket. My eyes focused on the screen for a long time before it registered who it was. I hadn't seen the name in so long I had forgotten it. I tossed my phone onto the seat. I didn't want to speak to her. I couldn't.

I stared at the phone as it vibrated again. *Why was she texting me now?* It had been a few years since I talked to Brianna. Not since the funeral. I had nothing to say to her, to any of them. There was nothing they could say to me that could be meaner or guilt inducing than I already said to myself every day.

I knew they blamed me for her murder. It was my fault. If I would have just stayed home with Delilah like she wanted it never would have happened. I glanced down at the phone again, it had stopped. Relief flooded my body, my hands loosened on the wheel. I didn't realize how tightly I gripped it until my fingers ached when I let go.

I picked up the phone and scrolled to the calendar. I knew it without looking, but part of me wanted to check, just to be sure. The anniversary was coming up. Her birthday and the day she was killed were in the same month. That was why she was calling. The anniversary of her death was coming up. Maybe she wanted to rub it in my face. Remind me of what I did.

I didn't have the time. I was working on a case. My forefinger brushed the screen when her number came up. "I should just block her. I should block all of them," I grumbled. If I did, I wouldn't have a minor heart attack every time their numbers flashed on the screen. It would have made sense and yet it was still something I couldn't bring myself to do.

I met Brianna at a coffee shop. She had just moved to the city from a small town in the Midwest. The second I saw her I knew she was from a small town. She had that wide-eyed, deer caught in the headlights look on her face. I had that look too when I had first gotten there. We became instant friends. I showed her around and then introduced her to some of my friends and then that was it. We became best friends from then on.

But now we were strangers, and I wasn't ready to change that. Not now. Not after I've tried so hard to get my life together. To pick up the pieces of my life after the funeral. If I didn't think about it, I was okay. The thought was like an open wound. It would scab over for a while, but every once and a while the wound opened up. Red and sore and a pain so blinding I couldn't think.

"I don't need this right now," I whispered to no one. When my phone started ringing, I was half tempted to ignore it. But thankfully, it was from Keith.

"Yeah...Okay." Keith wanted to see us at the morgue. He either found something or he finished his examination. Keith had become one of my favorite coroners we had ever had. We had one before him that was mildly annoying. Well, not mildly. Very annoying. He was an older man and the way he dealt with the victims reflected that. I had a rape case back then where the victim was raped and then killed. When he pulled up to the scene and saw her body, he made a remark about what she was wearing. She wore a short skirt and sandals and a low-cut top.

"What did she think was going to happen?" he said as soon as he saw her. They way he handled her body was different from some of the other victims he handled. All through the autopsy and in his notes, he made it seem like it was her fault and only her fault. "If she hadn't been out in this attire then this wouldn't have happened." He said this during his recording of the autopsy and he wrote it in his notes.

He was gone soon after that case. We went through a few more coroners before we found Keith. I hoped he wouldn't leave us until he was old and gray. He was respectful of the bodies and objective—which was what we needed.

My phone rang yet again when I got out of the car. A glance at the screen told me it was Brianna. I cancelled the call and headed inside. Before I reached the door to the morgue the door behind me opened. I knew it was Z without having to look behind me.

"You got here before me? A miracle."

I smiled despite myself. "I know. I know. I was already in the car when he called. Where were you?"

"At the house of a strange sex offender. She wasn't there. And nothing she owned was there, but someone else was. I'll explain it to you when we get back to the station." She stared at the door. "Did he tell you what he found? He didn't tell me anything, just to come down because he found something."

I shook my head. He had told me the same thing and nothing else. Usually that meant that he found something he couldn't explain. Or something he thought we would find interesting. It was always interesting. Always strange.

"I'm glad you came down so quickly." Keith stood next to an exam table eying a folder. "I wasn't sure if you two were together or not, or were in the middle of chasing down some suspect, so I called you both."

"Well it sounded important when you called. I figured we better hurry up. What did you find?"

Keith smiled. "I don't know if I would say important... it's interesting. It might help you solve the case, or it might be insignificant. I think it's important, though." There was that objectiveness again. "Okay let's start with the basics. By the time she was found she had been dead for a few days. She was likely killed Friday evening."

Zelina nodded. "That was the last time anyone saw her."

"I would say so." He opened a folder he had placed on the covered body. "She was tied to the tree before she was killed. I believe she was strangled with some kind of rope. Nylon rope. I found nylon fibers in the wound on her neck. Not enough force to kill her, but enough to make her pass out so they could tie her to the tree."

"Did you find anything from the killer? DNA or something."

"Killers."

"I'm sorry what now?" I inched forward. I wanted to grab the report out of his hands and stare at it myself.

"There was more than one killer."

"Are you sure?" I asked.

"Okay. Let me explain this." He took a deep breath. "The knife wounds are all different sizes and depths. Different amounts of force. Different angles. It only makes sense if there were other people were involved. The wound by her hip was at an angle, where the person had to be shorter than the person who stabbed her in the heart."

"Judging by the angles there were different killers."

He jerked his thumb upward before verbally explaining the answer. "She was stabbed multiple times in different places. All on her thighs, chest and torso. Some wounds were inflicted with so much force the blade pierced the tree trunk. But other than that, she wasn't harmed. I can say for certain she wasn't raped. She wasn't beaten. It was like they only wanted to stab her."

"What kind of weird shit is this?" I asked. It was better to think of one person killing her and not multiple. Who talked them into doing it?

Why would a group kill a news anchor? This shit wasn't making any sense. Had she pissed a group of people off?

When we got back to the station, Zelina told us all about who she found. The sex offender she had been chasing did not have anything of Olivia's, but he did have a sixteen-year-old girl, half naked and tied to his bed.

"Clearly he wasn't expecting guests," I said.

"Obviously. She's at the hospital and her parents have been contacted. He's in a cell back there."

"Well at least something good happened, today. Not a total bust."

CHAPTER THIRTEEN

Logan Elwood

I HAD BEEN THINKING ABOUT IT OVER AND OVER. THE THOUGHT danced around in my mind until I could no longer resist. My best bet of finding someone who knew about the fire was Facebook. I didn't really use social media much, but everyone was on Facebook, just about. Well, everyone from my generation, as Nicole so eloquently pointed out.

"My grandmother uses Facebook to contact people she hasn't seen in years. To keep up with her friends from school. It's where the old people hang out. For them it's easier to use than the others."

At the time I wasn't sure if she was calling me old, or if she was saying my chances of finding someone who worked at the school during that time was better on Facebook. The more I thought about it, she was definitely calling me old, but it was a good idea, so I was willing to overlook it.

"Are you sure this is a good idea?" Sac stared at me from across the dining room table.

"Don't you want to know what happened?"

"Of course. I love a good true crime story. That being said, I'm still not sure about you contacting survivors. Can't your cop friend do it, so you don't get… hurt in some way?"

"Riley is working on a case right now. You heard about the news anchor."

Sac cocked his head and stared at me. "The whole town is abuzz with what happened to her. I went to the coffee shop before work, and I heard people talking about it. Apparently, the way she was found was really gruesome."

I stopped scrolling and looked up. "What do you mean?" The news had stated where her body was found, and that she was dead, and who she was, but they skimped on the details. I thought it was out of respect for her family. If her death was extremely gruesome, I could understand why they would want to keep that information out of the news.

"Like, stabbed several times. I heard her throat was slit and she was found naked tied to a tree. Face so bloody they couldn't recognize her at the time. At least that's what people have been saying."

"You see, Riley is too busy to help me on this. Not to mention I don't need her help on this. I'm just looking up the list of names Bert gave me and seeing who wants to talk. That's all I'm doing."

His head tilted to the side slightly. "Also heard her mother found her body."

My fingers stilled over the keys. "That's messed up. She shouldn't have had to see her like that. How did she find her?"

"She was looking for her and knew she liked running in that park."

"Damn." I couldn't imagine seeing someone I loved like that. Instantly images of Marie stuck in the windshield of our car flashed in my mind. Her face cut up by glass. I shook the thought loose. "Wow. That's an image she'll never get out of her head."

"Nope." He stared at me for a long time. He still wasn't a fan of my idea, but I needed to do this. I believed that if Bert thought it was going to be dangerous, he never would have given me the list. We both believed that since these people wouldn't talk to him, maybe they would talk to me. Especially if I added that Jamie was my sister-in-law and I was worried she might do something dangerous.

Hearing her name might make them open up. Or it might make them hang up in my face and block my number. It was a risk I had to take.

"I get what you're saying. Just don't meet anyone without me."

"Riley suggested I take you with me if I meet anyone."

A smile passed over his lips. "You two hang out a lot."

I looked up. He threw his hands up.

"I'm just saying you two hang out a lot. It's good you have a friend." There was something about the way he said 'friend' that didn't sit right with me. I couldn't help but think he was trying to say something else. There was nothing going on with Riley and me. No matter how many times I said it, I felt like no one believed me. I wasn't ready to date. Not yet. All I needed right now was a friend and she was just that.

"I'm just saying, she's beautiful and smart—"

"Stop it and let me focus." I turned my attention back to the computer screen, scrolling through pictures and looking for the names on the list. I had searched several names from the list and hadn't found anyone yet. Maybe they didn't have Facebook.

Maybe they didn't like social media. Or maybe, for whatever reason they were already dead. Whatever the reason, I scrolled and searched for names for over three hours until one of the names I searched turned up a picture. I scrolled through many users named Bianca Lewis. Some had pictures, and some didn't, until I stopped at one. I stared at the picture on the screen and then at the pictures in the folder Bert had given me.

I was looking for anyone who either went to the school or worked there at some point. Bert had told me it was hard to find people from that time.

"Most of them probably changed their names, either through marriage or trying to disassociate themselves from the school. It's understandable. Especially if they lived in the same town. They would forever be known as a surviving victim of a fire that killed over thirty people. People in small towns have long memories. probably would never let them forget it."

"I still want the names so I can try to find someone. I might not find anyone, but I think it's worth a shot. I just want someone to tell me what happened that night and if Jamie was involved."

Bert had warned me of this the last time we talked about it: "I should warn you that this happened a long time ago and Jamie was a child at the time She might not get jail time. Especially if a lawyer can show that she was not in her right mind at the time. She did have some behavioral issues and that has been well documented. That being said, it could get an investigation rolling and they might find something else on her, or they might be able to find the missing victims that have changed their names or what have you. I just don't want you to get your hopes up." I was grateful for the advice, but it didn't change anything. Not on my end.

I felt like I had been looking for ever until one picture caught my eye. "I think I found one. Bianca Lewis."

"What are you going to do?" Sac leaned forward. "What kind of message do you send. Hey, you remember when your school burned down, and you barely made it out alive? I want to talk to you about that."

I looked at him. "Umm… I'm not going to say it like that." I didn't know what I was going to say actually. I didn't think I was going to be able to find anyone. But I had found her and now I needed to think of a way to contact her. "I think I'll see if she will *friend* me first." I clicked the button.

"Friending under false pretenses." Sac shook his head. "Shameful."

"Shouldn't you get to bed? Don't you have to work in the morning?" I leaned back on the sofa.

"Not in the morning. Afternoon shift. I think I like mornings better though."

"Why? Don't you have to get up earlier?"

"Yeah, but it's something about being there when it first opens. It's quiet and we're getting things ready. Cooking, listening to music, and then people start to trickle in. The afternoon shift, you're rushing around from the time you get there."

"Morning shifts are slower to start. You get to ease into it."

"Exactly. But one of the cooks called in sick, so here we are."

I smiled. "They know they can depend on you."

He rolled his eyes, but a smile slowly took shape. It was a great thing to see, Sac getting his life together. It was something I thought I was never going to see. I never thought we'd live in the same house again. But here we were getting along.

My computer dinged.

"What happened?"

"She approved my friend request. I'll message her and see what she says."

By the end of the night Bianca had not returned my message. It was late though, and Isaac suggested she had gone to bed or maybe to work.

While Isaac went to bed I continued searching and found two other students that went to the school. I sent them messages and friend requests before closing my laptop and heading to bed. Moving up the stairs was like walking through quicksand. My limbs were so heavy, I felt like I was fighting some unseen force trying to push me down.

I crawled into bed with my clothes on and hadn't even slid under the covers before I fell asleep.

When I woke up the next morning, I rolled out of bed and jumped in the shower. The smell of bacon wafted through my closed door. Sac must have gotten up and made breakfast.

I finished getting dressed and grabbed what I needed for work and headed downstairs.

Dani smiled and waved at me. "Hey papa. Uncle Sac is making breakfast."

"I smell the bacon." I kissed her forehead and tousled her dark curls.

She giggled "Papa don't mess up my hair!"

"My bad."

We ate breakfast and then we dispersed. I grabbed my laptop, kissed Dani goodbye, and told her to have a great day. Bonnie walked her to school while I headed in the opposite direction to the office.

Nicole was there before me as always. I said good morning to her, went into my office, and sank in my chair.

"Your first appointment isn't until ten, and we get our new secretary tomorrow."

I grinned. "That's good to hear."

She closed the door, and I leaned back in my chair. My eyes rested on my computer bag. I wondered if anyone messaged me back. I was hopeful, but I tried not to cling to it too tightly. Maybe no one would ever answer. It was probably one of the worst moments in their lives. Who would want to relive that? But I still needed answers, and talking to people who were there that night was my best way to get them. Isaac asked me why I couldn't just let it go.

"It's obvious that Jamie could never get custody. She's not stable. No judge would give her Dani. You don't have to dig into this. It's not necessary. So why keep doing it?"

It was a question I didn't know how to answer. I couldn't explain why I needed to do this. I needed an answer to the question that had been nagging at me since I heard about the fire. A question that wasn't about Jamie.

I opened my computer and went straight to Facebook, hoping someone messaged me back. My heart stalled in my chest when I saw I had one message. I clicked and there was Bianca, and she was online.

Bianca: Hi, how did you know to contact me?

Logan: My lawyer gave me your name. I just need to ask you a few questions about the fire. I'm not a reporter or anything. I promise.

Bianca: So, what do you want? Why do you need to know about it now?

Logan: You went to school with a girl named Jamie who got out before the fire started. She's my sister-in-law and she's trying to get custody of my daughter.

Bianca: What happened to Marie?

Logan: Marie was my wife. She died a few years ago.

Bianca: Oh. I'm really sorry.

Logan: That's why I'm concerned about Jamie. She wants custody of our daughter ever since Marie died.

Bianca: Sounds like her, to be honest. There was something wrong with her, even then.

Logan: Can we talk? On the phone or in person. I just want information. That's it. I'll do this on your terms, I just haven't found anyone else that's willing to talk to me.

Bianca: That's not surprising. Worst day of my life. I don't want to go back to that day ever… but Jamie shouldn't have access to any child. So, if this will help you stop that from happening, I'll talk to you. I'll send you my work address.

I was relieved that she even messaged me let alone agreed to meet with me. I wasn't sure if anyone would want to talk about the fire, I knew I wouldn't, so I understood. I wished I could let it go. Stop thinking about it and just let things happen the way they were meant to. But I couldn't. I couldn't let go of the thought. The suspicion. The wondering. I had been told by several people that Jamie was not going to get custody. Not now. Not after that mediation and what the social workers had to say.

Both worked out in my favor and made her look crazy. I knew that. I knew she wasn't getting custody. I told myself that over and over and over again. And yet the thought never stuck. It never stayed in my head no matter how many times I repeated it. But the thought of Jamie getting custody of Dani—that lingered. It had burrowed in my bones and would not let me go.

I had to ensure that she could never get her hands on Dani in any way. I didn't want her to have custody or visitation. I didn't want Jamie and her family coming over for dinner. I didn't want Dani playing with her children. No contact. The only way to ensure this was to make it impossible for Jamie to even be considered as a potential guardian for my daughter. If she was arrested for murdering at least thirty people in that fire, that would have helped my case.

But it wasn't just that. I wanted to know. I needed to know if Jamie did it. And I needed to know if Marie knew had known about it all that time and continued to allow Jamie to be in our lives. If she knew her sister was a killer, and never turned her in... that wasn't the Marie that I knew. That was what worried me. It wasn't just about Jamie. It was about Marie too. Did I ever really know her?

I couldn't shake the feeling that there was something more to this. I couldn't put my finger on it, and I didn't think I would know anything until I learned more about the fire.

CHAPTER FOURTEEN

Riley Quinn

THE LAST THING KEITH SAID STILL RANG IN MY HEAD. WHEN WE were on our way out, he stopped us, a pensive look on his face. "Before you two leave, I need to show you something. I don't know what it means, but I feel like it's something. Here's the peculiar thing I want to show you."

He pulled down the white sheet and exposed part of Olivia's chest. Near her collarbone, there was something carved into her skin.

"What is that?"

"I'm not sure. I think it's a sun. Someone carved a sun into her chest."

"What the hell is that about?" I glanced at Zelina who stared at the sun intently.

"Why do that unless they were marking her? Leaving their mark on her." Zelina turned away.

The mark was crude and carved in her skin deep. "Was she dead when this happened? I really hope that she was dead."

He sighed. "Sorry to say, she wasn't. Her heart was still pumping when someone made this mark."

I shook my head. "Can you send me your report when you're done? And," I stared at her face, "can you clean her up a little bit. Her parents will get here soon, and they need to formally identify the body."

"I'll get working on that and do the best I can."

"Thanks." I followed Zelina outside to the car.

"We should talk to her coworkers."

Zelina gave a half shrug. "Yeah, since she was stabbed by multiple people, I'm thinking maybe a group at work really didn't like her."

"Yeah, that was my thought. Though I find it strange if a group of people can all get talked into murder."

"Stranger things have happened," said Zelina.

I hated that she was right about that. "We should probably go back to the station and fill in the captain before we head to the news station.?

Back at the station, we spoke to the captain in his office. He sat at his desk flipping through a folder while he listened to us.

"A sun? Carved into the body? What the hell is that about?" He tapped his pen against the desk. "For some reason, that sounds familiar. I can't remember why, but it does. Any leads?"

I shook my head. "We are headed to the news station where she worked. Talk to coworkers, see what kind of person she was. If any of them had a problem with her."

"Okay. That's a good start. Keep me in the loop."

"Will do." I opened the door and walked out, followed by Z. Talking to her coworkers was going to be interesting. I definitely wanted to talk to Donna again since they were so close. She might be able to tell us if anyone in the office had a problem with Olivia.

The news station was lively. People were moving about all over the place. Rushing from one end to the next. I spotted Donna as soon as I cleared the front desk. She stopped talking to the man she was talking and rushed toward me.

"Have you found anything?"

"Is there a place we can talk?" I asked.

She looked around. "Umm... the break room is usually empty about this time. Follow me."

We followed her down a hallway and into a room with two round tables, chairs, and a strong smell of burnt coffee hanging in the air.

"Have you found anything?" Her voice sounded panicked.

"We haven't yet. We came here looking for leads. Is there anything you can tell us about Olivia?"

"What do you want to know?" Her arms folded across her chest as she stared through the doorway. Her demeanor was a little off-putting. At the station, she looked concerned, but here... it was like she was worried about someone seeing her talk to us.

"Did she have problems with anyone? Anyone who would have held a grudge against her?" asked Zelina. She leaned on the wall by the doorway, her arms folded mimicking Donna's stance.

Donna must have noticed it because she sat up straight. "You have to understand something about Olivia." She took a deep breath. "She was ambitious. Maybe a little *too* much."

"In what way?" I asked.

"She was shooting for the top. She made her jump to anchor *very* quickly. We knew she had her sights set on bigger and better cities, and she wasn't shy about making that fact known. This place was too small for her. Too limited."

"She would insult you guys to your face?" I asked incredulously.

Donna shook her head. "Not like that. More like we all kind of knew that none of us mattered to her more than getting ahead. Chasing the big story. Trying to get the big break that would bring her to a major media market. She could be nice, but once she got her sights set on a story, Lord help the person that gets in her way."

"Wow. Okay." I looked back at Zelina. "Is there anyone in particular that might have gotten in her way?"

She sighed. "I can think of a few people. There's Walter Norman, a news anchor who was passed over. He really hated her."

I jotted down the name. "Anyone else? Anyone she did a story on?"

She thought for a moment. "Look into a man named Terrell Rayner. He sent a bunch of angry voicemails to the station after her story on him. He thinks she did it intentionally."

"What do you think?"

She looked at Zelina for a long moment. "Honestly, I wouldn't put it past her, but I don't know for sure. Maybe someone else knows. Then there's Sherri, Melissa, and Yvonne. They are also reporters. Yvonne does a lot of our research. She might know something."

"Where can we find these women?" I asked.

"Follow me. Mr. Wilt said that you might want to speak with us and that we were supposed to make ourselves available." We followed her out of the room to the back space that was filled with fifteen cubicles.

"You guys are low on space?" asked Zelina.

"Takes an army to get the news to your televisions." She pointed to the back cubicles. "They're back there."

I interviewed Yvonne, while Zelina interviewed Melissa.

"Hello, Yvonne. Do you have a moment?" I held up my badge. Her cubicle smelled like vanilla and caramel.

"Mr. Wilt said you might want to talk to her coworkers. I can't believe this happened to her, but I'm not too surprised." She closed the folder on her desk and pushed it away. "Please have a seat."

Yvonne's cubicle was clean. Everything was in its place and the trash can was empty. I wished my desk was that clean. My desk was littered with folders from cases I still needed to finish reports on. It seemed like as soon as I started to write one up, another case came along begging for my attention.

"So what do you want to know?" She smiled. Yvonne was a beautiful black woman with honey brown hair, big hazel eyes. She was even more stunning in person than she was on TV, and she looked beautiful on TV.

"Well, why aren't you that surprised? Did you have a problem with her?"

She inhaled sharply. "Olivia was an amazing reporter. She was great at getting to the truth and figuring things out. She was also great at research. She was the prefect news anchor."

"I sense a but coming," Zelina said.

"If you were on camera, she was wonderful. But behind the camera, she just… if you couldn't help her, she had no time for you."

"Really?"

She nodded. "Yeah, really. If you couldn't help her with a story or help her figure out an angle, she didn't need you. Her people skills sucked. She couldn't read a room. She couldn't sympathize with her coworkers, like she could with victims of a crime."

"Is there a specific instance where she couldn't read the room?" Reading the room could be hard for anyone. Sometimes I had a hard time myself.

"One of our anchors was celebrating his first big piece that he had done himself. He was so excited. I had worked with him myself and was so proud of him. Olivia found a way to shit all over him. Everyone was happy for him and patting him on the back. She walks in and sees how happy we are and assumes that he's being fired. She turned to him and said, "Oh, did Mr. Wilt finally fire you? He said he would a couple of weeks ago if you couldn't prove your usefulness. And you haven't done that yet."

"Wow. That's—wow."

"Rude as hell. He transferred out of here a few months later, and almost definitely because of her. Great journalist, good attention to detail, but he was too slow to work here. He was better off at a newspaper or magazine."

"Is he still in town?"

She shook her head. "He lives in New York, now. Got a job at a publishing house. He's doing great."

"Can you think of anyone that might have wanted to hurt her?"

A low chuckle cut through the silence. "Most people that met her. She was nice until you get in her way and then the claws came out. She didn't stop until she drew blood."

Zelina heard pretty much the same thing from Melissa. We both spoke to Sherri, and she seemed annoyed by our questions.

"I can't imagine anyone in this office killing her. Not like that."

"We heard she wasn't the best person to get along with," I said.

"Huh, that's an understatement. I brought in a story I wanted to cover. Witnesses came to me and said they would only speak to me about it. I took it to Wilt. I don't know how she heard about it—I really don't, but..." She took in a long deep breath. "When I got it approved and went to interview the witness, she's already there. I still don't know what she told him, but he wouldn't even look at me."

"She bad mouthed you?" asked Zelina.

She laughed. "Yeah, she did. He would only talk to her, and she got the story, and then she became a news anchor."

I leaned back in the chair. "I wasn't expecting to hear you say that." Usually when we were investigating a missing person the people in their lives always talked about how great they were and how good and nice... but not these people. They weren't holding back. "Thank you for speaking with us. If you think of anything else, please let us know." I handed her my card.

She smiled. "I will."

As I walked away, I doubted she would call us if she thought of anything that might help us. This was one of the few cases where we interviewed people who knew the victim and they didn't try to make it seem like the person was perfect. Like they could do no wrong, and would never have done anything that would make someone want to kill them.

Her coworkers were brutally honest. A complete contrast to what her mother and father said. She was ambitious, but I believed you could still do so without being ruthless and cruel. Olivia hadn't gotten that message. On one hand, her commitment to the truth was commendable. Many journalists and reporters just wanted a story that would get them noticed. They didn't care if they had to make it up as long as it got attention.

CHAPTER FIFTEEN

Logan Elwood

"SO WE ARE GOING ON A ROAD TRIP?" ISAAC SIPPED HIS COFFEE, regarding the question.

"I want to go on a road trip!"

"You have to go to school, Dani." I placed another piece of sausage on her plate.

"Uncle Sac has to go to work. If he can miss a day, why can't I?"

"Solid point," said Sac before he took another sip.

"Both of you, stop being difficult." His lips curled into a smile. Riley told me not to go by myself. That's what I was trying to do. She suggested that I take Isaac with me because he could handle himself. "The detective you like so much told me to take you with me."

His smile got wider. "Well since she suggested it, I guess I'll go and back you up."

"And me saying it meant nothing?"

"I wouldn't say nothing."

"You guys are so funny." Dani finished her bacon and placed her plate in the sink. "Really, really weird."

I laughed as she walked away. "I guess we are a little strange." I was relieved that Sac agreed to go with me. I would never tell him that, but it did make me feel better about going. I would go on my own, but it was nice knowing I didn't have to.

I was eager to meet Bianca, and I didn't think that she was going to hurt me or set me up or anything. That being said, I had a bad feeling. Like she was going to tell me something that would be hard to hear. I felt it in my bones that day was not going to go well. It'd be nice to have someone there with me. Someone I could lean on for support.

We left after Dani went to school. I could tell by the look in Bonnie's eyes she didn't think we should go.

"I understand you *want* answers, but you don't need them. You don't have to know about the fire. That girl is not getting custody of Dani." She looked at Isaac. "You two shouldn't go."

"Don't worry." Isaac clapped a hand on my back. "I'll take care of him. I promise."

She shook her head. "That's not what I'm worried about." She sighed as she stepped away from the door. I hugged her before we left. I had the same worries, so I understood where she was coming from. And I knew that I didn't have to go looking for answers, but I needed to know. It was like a compulsion at this point. I had to know.

Isaac typed the address into his phone. The GPS lady blurted out directions as we pulled out of the driveway. Bianca lived in a small town a four-hour drive from my house. I hoped it was worth it.

"Is this really about Jamie?" asked Isaac as we drove .

"It's about a lot of things. I just can't wrap my head around this. I have a lot of questions."

"About Jamie? Or Marie?"

Silence hung in the air like smoke, thick and suffocating. I didn't know how to answer. "Both, I guess. I don't know. Knowing Jamie might have been involved makes me wonder if Marie knew or not. And if she did, how could she protect her for all these years?"

"They were sisters. You protect the people you love."

I shook my head. "Not if they committed murder. You don't protect them for that."

"What, you wouldn't protect me if I murdered someone? Damn, I was counting on you ..."

I rolled my eyes. "I'm serious, Sac."

We laughed a bit about it, but it hung heavy in the car around us. Isaac's fingers gripped the wheel for a moment and then relaxed. Silence clawed back into the car as our conversations tapered off.

After four hours in the car we pulled into the parking lot of the salon Bianca worked at. I sent her a text and then got out of the truck. "Wait here. I told her I'd be alone."

Isaac drew in a long slow breath, and I closed the car door. It was clear he didn't like the idea of me going in alone, but I didn't want to overwhelm her. Just as I neared the door a woman stuck her head out. "I take it you're Logan?"

I nodded. She ushered me inside. "Come back here." The salon was virtually empty with three customers getting their hair washed. I followed her out of the salon area, down a short hallway, and into what I assumed was the employee break room. It was filled with all kinds of snacks and had a coffee maker on the counter. I sat at one of the small round tables. She sat across from me.

Once we were seated, I could finally get a good look at her. Bianca had been in the fire. Part of her neck still had the scars. The scarred flesh formed a point right next to her ear.

"So Jamie is your sister-in-law?" She shook her head. "That's rough."

"Tell me about it. It wasn't good even when Marie was alive."

"Is that why you're looking into it?"

"I guess so," I said. "I know it must be hard, but... I have to know what happened."

"I don't know a lot," she started. "Once I got out and saw the fire trucks they whisked me away. I didn't even notice I was burned until I got out. Only then did it feel like my body was on fire." She took a long deep breath. "So... on that night, everything seemed like business as usual. At night before bed, they forced us to go to the chapel and pray. So I did that. They had us divided by age. Jamie was in my group. She and her roommate slept across the hall. I didn't see her in the chapel, which was odd because it was mandatory. The nuns watched us constantly. Sister Isabella noticed Jamie wasn't there and asked us about her, but no one had seen her since dinner. She left to look for her. She was pissed too."

"Did Jamie get into trouble often?"

A ghost of a smile touched her lips. "She did. She was always getting into something. And she could never just sit still. It was obvious she didn't want to be there. None of us did. After prayer we went back to our rooms. Lights out by nine. Only... I got up to go to the bathroom and the door was open, my roommate was in the hallway. I asked her what was going on and she said she heard someone screaming. I waited a few minutes and didn't hear anything, so I went to the bathroom. The bathroom on our floor was out of order, so I had to go down two floors. I rounded the corner and heard arguing, I couldn't tell who it was though, and I really had to pee, so I did my business. When I got out, I saw the smoke."

"That means it started on the bottom floors?"

"Right. It was in the middle of the night, and I was confused. I thought one of the nuns might have left the oven on and fallen asleep. I headed toward the kitchen, and as soon as I opened the door, I saw the fire. I mean, it was everywhere. I thought I saw someone on the ground, and I tried to go in, but someone grabbed me by the back of my shirt and pulled me out. It was one of the nuns. She pointed down the hallway when I tried to tell her there was someone in there. There were flames on the ceiling. It was so hot. So hot. She said we need to warn who we can. I ran back upstairs and started banging on doors, screaming about the fire. I started at the top and worked my way down, screaming and banging and trying to help who I could. She did the same for the nuns and the other workers. Girls left their rooms, smelled the smoke. I screamed for them to run, and they did. I made it out, but Sister Susan didn't. She never made it out of the nuns' quarters. She saved a lot of people though."

Her voice trailed off for a moment as she took a minute to remember the woman that saved her life.

"When I got outside, I didn't notice that my nightdress had been burned. I was just running trying to get the girls out. When I got outside, off to the left I saw Jamie. I never liked her. She leaned way too hard on her sister. Marie protected her. I don't know if it was because of the age gap, and she viewed Jamie as... I don't know... a child that needed protecting, or if it was because Marie knew what it was like in that school and felt sorry for her. But I saw them. Marie had her arms wrapped around Jamie, and Jamie was crying."

I blinked. my back straightened immediately. "Marie was there?"

Her shoulders tensed. "I don't know how or when she got there. She might have seen the fire, because by the time I got out the sky was lit up with the flames. People started coming in from the surrounding areas. I thought it was nice of them to try to help, but by then it was too late."

"When you pounded on the rooms on your floor, was Jamie in her room?"

She shook her head. "Her roommate was there by herself, and she hadn't seen her." She stared at the table for a long minute. "I should also mention that the nun they found in the kitchen was Sister Isabella, the one who went looking for her. I never thought that was a coincidence. I had no proof she did anything. None of us did, but I always felt like she knew something, or did something. Marie vouched for her though."

"What do you mean she vouched for her?"

She sighed. "Marie said that Jamie was with her. She said she came there that night because she missed her sister and wanted to see her. That Jamie missed her too, and didn't like being there. She said Jamie was outside with her, and that was why she didn't have any soot or smoke or anything on her. But the night you come to see your sister just happens to be the night the place is burned down? That bothered me."

"That is curious. Who called the fire department?"

"I don't think they ever figured that out. There was a payphone not far from the school, they thought someone used that to call them. The call didn't come from the school. I think everyone was just trying to get out."

"Understandable. I never knew she was there that night. I just learned about the fire a few weeks ago."

"Marie never mentioned it? That's odd, but in a way I kind of understand it. I don't mention it too often either. It was a horrible night. Horrible. I'd try to forget it, but it's pretty much seared into my flesh."

"I'm so sorry that happened to you."

She waved her hand dismissively. "I don't have any proof that Jamie started that fire. I always thought she did and if she didn't, she knows how it started. She knows what happened and just refused to say it. But it gave her what she wanted. She hated being there. She hated being away from her sister... I tell you her obsession with Marie was... it knew no bounds. Because of the fire she was able to go home."

I shook my head. "Even back then? She was always obsessed with Marie when we were together too."

Bianca nodded. "She always had to be up under her. For starters, I heard Marie got a boyfriend which was surprising because she didn't really like talking to people or being touched. One night, I heard they were fooling around in the back of his truck, and Jamie was watching them. Marie caught her peering into the car while they were doing it."

I leaned back in my chair. I was surprised, but I wasn't surprised. It was exactly what I expected Jamie to do. "What did Marie do?"

"I heard she gave her a show and before they finished, Jamie stalked off back to the house. Jamie didn't talk to her for a week."

"She wanted all of Marie's attention. She never wanted her to care about anyone but her."

"Exactly. It was a bizarre ass relationship. I love my sister too, but everybody needs their space every now and then. Jamie just couldn't understand that." She checked her watch. "That's it for my break."

I stood up. "Thank you so much for talking to me. I really appreciate it. No one else will."

She shrugged. "I know. They just want to forget that night ever happened. And some of them are dead."

"I thought a lot of you survived the fire."

She inched toward the doorway. "Initially we did. But the death toll went from thirty to sixty-five over the years. Smoke inhalation. Lung cancer from breathing in the smoke and other fumes. I mean, the building was mostly asbestos. Some died from their injuries. It took a while, but eventually the fire killed sixty-five people."

My mouth hung open. That was something I didn't know. "Thank you so much for speaking with me." She nodded. I followed her out of the room and back from where I came. Isaac straightened up when I neared the truck. He was on the phone.

"I got to go. I'll call you later." He hung up as I climbed in.

"How's Nicole?"

"She's good. Wanted to check on you."

I sighed. "We need to stop somewhere to eat, and I'll tell you everything she told me." I shook my head. I felt his eyes on me, so I looked out the window. I didn't want to talk about it now. I still needed time to process my thoughts. I couldn't believe most of what she said. Marie was there that night? That couldn't have been right. Maybe it was just someone that looked like her. I would have said that earlier, but I didn't want to challenge her memory and make her defensive. But if Marie had seen that fire and knew Jamie did it, how could she not say anything?

CHAPTER SIXTEEN

Riley Quinn

B ASED ON WHAT WE WERE TOLD BY OLIVIA'S COWORKERS WE HAD
new leads to chase. Her coworker Walter—who resented her over a
promotion she received that he felt he was entitled to—was easy to
find, and he wasn't happy to see us. Walter sat on the sofa in his home
drinking a cup of coffee.

"I'm surprised someone actually had the balls to kill her. They did
the world a favor."

"You're making yourself an even bigger suspect when you talk like
that, Walt." His wife sat next to him, shaking her head and sighing.
Judging by the look on her face when we stopped by, she expected to
hear from us. It was like she was waiting for us to arrive. On the coffee
table were coffee and pastries she had set out for us.

"You should listen to your wife," I said. "We just want to ask you a
few questions about Olivia. To start: why do you hate her so much?"

She leaned back on the sofa and sighed. I was sure she had heard this story a thousand times. Walter seemed like the kind of guy to harp on things. Even though he no longer worked at the news station, he probably talked about it at length, and his wife was the only one around that could hear him.

"She stole my promotion," he spat. "That's what she was... a thief. She stole stories, witnesses."

"Yeah, we heard about an instance when she did that," I said.

He laughed. "An instance! I brought in a story I really, really wanted to work on. I found a few sources and had most of it written. And then here she comes. I don't know how she knew about it. Well, she might have seen it on my desk. But anyway, she talked to my sources, and I don't know what she said to them, but they stopped returning my calls. Next thing I know she was doing the piece. She changed it around, but it was my story."

"Did you call her out on it?" asked Zelina. That was exactly what she would have done. Zelina would have called her out on her shit in front of everyone. She might have even done it on air.

"I tried. She told me I was exaggerating. She told me my story was missing key facts that my sources tried to tell me, but I wasn't listening. She said she made the story better. That it should have been told from a younger perspective to really get the point across."

"Damn," said Zelina.

He gestured wildly. "That's what I said! No one came to my defense. They agreed with her, the younger perspective made the story better. They told me to let it go. And it was that story that got her the anchor job. I busted my ass for years trying to get that job and here comes this rookie with a pretty face and takes the job that I should have gotten!"

His wife's eyes darted my way for a brief second, then she went back to staring out the window. A smile pulled at the corner of my mouth, and I tried my best to push it down. Apparently, she thought he should let it go too.

"So... did you kill her?" I asked.

The look of shock and disgusted embedded in his face and eyes. "Of course not. I waws furious at her, but I wouldn't kill anyone. Least of all her. I just hated the way she worked. There was no respect. No honor. No talking to me, person to person. She saw a story and nothing else. As long as she got the story, everyone else be damned. And that might work in a big city where everyone is fighting to get to the top, but this is a small town with small news problems. It wasn't worth all that."

STRANGERS IN THE PINES

I didn't like him when I walked in, and I really didn't like him now. But that being said, he made a few good points and reiterated some talking points her other coworkers said.

"Olivia was like a dog with a bone when she got a good story. Not even a good story, any story," he continued. "She was focused on getting to the truth, and while that made her a great journalist, it made her horrible to work with."

"Well, we have to ask, where were you Friday night?"

He glared at me and then his eyes softened. "I know. I know how this works. My wife's book club meets on Friday night at the house, and I went to my poker club. I'll give you their names and numbers."

"That would be great, thank you."

He got up to get the information and as he left, his wife leaned forward. She opened her mouth to say something. Walter entered the room, and she leaned back. He returned to the living room with a slip of paper. "These are the guys, and I was there until a little after midnight."

I took the paper and glanced on it. "Okay. We'll check this out. Who do you think might have killed her?"

"Someone she pissed off. Someone she did wrong. That's a long list, I imagine."

"But not you."

"I swear, it wasn't me," he insisted.

"I'll walk you out. Want any pastries for the road?" His wife did her best to keep the peace.

I took one of the blueberry Danishes and Zelina took a butter cookie. She followed us to the door, while Walter stayed in the living room. She walked us out and pulled the door behind her.

"There's something else you should know," she whispered. "It was more than just stealing the story. She got the promotion because she was more personable than him, and likable. My husband was good at his job, but the camera and the audience like her approach better. He was never going to get the anchor job because the viewers didn't trust him. That's why she got the promotion, but he hates for anyone to bring that up."

I ran my hand through my hair. "Thank you."

She ducked back inside the house and locked the door. Now what his wife said made a lot of sense. He didn't seem that personable or likable in person. I couldn't imagine how much that translated on camera.

"Okay. Who's next?"

"Let's check out Terrell Rayner. Apparently he left a bunch of angry and threatening voicemails to the station after her story on him released," Zelina said. "I listened to the messages, and they were … pretty rough."

"What was the story about?" I asked as we got back in the car.

"She interviewed him because his wife went missing," she explained. "But listening to the voicemails, it seems he was pretty unhappy with how it came out on the show in the end."

"Sounds like we need to watch that tape," I said.

We went back to the station after getting the taped interview with Terrell Rayner from the news station. I was eager to see it. We set it up in the conference room and pressed play. We huddled around the TV and even Captain Williams came to watch it.

It was hard to watch. Terrell was barely holding back tears as Olivia interviewed him as they sat on sofas across from each other. At first, she was sympathetic. His wife had gone missing and he wanted to get the word out, hoping someone had seen her or knew anything. He was desperate, truly trying to get any information he could.

Olivia put on the perfect face. She was comforting, sincere, and sympathetic. But I could see the coldness in her eyes.

"Mr. Rayner, some of the rumors around town are saying that you killed your wife. Do you care to comment on that?"

"What?"

"I have information from a reliable source that says that the alibi you provided to police was a lie. You claim that you went out for a drink at Ricky's Bar that night, but no witnesses have been able to corroborate this."

Terrell's face flared in anger. "How dare you! I don't know what you're talking about—"

"Do you care to provide an explanation for this discrepancy? On the record?" Olivia smiled sweetly. Cruelly.

"I—I—I swear, I was at Buddy's!" he said. "And when I came home, she was gone!"

"Do you care to explain why there's no security footage of you at the bar that night?"

He threw up his hands. "How should I know? I don't work there!"

"That's a little convenient, isn't it?" Olivia pressed.

"Where are you getting this information?" he demanded. "Jasmine is missing and … and you're trying to act like I did something? What the hell is wrong with you?"

Terrell was getting visibly agitated now. He was clenching and unclenching his fists and breathing heavily.

"I'm just looking for the truth, Mr. Rayner."

"I can't believe this. I thought you could help me. This interview is over." He ripped the microphone clip from his shirt and stormed away, leaving the station in a huff.

"Sir—"

Terrell released a storm of curse words that were loud enough that, even without his microphone, they had to bleep them out.

Olivia shook her head and turned to the camera. "And there you have it, folks. Reporting the truth, and only the truth. This has been Olivia Tucker for Channel Seven News."

"Damn... she really made him look guilty," I said when I turned off the video. "I mean... he really seemed guilty." I knew better than to listen to rumors and base investigations off of them, but she painted a pretty damning picture.

"I wonder if she did that on purpose?" Zelina leaned back. "Like she edited things to make it seem even worse than it was."

"It would make for a better story than a man that loves, and is worried about, his wife. Especially with all the true crime docs out there."

My fingers drummed against the table. I could see why he would be upset. "We need to talk to him."

Terrell let us in his house and threw himself down in the same chair as he did in the video. Only this time there were four beer bottles on the table next to him and one in his hand.

"What do the police want?" His words came out slow and jumbled.

"Well, we wanted to ask you a few questions about your interview with Olivia Tucker—"

"I didn't kill that bitch!"

"Okay," I said slowly. "Good to know." I wanted to sit down, but there was nowhere to sit. The sofa was covered in newspaper clippings. Bottles were strewn all over the floor. He had become a drunk after the interview. Actually, I wasn't sure if he had started drinking after the interview or when his wife went missing. "I watched the interview, and I have to ask, why did you do it? She made you look pretty bad."

"You don't think I know that? She told me she wanted to help get the word out about Jasmine. Get someone looking for her." He lifted the beer to his lips and drank deep. "I thought she was going to help me. She was so nice, but then she started asking me all the questions, and I got flustered and confused and I wanted to stop. But she said that if I did people would think that I had something to hide. It didn't matter though. People think that anyway."

"She thought I killed Jasmine the second she walked through the door. She just used the interview to push her agenda."

"We noticed. Have you had any contact with her?"

He finished his beer. "I tried. I called the station a bunch."

"We noticed," Zelina said. "Some of the messages you left were... interesting."

"I was drunk and angry at her, okay? I said some shit in those messages but I wouldn't have killed her."

I had to give him credit for that. The messages had been filled with insults and cursing, but there was never any threats.

"She answered one call and said she was just making the kind of story people wanted to see. And that I couldn't sue her because she never said I killed my wife. She just asked questions, and I answered them. If I looked like a killer that meant that I made myself look like a killer."

"Has your wife been found?"

He laughed bitterly. "You wanna hear something funny? She left me. Jasmine wasn't missing or killed or kidnapped. None of it. She packed her shit and left and didn't say anything. Her mother found out she was in Canada with her boyfriend, who she was dating while we were married."

My jaw fell open. That wasn't the answer I was expecting. "I don't know what to say to that."

"Yeah... I didn't either. She could have left me a note or something. Sent me a text after she left."

"How long did it take for the police to get that information?" asked Zelina.

"A year. She was gone for a *year* and never thought to say anything, and that's what I still don't understand. They were looking at me for her murder. How did she not know I was a suspect and why didn't she say anything? And in the end, she didn't come forward, her mother did. I didn't know she hated me that much."

"Was that information released?" asked Zelina.

He laughed bitterly. "Didn't matter. It was a year later. Everyone, all my friends and so-called family had already deserted me. I can't understand that anyone in my life thought I could have done something like that."

I sighed. I felt sorry for him. He got screwed in every direction "I still have to ask for your alibi last Friday night."

He smiled. "Well that's easy. I was at Ricky's bar. I'm there most nights until closing."

"Thank you. We'll check that."

I felt so bad for him when we left. To be honest, I hoped it ended better than the last time he'd used Ricky's Bar as an alibi.

"I wonder what would make his wife leave him like that without a word, and not come forward when he was on the verge of being arrested,." I said to Zelina at we left.

"Maybe she thought he wouldn't actually get arrested because there was no evidence. There was no blood or evidence left behind, which was why they didn't arrest him right off. She might have figured he would never go to prison for it so there was no point in coming forward."

"Good point." My forefinger tapped my knee. "She might... I'm guessing she didn't want him to know where she ran off to, and if she came forward, he'd have to be told. She's probably not even in Canada anymore."

CHAPTER SEVENTEEN

Riley Quinn

FROM TERRELL, WHO WAS STILL A PLAUSIBLE SUSPECT—TO ME AT least—we learned that Olivia had a few stalkers. When I asked him how he knew, that he said it was because she told him.

"We talked about all kinds of things before the camera started rolling. I told her how I had to avoid certain places now because I felt like people who thought I was responsible for my wife's disappearance were following me. She mentioned she had a couple of stalkers who followed her around too. She didn't think it was anything to worry about."

I half believed what he said. Many people with stalkers initially believe that it's no big deal. They think that the person will get tired or they'll just go away given time. And sometimes that's the case, but most of the time it isn't.

Celebrity stalkers often get violent believing that the person was their friend. Sometimes they try to kidnap them. Olivia wasn't a celebrity on a large scale, but she was a local celebrity. We went back to the station and asked for any letters or information on her stalkers. We were giving letters that made my skin crawl, but after searching through the depraved madness we found two promising suspects. A woman and a man. The woman surprised me. I knew that women could be stalkers, but usually, they were after men.

Our female suspect was right where we thought she was going to be: in front of Olivia's home. Her car was parked across the street two houses down.

Julie Collier was either waiting for Olivia to come home or she was waiting for the strong police presence in the area to leave.

Olivia was dead, so she was waiting for us to leave. My question was why? Why wait for all the cops to go away unless you needed to get something from the house, or you forgot something? Olivia was not killed inside her home so that thought was a bust.

I walked up to the car and tapped on the window. She jumped and stared at me for a long moment before rolling down the window.

"Yes?"

"Could you get out of the car?" I held up my badge. Zelina positioned herself in front of the car so she couldn't drive away. Julie's grip tightened on the wheel and for a second, I thought she was going to drive off anyway. Run Zelina down. But then sense took over and she took the key out of the ignition. It might have been the witnesses or maybe it was my hand on my gun. The car door opened, and she stepped out.

"I wasn't doing anything illegal."

"True." I glanced back at the house. "Not yet anyway. We were just curious as to why you were sitting out here like you're waiting for something."

She shoved her hands in her pockets. "I was just waiting."

"Well, my partner thought you might be waiting for officers to leave so you can enter the house and take something or plant something."

"Which is it?" asked Zelina.

"I haven't done anything."

"And yet we need you to come down to the station all the same."

"For what?"

"Well, we know that you stalked Olivia. You sent her creepy letters, and even followed her when she went on her runs. And we need to talk to you about that at the station."

Julie stared at me in disbelief like she couldn't believe we already knew who she was.

"Just for a talk, and if it turns out you had nothing to do with it, we'll bring you back to your car." I slammed the car door and guided her back to our car. She was reluctant at first, but we didn't really give her an option.

Back at the station she sat in an interrogation room visibly annoyed that she had to be there.

"I would never hurt Olivia. I loved her. She was my best friend."

My eyebrows lifted slightly. *Her best friend? Really?* "I see. Are you sure she was your best friend?"

"Of course. We talked all the time, and we went running together."

"Okay. That's good to know. Olivia could really use a friend right now. We need you to tell us everything you know about her, because right now people are saying a lot of mean things."

"About Liv? She didn't have a mean bone in her body. She was so kind. She just wanted to get to the truth and sometimes that made people angry. But it wasn't her fault."

"Right. Can you think of an instance? When she got so focused on the truth and someone was mad at her?"

Julie fidgeted with her fingers. "It happened all the time. She was always on a mission to get to the bottom of things. That's what made her special. I remember seeing her on the news covering this missing woman, and her husband was of course the prime suspect. When I finished watching I knew he did it. I knew. But he was pretty pissed because he said it made him look guilty. I just think it revealed his true self to the town. That's what she did, she revealed the truth. She was like a mirror." The way her lips curled into a smile was unnerving. She was truly obsessed with Olivia and believed she was her friend.

"Did you and Olvia go for a run Friday night?"

She shook her head. "Unfortunately, I was in the emergency room."

"What happened?"

She rolled her eyes. "I was helping my sister move. I didn't want to, but I had promised her so I kind of had to. We were moving her dresser down the stairs, and I slipped. I thought I broke my ankle. It was just sprained, but then it blew up and I couldn't get it in my shoe. She took me to the emergency room. Took all night."

"How is it now?"

"It's wrapped up. Right now it feels okay."

While she talked, I sent a text to Zelina so she could check her alibi. "Okay. I'm going to make sure you were where you said you were, and if so, I'll get an officer to take you back to your car. But I need you to go home. No more sitting outside her house. She isn't there anymore. And I don't want you disturbing anything in her home."

Her head lowered like a child getting scolded by a parent. I walked out of the room and back to my desk. I didn't peg her for a killer. She was strange. Very strange, but a murderer? I wasn't sure. She seemed more childlike than anything.

"You checking her alibi?"

"Yep."

"Okay, while you do that, I'll start looking for Alexander Choi." He was her other stalker, but a bit more elusive. We hadn't been able to find him, which immediately made me suspicious. He did have a record, and according to his neighbors, he was a peeping tom. I went to his home with a few officers, to speak to his neighbors, while Zelina went to get a warrant for his home.

"I heard he was peeping on some of his neighbors."

The neighbor to his left was the only one home. She eyed me for a long moment behind her screen door before opening it and leaning on the door frame. "That man is a menace. It's about time you did something about him."

"What has he done?"

"What hasn't he done?" She recounted several instances where Alex spied on her and her daughter. How he spied on the neighbors across the street and watched the women sitting poolside on his other neighbor's patio. "He's always watching. He told me that when I moved in and I thought great, you know. It's good to have someone watching out for us, but that wasn't what he meant. He was watching *us*—not looking for intruders. Just watching us. It's so creepy I want to move, but I have nowhere to go."

"Have you seen him the past few days?"

"Not for the last couple of days, and I've been looking for him. I got two teenage girls, and I don't let them go out in the backyard or to the pool next door if he's home."

"That's understandable."

"It's been nice here the past couple of days because he hasn't been here. Felt like we could actually breathe and have fun. It won't last though. He'll come back eventually."

"When was the last time you saw him?"

Her fingers drummed against the screen door. "Um, Sunday. I got excited because I saw him loading bags in his car. I thought he was going on a trip or something."

"Okay. Thank you for speaking with me." I handed her my card and told her that if he did come back to the house to give me a call.

"What did he do?"

"We aren't sure yet, but we need to ask him a few questions."

She tucked a clump of auburn hair behind her ear as she eyed the street. She looked at our cars for a moment more before stepping back into her house and closing the door. Just as I reached the driveway of Alex's house, Zelina pulled up. She jumped out of the car, her lips pressed into a thin hard line.

"Julie was at the emergency room, and she didn't leave until almost ten. They were backed up. As for the warrant," she held up a slip of paper. "Only things that are in plain sight."

"Got it."

I didn't want to search Alex's home. One look at it turned my stomach. I would let the officers handle it. I mostly just looked at things. His home was sparsely decorated. There was only enough there for one person. One bed. One set of sheets. Three, maybe four bath towels. One bowl, plate, cutlery, and glass. All the food in his fridge was spoiled, but his liquor cabinet was well stocked. "More concerned with drinking than eating. Not a good sign."

CHAPTER EIGHTEEN

Logan Elwood

WE STOPPED AT A STEAKHOUSE ON OUR WAY HOME. THE CAR RIDE was relatively silent. What Bianca told me percolated in my mind over and over again. I followed Isaac into the steakhouse. We were seated right away, as the place was practically vacant. It was late, but it smelled like the kitchen was still open, and the waitress seemed nice. She didn't look at us as if we were ruining her night for coming in so late.

Isaac commented on that fact once she walked away to give us time to look through the menu. "I don't think they were close to closing."

"How do you know?" I flipped through the menu looking for something that wasn't too heavy or too light. I was already tired, and I didn't think my stomach could handle anything heavy before the big drive home.

"I know that look. I've given it myself a few times. When we're closing down for the night, and someone walks in five minutes before we lock the doors... you can feel the anger pulsing through the room. Customers never seem to take the hint though."

After the waitress took our orders and brought our drinks, only then did I start talking, really talking. I told him everything Bianca told me, and in the order she told it to me. Isaac sipped his drink slowly. He had stopped drinking so much a while ago and now he kept it to two beers or one strong drink.

He sipped his bourbon while I talked, and when I was quiet, he leaned back in his chair and sighed. "I don't know what to say. I didn't think you were going to find anything, honestly. And I'm still not sure what to make of it."

Silence stretched between us for a long time, enveloping us like a cocoon. We ate in silence. Only after I finished my steak and mushroom burger did I feel human again. I had been careful not to eat anything before we left, even though I was hungry. My nerves were shot. I didn't think I could put anything on my stomach. The uncertainty of how the conversation would play out frayed my nerves. Thankfully it was better than I expected. Bianca was nicer than I thought she would be. I mean here I was, someone she didn't know that just burst into her life asking questions about a horrific night in her teens.

I wasn't sure if I would have talked to me, but I was glad she did. Neither of us knew what to say or what to do with the information. My mind was still processing everything when Isaac paid for the check. That surprised me. I felt my eyebrows lift when he placed his debit card on the check.

"Look at you."

He grinned. "Well, it's the least I could do." We settled back into a comfortable silence on the way home. I tried calling Everly again when we pulled into the driveway. She still wasn't answering. I left a voicemail telling her how much I needed to talk to her. I had a few questions I wanted to ask her.

"Maybe she's washed her hands of the whole thing," said Isaac as he opened the front door. "I wouldn't blame her. This shit is a lot."

"Yeah, me either." I sighed as I strolled into the living room. I wouldn't have been upset if that was what she had decided to do. She knew she couldn't talk Jamie out of it and the frustration might have gotten the better of her. Everly didn't have to babysit her daughter anymore or try to get her out of trouble. Jamie was an adult, responsible for her own actions, and needed to be held accountable. I didn't want to talk her into coming back or try to get her to deal with Jamie. I mostly wanted to make sure she was okay because I hadn't heard from

STRANGERS IN THE PINES

her since the mediation. There was also the matter of the million questions I needed to ask her about her daughters. Those two things were my main priority.

Bonnie sat on the sofa knitting. She smiled at me when I sat in the chair across from her. Her smile wavered for a second before disappearing completely.

"I take it things didn't turn out well."

For the second time, I knew it wouldn't be the last I repeated what Bianca had told me. Word for word and in the order she said it.

Her fingers stopped moving, the blanket or whatever she was making, pooled in her lap.

"What I keep moving around in my mind is why she was crying. Bianca said Jamie was hugging Marie and crying. Why?" I struggled to puzzle through it.

Isaac joined us. "I thought about that too. I was wondering what made her cry. People dying in the fire would make most people cry, but I have a difficult time believing Jamie would cry over anyone but herself. Maybe Marie confronted her about the fire, and she turned on the waterworks."

"That seems plausible." My fingers drummed against my knee. "Something irks me about Marie being there, and I can't put my finger on it. It just doesn't feel right. How did she get there? Was her house close enough for her to walk? Did she have a car? These are the questions I want to ask her mother."

"You protect family," said Bonnie. "Even if that girl told Marie what went down, that's her little sister and she's going to protect her. No matter how she feels about her, she'll protect her. That might be why she never said anything."

I kind of understood that, but not fully. It wasn't something we did in my family. We didn't protect each other. My mother worked hard for years turning Isaac and me against each other. She liked it when we were fighting. If we weren't talking to each other, we were talking to her. I didn't think I would have protected Isaac like that when we were younger. Maybe now, but not then.

While Bonnie might have been right, it still left a bad taste in my mouth. I couldn't imagine Marie keeping it to herself. She was the most honest person I had ever known. She hated lying so much she couldn't do it. It didn't make sense, and no one could convince me otherwise.

We sat in the living room and talked quietly for a long time. Bonnie went to bed first and then it was just Sac and me. "You came in pretty late the other night and a couple of nights before that one." My eyebrow raised on its own. "Something you want to talk about?" I waited for him to tell me he had met someone. Or he and Nicole were hanging out more.

"Umm...yeah. Sometimes I go for a meeting after work. Sometimes it goes pretty late."

I leaned back and stared at him. *Meeting? What meeting?* He must have guessed I didn't know what he was talking about by the look on my face. He fidgeted in his seat for a moment.

"NA."

My body straightened immediately. My arms went rigid at my sides. "I didn't know you were in Narcotics Anonymous."

"I know. I was going to tell you, but never found the right time. Then things were going so well between us I didn't want to screw it up."

"How long have you been clean?"

"A few years. Four to be exact."

"I see." I didn't know what to say. I know Isaac had his problems, but I never knew concretely what they were. My mother would mention things here and there, but I was never sure whether to believe her or not. She was known to lie to one brother about the other. She was never to be trusted. "How's it going?"

"It's always difficult, but we push through. You know, one day at a time and all that. I found a nice group of people here during the meetings that have helped. Still looking for a sponsor here though. Mine is in the UK. But other than all that, I'm doing okay."

"Stressful situations make it worse, right?"

Isaac nodded slightly. "They do."

"This has been a stressful time."

He chuckled. "Yeah, but I've had worse. If it gets too much, I'll let you know. And then I'll go to a meeting."

"If you need anything, let me know. Even if it's just someone to talk to. I'm always here if you need me."

"That's good to know." Isaac stood up. "Good night. Don't stay up too late worrying about things you can't change."

I scoffed. "I'll do my best. Can't make any promises though."

He grinned and walked away. And then it was just me. I fought the urge to call Riley and tell her what I found. I wanted to, but I hadn't told her I was going, and I felt like she had a lecture brewing. I didn't want a lecture, I wanted answers, and I wanted people to stop telling me it didn't mean anything. It did. It had to.

If Jamie was responsible for a fire that killed over sixty people, I wanted to know. I needed to know. I needed her put away, for my safety. For Dani's safety.

Maybe I could call some of Marie's friends. I hadn't spoken to them in a while. After Marie died, our only reason for hanging out died with her. I still got Christmas cards and birthday cards for Dani, but that was a about it for most of them. There were two that checked in monthly to make sure that we were okay. Kay and Pen. If I needed to know anything about Marie's past they would tell me. I turned the conversation over and over in my mind while I sent both women a text and then went upstairs to bed. Bianca said Marie was no saint. And she talked about her like she knew her. Like they were friends or something.

Did Marie go to the school too? Was that how she knew exactly where to go and how to get there? The more I learned about Jamie the more curious I became of Marie's past. She never talked about these things with me. Or she kept her answers short and sweet.

Why hadn't I noticed it before?

I tossed and turned all night until finally I fell asleep. It felt like no sooner had I gone to sleep than it was time to get up. I checked my phone before my feet touched the ground. Kay had sent me a text back

I was just thinking about you guys. Would love to come out and see Dani. Hope you both are taking care of yourselves. Sure we can talk about Marie's past… what do you want to know? Better yet what brought this on?

I didn't know what to text back. I played with a few ideas, typing them out and then quickly discarding them. I settled on the truth. I told her about Jamie and what she was trying to do.

I will call you tomorrow!

Waiting around for the phone call was agonizing. I wanted to know what she knew, but I still had work to do. The patients I had to see seemed to drag on and on. I thought it was never going to stop.

Finally, noon came around and my phone rang. "Hey!"

"Jamie wants custody of Dani?"

Kay was the most direct of Marie's friends. She always said what was on her mind no matter the consequences. It was why I liked her. You always knew where you stood with her. I explained everything and included the mediation. She got really for a long moment.

"They will never give her custody. She has to know that."

"She still thinks there is a shot if she can show that I'm an unfit parent."

"You're not." She sighed. "I don't know a lot about Marie's life when she was a kid. She didn't talk about it much. Said it was a time in her life she'd rather forget. And that was her right, so I didn't push, but…"

to be real, I never liked Jamie. I don't think any of us did. She refused to let Marie breathe. Like if she didn't see or talk to her every day, Marie would forget about her. And Marie took care of Jamie. No matter what. Even when she didn't want to. Even when she was getting on her nerves."

"Yeah, I know."

"I do know that Jamie went to that school that burned down. And I know that afterwards, things were tense between them. It was the only time Jamie wasn't talking to Marie. And the way Pen explained it was that Marie was trying to get her attention. It was like they fed off each other. They needed the attention of the other to survive. Like a symbiotic relationship or something."

"I didn't know that. Pen would know more about Marie's past?"

"Yeah. She's known her the longest. I'll tell her you need to speak with her and it's dire. She'll call you. I can't believe Jamie—wait, yeah—I can. To her Dani is an extension of Marie. If she can't have one, she'll take the other."

"That's what I was thinking. It's just so strange. I mean, I love my brother, but not that much."

I heard the smile in her voice. "You two talking again?"

"Yeah. He's here with us. Dani loves him."

"That's so good. Marie always wanted you two to make up and be close again. She hated you two weren't close anymore. It made her sad sometimes. I'm glad you two are getting along."

"Yeah, it's been nice having him around." I would never say it out loud to him, but it actually was nice being able to sit and talk to him every day. We still had our moments of silence, but it was nowhere near how it used to be. I was thankful for that although I wasn't sure how he felt about it. "Thanks for speaking with me. So few people want to talk about Jamie."

She laughed. "I bet. From what I heard she was a little hellraiser. She was not a fan of people or animals. Pen said there were rumors that she killed some of the dogs in the neighborhood and that she hurt some kids her age. She did something to one kid had the whole family moving in the middle of the night."

"That doesn't surprise me."

"Me either." She inhaled sharply. "I have to go. Back to work. I'll be sure to give Pen your message and phone number."

"Thanks." I hung up the phone and sat back in my chair. *Wasn't killing animals the sign of a serial killer?*

It was a little concerning when I thought about it. I hadn't watched a lot of serial killer docs, but Nicole was well versed in psychopaths. So I brought it up to her.

"Killing animals is an early sign of serial killers. If you research any of them chances are that's where they started," she told me.

"I never knew that about her, and yet I'm still not surprised by it. I wonder if Marie knew about it. If she cared. If she was worried about it. I can't imagine her wanting Jamie anywhere near Dani if she knew what she was up to. I just can't see it."

Nicole shook her head and sat down in the chair across from my desk. "People are often blind when it comes to their own families. They don't want to see the bad. Marie probably did the same thing. She didn't want to think her sister was a bad person. But now you know, and you need to protect Dani."

I sighed. She was right. I needed to protect Dani now that Marie couldn't—or wouldn't, had she still been alive. It felt like the more I learned about Jamie, the more I learned about Marie. That was what I wanted. I never understood their relationship. But maybe now I was getting to some of the secrets that had been buried for a long time.

CHAPTER NINETEEN

Riley Quinn

THE SEARCH OF THE HOUSE TURNED UP NOTHING. EITHER ALEX Choi was a messy person, or he left in a hurry. Clothes strewn all over the bedroom. Balled up papers everywhere. Different pairs of shoes on the stairs. He packed as fast as he could and left. Who was after him? What if he thought it was only a matter of time before we figured out he had something to do with it.

"You stay here and continue going through the house. Maybe he forgot something. I'm going to talk to his ex-wife. Maybe she knows where he might have gone."

Zelina's head bobbed slightly before she followed a tech up the stairs.

The previous Mrs. Choi sat on her front porch as I pulled up in front of her house. I got out and her posture changed. She leaned forward her hands on the railing in front of her like she was ready to run back inside if need be. I held up my badge. Her shoulders relaxed slightly. She didn't lean back.

"I need to talk to you about your husband." I walked up the stairs.

"Ex…"

"Right, sorry. Your ex-husband. Are you two still close?"

She rolled her eyes. "Hell no. I see him in the grocery store? I leave my cart, and I walk out. We're not close. We have no reason to talk to each other because we don't have any children together. And yet he still calls me."

"I take it you don't answer."

"Of course not." She leaned back. "What is this about?"

"We're looking for him. Need to ask him a few questions about a case I'm working. Went to his house and he wasn't there. Neighbors said he left with a suitcase."

She laughed. "He doesn't have the money to go anywhere out of town, let alone out of state." She stood up. "I'll write down a few places he has been known to go. She returned with a slip of paper. Some of the places on the paper I recognized.

"Is this about that news anchor being murdered?"

I sighed. "I'm not allowed to discuss an ongoing investigation."

"So that's a yes then. I'm not surprised if he did kill her. He was obsessed with her. He wouldn't watch any other news station. He wrote her letters. She never wrote him back."

"Do you know why he was obsessed with her?"

She chuckled. "Alex was one of those guys that never got lucky in high school and fifteen years later still couldn't let it go."

"I see."

"He asked her out to a dance or something. I don't think it was prom, but it was a dance the school was having, and she declined. He thought she had a date, but she turned up at the dance by herself. And that seemed to really piss him off. Like he thought going with him would have been better than going by herself. It was so stupid. He never let it go. It was like he thought if she had said yes then maybe they would still be together, and his life would have turned out differently."

"Wow. Now that I didn't know."

"He tells people they were close in high school. If she wasn't dead, I'd say she wouldn't even be able to pick him out of a line up. Now his brother, well, he's a little… strange. That might be an understatement, but he is. I don't think he would hurt anyone, but if Alex needed some-one to take him in, he would do it."

"Thanks."

"I'd check out the bar first. He's there every day."

The bar was smoky inside. The bartender stared at me as soon as I walked in. I walked over.

"Haven't seen you in here?"

"I don't frequent bars." I held up my badge. "Have you seen Alex Choi?"

His lips curled into a smile. "Ma'am, he's here every day. Almost here more than me. He hasn't come in today, though. Which isn't like him."

"What do you mean?"

He shook his head. "He's an alcoholic, ma'am. Some days he's here from sun-up to closing. You can almost set your watch by him." He looked down at his watch. "He should have been here by now."

I looked around the room. It was pretty sparse. A woman and a man sat at a table near the stage talking and nursing their drinks. A man sat on the other side staring up at the ceiling as if he was contemplating his whole life.

I slid my card across the bar. "If you see him, please give me a call."

"Of course. And if you ever want a drink, you should come in. On the house of course."

I smiled despite myself as I walked out. Now where could he be? I scanned the area, my eyes settled on a motel. It was close to the bar and if he was hiding out it might be somewhere he thought no one would look for him. I stopped in and showed the clerk a picture of Alex on my phone.

"Nope. I mean—sometimes he stays here when he's too drunk to drive or walk home and no one will give him a ride. But he's not here now."

"Okay. Thank you."

My next stop was his brother's place. Before I left his ex-wife, she had told me all about how the brothers would drink together.

His brother Allan lived in a nice house. It appeared that he took care of it. The lawn was freshly cut, and the flowerbeds were neat and mulched. Nothing was out of place. I knocked on the door. I knocked again and the door creaked open. My heart sank into my feet. Something was wrong. My pulse rushed in my ears as I drew my weapon.

"Alex Choi! You in there?"

I pushed the door open a little further. The house was silent. I pushed the door open a little further. The house was silent. So still and dark. The hairs on the back of my neck stood straight up. A metallic taste stung the back of my throat.

The front door opened up into the living room and a long hallway. I needed to call for backup. Before I could reach into my back pocket I heard a noise. My head twisted to the left. There was a doorway without a door. Probably led to the kitchen. I inched forward, slowly with my gun drawn.

I peered into the doorway first before I walked through. When I looked into the room, it was the kitchen, and Alex stood near the kitchen table with a gun.

"You need to leave."

I walked into the kitchen. His brother sat at the kitchen table, his hands on the table. My heart stuttered in my chest. I should have called for backup before I entered. This was so stupid. I didn't know how many people were in the house. I didn't know how many weapons were in the home. *Stupid!*

"I can't do that, Alex. I just want to ask you a few questions."

"Bullshit! You think I killed Liv. You're here to kill me."

"No, I'm not. I just have a few questions for you, and if you didn't kill her and your alibi checks out, I'll be on my way. But first you need to drop the gun."

"No. You're here to kill me."

"Alex! If you're gonna shoot her then do it already. Before her backup comes! We can get out of here."

I looked at his brother. It was clear he was not on my side. I thought for a split second he might have some sense, but apparently whatever Alex was on, they were in it together.

"We can talk about this like normal people. No guns. Calmly."

"No. You're going to kill me, and I won't let that happen. Not now."

I watched his finger twitch near the trigger. Before he could pull the trigger, I did. My bullet blew through his thigh. He screamed and fell to the ground. I kicked the gun away from him. He groaned even louder.

"You shot me!"

"Don't you move." I pointed my gun at his brother who had jumped up from the table. He threw his hands up. Then I reached into my pocket and called for backup and an ambulance.

While we waited, I cuffed Alex to make sure he didn't run and get another gun, and then I bagged Alex's gun so no one else could get to it. When I was done, I leaned against the counter. My heart rocked against my ribs. It was hard to breathe. Not just because of the adrenaline coursing through my veins, but the house... there was a strong smell. Like something was rotting. A rat in the walls or something. Or several rats. The smell was strong. Too strong.

I yanked Alex to his feet and pushed him and his brother outside so I could breathe.

"I can't walk on my leg. You shot me."

"And I can't breathe in this house. How do you live here?"

"It's a roof," said his brother. "That's all I need."

I gulped in air. A moment later, officers pulled up followed by an ambulance.

"Finally. I'm bleeding to death here."

"No you're not. I didn't hit any major arteries."

"How do you know?"

"You'd be dead."

Paramedics jumped out of the ambulance and sprang into action. They tended to Alex while he whined about life being unfair and that he didn't do anything. His brother was quiet as officers led him to a car.

"You okay, Detective?"

I nodded. "Yeah, he didn't get a shot off. I want units to search the house. I think there's something dead in there. Might be a rat. Might not be. You'll have to search because it's dirty. I'll follow the ambulance to the hospital."

"Yes ma'am." The officer walked back to his car and picked up his radio.

I got in my car and followed the ambulance to the hospital. I had so many questions for Alex—the first one being if he didn't kill her, then why did he run? Guilty people, in most cases, don't take off before the police have a chance to ask them questions. Or before they even know they are on our radar. He was hiding something, and I was determined to figure out what that was.

I had to wait about thirty minutes before I could see him. At that time, Zelina called me to find out if I was okay and if I needed her.

"You always get into trouble when I'm not with you."

I shrugged even though I knew she couldn't see me. "I am seeing a pattern. But I'm okay. He didn't get any shots off and I just nicked him in the leg. He'll be fine, I think."

She laughed. "Okay. Meet me at the station when you're done."

"I will."

When I hung up the phone a nurse pointed at me. "You can see him now." She rolled her eyes before walking away.

He had only been in the hospital for thirty minutes and he was already getting on her nerves. I walked into the examination room. Alex was on the bed with a nurse to his left. She was taking his pulse and then she put a blood pressure cuff on his arm. "Don't take this off." She turned around and looked at me. She sighed before walking out the door and closing it behind her.

"You need to be nicer to the nurses or you might not make it out of here." I moved toward the bed. His right wrist was cuffed to the bed.

"What do you mean?"

"That was the second nurse I've seen that has rolled their eyes in reference to you."

He sputtered. "I'm in pain... you shot me!"

"And you'll note I didn't kill you, because I wasn't there to kill you."

He opened his mouth to fight back, but then closed it. "Well. You still shot me."

"I did. But back to why I am here. I need your alibi for last Friday."

I looked at the wall. "I didn't kill Liv. And you should know where I was since I was in holding."

I stared at him for a long moment before the words crawled out of my mouth. "What do you mean?"

"I was in holding. One of my neighbors called the cops on me. I don't know why; I wasn't doing anything. But they arrested me. I was there all night."

I rocked back on my heels. "Why did you run?!" My voice went several octaves higher than planned, but he was so infuriating. "If you knew you had an alibi why run from the cops? Why try to shoot me?"

"I don't know. Force of habit, I guess. I knew people would think I killed her as soon as I heard she was murdered. I know my ex-wife does."

"I'm so pissed at you. I could have killed you because of nothing. And why do you keep peeping on your neighbors? Either move or leave those people alone."

"I'm just lonely."

"If you stopped peeping on people, you might get some real friends. People might want to spend time with you."

He wrapped his left arm around himself and rolled onto his side. "Just leave me alone."

I sighed. "Get some therapy," I said on my way out the door.

CHAPTER TWENTY

Jamie Washington

JAMIE STARTED HER MORNING WITH A FRESH POT OF COFFEE AND A game plan. She would divide and conquer. She would follow a different target each day. It made things easier than trying to follow all of them during the day.

She started with Logan. After she finished her coffee, she stuffed two bottles of water into her backpack and headed out the door. Her phone vibrated in her back pocket, but she paid no mind to it. She didn't want to talk to anyone. She knew it was probably her husband anyway, and he was of no help to her right now, so she didn't have time for him.

She debated walking around to follow him, but he would be able to pick her out in a crowd. She drove instead, and since her windows were tinted, she was more relaxed. She stayed two cars behind him as he drove to work. He got out of his truck and went straight to work. A young black woman followed after him in purple scrubs.

Jamie sat out in her car drinking a bottle of water and reading a book, waiting for him to walk out. He had a lot of patients, young and old. They seemed upbeat when they left. Around noon, Logan and his nurse walked out of the office. Logan grinned when he saw the female cop he had become friendly with. Jamie didn't like it. He was already trying to replace her sister. Just that easy. Marie would be pissed if she could see him right now. She'd smack the shit out of him. Part of her wanted to walk up to them and smack both of them. That would have made her happy.

They flirted a little bit. She knew that was what they were doing even though she couldn't hear what they were saying. It was their body language. She leaned into him a little and he didn't pull away. A lot of eye contact and laughing. The group walked into the diner. Jamie rolled her eyes. It was going to be a long day.

Logan didn't do anything but work. Work and home. That was his life. Jamie followed him home and then back to work. One night he did something different, though. He took Dani to the beach. There was the cop and an older woman. *The nanny.* The two talked while Dani and the woman picked up shells along the beach.

Now he's involving Dani?

As if that cop could replace her mother. Jamie's blood boiled. He was trying to make her forget Marie. He was trying to replace her. Pretty soon Dani wouldn't know anything about her mother. She wouldn't even know what she looked like.

When Logan went to work, she was tired of staying in the car, so she sat on a bench across from the office. Her baseball cap pulled low, she doubted he'd even take a second look at her. She folded her arms and watched the people of the town walk around.

She saw Bonnie and Dani walking around. Jamie instantly straightened. She wanted to walk over to the girl and say hello, but the nanny would get in the way.

Instead, she just watched them. Logan joined them, and then the cop walked over to them while they looked at the pastries in the window of the bakery. Jamie's hands balled into fists. She squeezed so tight she thought she might have drawn blood. "What is he doing?"

Anger pulsed though her body. She didn't like the idea of Logan trying to replace Marie in Dani's life. To her, it was clear that was his intention. She couldn't make out what they were saying, but the flirting was clear as day. It wasn't just the cop that surprised her. She had thought Logan wasn't ready to date yet, not so soon after Marie died. At least that was how he acted. like the heartbroken widower who would never love another person again. He acted like he was still stuck on Marie. Like he couldn't live without her. But there he was, already grinning at another woman. Leaning in to talk to her. His arm brushed against her shoulder. Jamie rolled her eyes. The *detective* was around him a lot. She noticed how they ate lunch together most days. Even though the diner was nearly empty, with several open booths and tables, they always seemed to go out of their way to sit together.

That annoyed her. It irritated her that Logan was speaking to other women so soon after Marie died and that this woman thought she could take Marie's place. It was clear to Jamie that those were her intentions. The longer she stared at them the stronger her resolve to get Dani away from him and her.

"Why are you always around?" she whispered aloud.

She eyed the detective, a scowl deepening on her face.

"You okay?"

Jamie looked up. An older woman stood next to her. "Umm, yes. I'm fine. Just thinking."

"I talk to myself too when I'm thinking. It helps me sort through things."

"It does."

"Why don't you come to the coffee shop and get something to eat? Or just some coffee. Coffee helps me think too."

Jamie looked up and noticed that both parties were gone. She hadn't seen where they went, but she had an idea. Logan probably went back to work while the detective went somewhere else. She considered the offer. While he was at work she would have some free time.

"Sure. I could use something sweet." She stood up slowly and followed the woman across the street to the coffee shop. It smelled like coffee and a variety of sweets, with notes of vanilla, butter and chocolate. Her mouth watered instantly. She couldn't remember the last time she'd eaten. Had it been dinner with her neighbors? How many days ago was that?

The woman moved behind the counter while Jamie eyed the display case. She could pick out a few recognizable pastries, apple turnovers, cheese Danish, croissants, and an assortment of cakes. But there were a few she was not familiar with. "What is that?" Jamie pointed at a cake with nuts on the outside and a golden-brown frosting.

"That is a caramel crunch cake. Pecans and caramel frosting on the outside, vanilla bean cake underneath."

"That sounds good."

STRANGERS IN THE PINES

The woman smiled. "It is a best seller. If you're not in the mood for something sweet, we have a ham and cheese croissant, smoked salmon and brie croissant with apricot spread and red onions. I like that one because it's salty, sweet, and buttery all at the same time. We also have bacon, egg, and cheese sandwich on a brioche bun. We have some other savory items, but those are our popular favorites."

Jamie ordered the smoked salmon croissant, an apple and cheese Danish and an apple and oat milk latte. She chose a seat all the way in the back so she could watch who came through the door while she waited for her food. If she had known she was going to spend time in the coffee shop, she would have brought her laptop with her. She had a lot of preparations she needed to make before she could take Dani with her.

"I'm April Quinn, by the way." She set the plates of pastry and the large cup of coffee on the round table in front of Jamie. "You must be new to town. I don't recall seeing you here before."

Jamie shrugged. "I am fairly new. Not sure about staying just yet."

April pulled out the chair across from her and sat down. "Some people don't like small towns. Say there's not much to do and that is true in most cases, but Pine Brooke has its charms."

Jamie gave her best smile. "It does have its charms; I'm just not convinced yet." She turned the name April Quinn over and over in her mind while she took a bite of the croissant. It was flaky, and buttery, with a slight sweet and saltiness. She understood why it was a customer favorite. She had heard the name April Quinn before.

"I've lived in this town my whole life. Never lived in a large city although I've visited a few times. My father, he died when I was younger, loved this town. He never wanted to live anywhere else which slightly annoyed my mother. She said small town people were too nosey. But once he passed, the town really helped us out when we needed it. That wouldn't have happened in the city, so she stayed."

Something clicked in Jamie's mind. The officer that killed himself had a daughter named April. She stared at the woman in front of her, it could have been her. She looked old enough.

"What happened to your father?" Jamie paused for a moment. "I'm sorry, excuse me for asking. It's none of my business."

April waved a hand dismissively. "No matter. You live here long enough you'll hear the story eventually." She took a deep breath. "My father allegedly took some money from the station and then he killed himself in his patrol car before he left town."

"That doesn't make any sense. Why take the money and then kill yourself before you have time to leave?"

The corners of April's mouth turned upward slightly. "You sound like my mom. She never believed it, but she never said anything in his defense. She never questioned it or tried to get them to actually investigate his suicide. We were at the mercy of the town then, and she was pregnant with my brother at the time. The town helped us immensely, and she didn't want to ruffle any feathers. But she never believed it happened the way they said it did."

"What do you think?" Jamie sipped her coffee while she waited for an answer.

April sat back. "I don't know. It didn't seem like it was something he would have done. My brother said he was framed even though he wasn't born until after it happened. He was adamant and promised my mother he would figure it out and clear his name. I could never understand why someone would frame him for anything."

"Your brother figured it out?" Jamie realized she had touched a nerve by the way April's shoulders deflated and her expression hardened. "Sorry."

April shook her head like she was shaking a thought loose. When she stopped her smile returned. "No, I don't think so. He was a patrol officer for a while trying to work his way up to detective. He was really good at his job and the people in this town loved him because he really cared about them. Just like our father. He became detective, and then three months later he was killed in the line of duty. Shot while trying to apprehend a suspect."

Jamie straightened in her chair. It didn't sound right to her. Sure, it could have been a coincidence, but... it was a strange one. Both father and son killed in mysterious circumstances? Strange coincidence.

"It could just be a coincidence, but... I don't really believe in those. When my daughter said she wanted to join the police force I was a little worried, but she's stubborn and does not like being told what to do. I made her promise me she would never look into either of their cases. I had no proof they were linked, but I had a hunch. She had the same hunch apparently because she said she had already told herself she was not going to touch it."

"That's good. Might just be a coincidence, but better not to risk it."

She smiled. "I didn't mean to tell you all of that. I usually don't ramble like that."

"I've been told I bring that out in people." Jamie returned her smile. It wasn't a lie. She had been told by many people that she was a great listener. Easy to talk to. Jamie didn't know why people said that, considering most of the time she wasn't listening, but they never seemed to notice. But this time she was actually listening to April because she was interested in what she was saying. *This town might be more interesting than I thought.*

"Any of your other children in law enforcement?"

"I have a son that's a coroner, but that's about it. I'm glad too because I worry about my daughter a lot and I don't think I have the nerves or the strength for all of them to be cops."

"Seems to be the family profession. At least you worry about her. My parents never seem to worry about me."

April's eyebrow rose slightly. "I doubt that. All parents worry about their children whether they want to or not. We usually don't tell you. I never mention it to Riley because I don't want to annoy her. Also don't want to hover... she hates that. But I do worry, silently. Drive by her house at night until I see her car in the driveway, that way I know she's made it home safe."

"That's sweet." April's words were like a knife in Jamie's heart. Her mother never seemed to worry about her or cared about what she was doing. Not like this. April wanted to make sure her daughter was okay. Everly only wanted to make sure Jamie wasn't hurting other people. Marie only wanted to make sure Jamie didn't disrupt her life too often. Their concern was more about themselves than her. Having a mother that actually cared must have been an amazing feeling.

"Is your mother here with you or does she live in town?"

Jamie fought back a smile. Technically her mother did live in town now. Underground, but still in town. And she was there with her. Both of these were true, but not in the way April was thinking. "No. She lives in Dallas now."

"That's pretty far away."

"She never wanted to be too close to me."

"I can't believe that. She's your mother."

Jamie took a long slow sip of coffee before she commented. "You can't believe that because you are a good mother. Her ways wouldn't make sense to you and that's great for your children."

April frowned. "Well, maybe then it is better that she lives in Dallas and now you can have your own life."

Jamie smiled at the comment for a variety of reasons that she kept to herself. Off and on, April and Jamie talked throughout the day. April would leave to deal with a customer or two and then she would return. They talked about their families and their lives up to this point. The more she learned about April and her family the more she realized what she missed out on growing up and how much that hurt.

At the end of the day, when Jamie was sure Logan was done working, she left the coffee shop. She and April said their goodbyes and she hurried to her car a few seconds before Logan walked out of his office. She watched him get in his car and head home. Once she was sure he was home she drove back to the diner and waited for Isaac to get off.

Logan's schedule was more concrete. He went to work, to lunch and then home. Sometimes he stopped by the store, but that was about it. Isaac on the other hand was a mystery. His hours changed depending on the day. Sometimes he left in the morning and spent time somewhere else before going to work. Other times he got off work and did not go straight home. Jamie needed to know where he was going to better create a schedule for the family.

She needed Dani to be alone so she could take her. Bonnie could be there. She knew the older lady wouldn't give her much of a fight. But no one else, especially not Isaac or Logan. And definitely not at the same time.

It had been dark for a long while before Isaac walked out of the diner followed by three other people, two men and one woman. Laughter floated across the street. The four of them walked together laughing and talking until they neared their cars. They dispersed after short goodbyes and reminders that they would see each other tomorrow.

Isaac got in his truck. He waited until the others were in their vehicles and drove off before he stuck the key in the ignition. The truck was loud. She could hear the roar of the engine all the way across the street. She waited a minute or two before she started her car and followed. His truck was so loud she could pinpoint its location without seeing it. She had to be careful while following him. It was late, so there weren't that many people on the street. It would have been easy for him to spot her, so she kept her distance. She watched as he turned left and pulled into a church parking lot. Jamie kept going before parking across the street. She glanced down at her watch when she turned the car off. It was too late for a church service.

"What are you doing?" She didn't know that Isaac was religious, let alone went to church. It surprised her. She thought he was too much of a heathen to even step foot in one without erupting in flames. She watched him enter the building before she got out of her car and followed.

The church smelled like coffee. Burnt coffee to be exact. She followed a tall man walking in front of her who moved like he knew where he was going. She scanned the room and did not see Isaac. They walked through a doorway into another room with beige-colored tile and a stage at the front of the room. They walked through another doorway and entered a room filled with voices.

Jamie was about to round the corner and continue following the man but stopped short when she saw Isaac. Near the front of the room, there were several folding chairs and a microphone stand. At the back of the room there was a long table with coffee, cups and pastries.

She looked all around the room, understanding settling over her like a weight. She knew Isaac had had his problems, but she didn't think drinking was one of them. Actually, she wasn't sure what his problems were. Marie never talked about them, just said that he was having a hard time in some areas of his life. *He was a drunk. Explains a few things.* She stayed behind the corner watching the room until a man walked to the front.

"Alright, it's time to start. Everyone have a seat."

Everyone found a spot and sat down. Isaac was at the front of the room. Jamie weighed whether to stay in the back or find somewhere to sit. Standing behind the corner and sticking her head out every once in a while, was sure to bring some unwanted attention her way.

A heavyset man, a head taller than everyone else in the room, sat in the second to the last row. She sat in the last row, allowing some of his girth to hide her from view of the front.

"Welcome to NA. Most of the faces I see around here are old timers, but I do see a couple of new faces. We welcome you. You don't have to share if you don't want to, but we hope one day you will. That being said is there anyone who would like to start?"

Isaac stood up and walked toward the front. Jamie wondered what drug he had a problem with. She didn't know him well enough to guess. She wondered if Logan knew. She doubted he would have Isaac in his home around his daughter if he knew he was a drug addict. She thought about telling him. The thought brought a smile to her lips.

"Hello. My name is Isaac, and I am a recovering drug addict."

"Hi Isaac!" said the group.

"I've had a fairly good week. It hasn't crossed my mind all week, which is a first since I quit. I want to say that has made this week easier to push through, but that would be a lie. If anything, it has made this week excruciating. Since I wasn't thinking about it, I was thinking about other things. People, mostly. The ones I've hurt. Those faces have been plaguing my mind all week and I really wish they weren't."

Isaac stared at his hands for a long moment. "I've hurt a lot of people in my life. Some names I remember and some I don't. I've finally started repairing my relationship with my brother. At times it's difficult, but we push on. I… I know he's not the same person he was when we were younger and neither am I, but sometimes it's hard." He sighed and then paused for a long moment. "The last time I used I was in London with some friends. Well, some of them were my friends, others were just there for the drugs. A friend of mine had never done drugs before and I kept pushing her to try it. I didn't think it could hurt. It was a small dose anyway."

He paused and slid his hands into his pockets. "But I was wrong. She overdosed off of just one hit. And we were too high to notice. She was lying on the floor; I was on the sofa, and I didn't think to look down. No one did. No one noticed the foam coming out of her mouth either. There was evidence of a seizure, violent convulsions but it wasn't those that killed her. She was alive for a long time afterward. I remember stepping over her to get to the kitchen table and get another hit. She was still alive then. I thought she was sleeping... I can still see her face just like it was the next morning. Pale and rubbery. Dried puke on her chin."

His voice trailed off like he could see her right in front of him while he talked. A moment later he snapped back, realizing he was still in a room filled with people staring up at him.

"This is one of the biggest regrets of my life. If I hadn't talked her into it, she'd still be alive today. That was the catalyst that forced me to get clean. I was the only one in the group that took it that way. When I got clean, I did what she should have done. I cut all ties with my addict friends. Got all the bad people out of my life that didn't approve of me changing my life around. I've been thinking about her all week and her family. And the way her mother looked at me at hospital. The hatred in her eyes. She looked like she wanted to kill me. There was a time I would have let her. I know that making amends is part of the program. I just don't know how I will ever be able to do that with her, but someday I would like to try. I owe her an apology, but she doesn't owe me her forgiveness. I guess that's what I've been struggling with and why I've been thinking about it. I owe so many people an apology, and I just don't know if I'll ever be able to do it." Isaac stopped and looked up. "I'm sorry this took such a dark turn. I didn't mean to say all of that. But thank you for listening."

Isaac walked away from the podium and sat down in his seat to the sound of sympathetic applause. Jamie stood up and walked out before anyone noticed. She slipped out of the building and hurried to her car. She didn't hear any footsteps behind her. Isaac must not have seen her. She got in her car and sat there for a long moment. She didn't know much about Isaac, but she never would have guessed what he said.

She was more surprised by her reaction to what he said. She didn't see the situation the same way he did. To Jamie, he was not responsible for his friend's death. Isaac hadn't forced her to take the drugs. It was a decision she made herself. Just because someone tried to talk you into doing something didn't mean you had to do it. He didn't force those drugs down her throat.

Jamie didn't see it as his fault, nor did she feel like he should hold himself responsible. She was in a comparable situation with her sister and yet she didn't blame herself for her death. But he was softer than her and therefore more susceptible to guilt.

CHAPTER TWENTY-ONE

Riley Quinn

W HEN I LEFT THE HOSPITAL, MY ADRENALINE HADN'T QUITE
come down yet. It was late, so I headed home, but I couldn't get a
good night's sleep. I tossed and turned, and my heart hammered
against my ribs so hard it was difficult to breathe. Alex Choi was so stupid. I could have killed him and for what? That's what infuriated me. I
could have killed both of them and then that would have been on my
conscience. I had enough of that already.

What the hell was he thinking?

Just the thought of how things could have gone pissed me off. I
didn't take shooting suspects lightly. Every time I had to it was a like a
knife to the chest. Sure they were deplorable people, but they deserved
the chance to make things right. For rehabilitation, those that could
anyway. Rapists and pedophiles were not high on that list.

My mind whirred so much that I thought about calling Logan to talk about it. But I didn't want to bother him. I couldn't wait to tell Zelina, either.

I must have drifted off to sleep eventually, because I was jolted awake by a call from Zelina at six the next morning.

I groaned. "I was just thinking about you."

"Well, hold that thought. We have another body."

My chest constricted like something had wrapped around it and tightened with each breath. Another body? We were still working on the first one and were no closer to finding answers than we were days ago. We had no suspects. Zelina wouldn't have been at that crime scene if she didn't think it was related to Olivia's case. If it was, probably wasn't a coworker. She might have been killed for a different reason.

I was curious about the circumstances, but Zelina didn't give me any details. She gave me the address and I told her I was on my way. It wasn't until I hung up the phone that I realized how close the address was to my home. Alarmingly close. Just along the river. A murder being so close to home gave me pause. A murder could happen anywhere, but it was still strange that one happened so close to a detective's home.

I pulled up behind the coroner's van. Police cars blocked the body from view of the road. I stooped under the crime scene tape.

"So you found Alex?"

Zelina stood next to the lake. I walked over to her and shrugged.

"Technically I did, but a lot happened since I did. I'll explain all that to you later. What do we have here?" I'd have to tell her that story in one sitting when we got to the station. I didn't want to leave anything out. We strolled to the body where Keith and the crime scene techs buzzed around it like bees circling their hive. Flashes went off in all directions. I took stock of the scene. A man sat in a folding chair near the edge of the lake. His fishing pole inches away. His shirt soaked in blood. His eyes staring up at the sky blankly.

By the looks of it, someone caught him off guard. I slipped on my gloves and then pulled down his shirt collar. He had the same thin red line across his neck as Olivia. Judging by the front of his shirt he was stabbed multiple times just like her too.

Keith gave me a small nod. "You probably already guessed it, but I think this murder is related to Olivia Tucker's. Stabbed several times, strangled. He wasn't tied to a tree like her, so that's something. But everything else seems consistent. I'll know more once I get him on the table."

"Did you find a wallet?" I asked. While he was working on the autopsy, with his name we could start our investigation.

He leaned over the body and checked his pockets. "Here you go."

I took the wallet. "Well, at least there was a wallet on the body." I walked over to Zelina before I opened the wallet.

"Oh!" I spun around and stared at Keith. "Find something?"

Keith lifted his head. "He has the same gash on the back of his head as Olivia."

"She had a gash on her head?" asked Zelina.

"Yes, I put it in my report that I sent over to you this morning. Something or someone hit her in the head with something."

"Really?"

"It would have happened when she was strangled, and she fell to the ground and hit her head on something. The wound isn't clear enough for me to tell you what it was. But this one..." He twisted the man's head slightly to get a better look. "I might be able to get an impression from this wound. Can't say if the same implement was used."

I would take any bit of information that I could get. We knew nothing at this point so anything would be helpful no matter how small. I opened the wallet.

"Mark Davis. Why does that sound familiar?" I searched his wallet. Cash was still there along with his credit card and debit card. I handed it to Zelina.

"Let's walk through the scene and then go to his house and see what we find." I glanced at all the techs combing the grass around his body. People came to that area to fish all the time, so his presence wasn't too unusual. Those same people didn't usually die though, so that was out of the ordinary.

I looked at the lake and then at the area around the body. To me, it looked like Mr. Davis was fishing when someone came up behind him and used some kind of cord to strangle him. He tried to fight back, but he couldn't. His fishing pole fell out of his hand, his shoes dug into the ground. I doubted he even saw his attacker. It must have happened so quickly to catch him off guard like that.

"The techs will continue looking through everything. They are going to search the grass in the area. I wonder if they should search the lake."

I looked at the lake and then back to Zelina. "I doubt they'll be able to do that. Right now, we need a reason to expend the resources to make that happen and we don't have a reason. As the captain says a hunch is not a reason. Also, if they are as smart as they seem to be, they probably didn't throw anything in the lake because they knew it would be the first place we searched. I wouldn't have."

Zelina sighed. "Fair point. Let's go to his house and see what we can find there."

It was a nice cottage-style home with a beautiful garden. It wasn't far from my house. A beautiful cottage by the lake. There was one car in the driveway that could have been his. I didn't see any other vehicles at the scene except for ours. It was a manageable walking distance to where he was killed. I opened the door with his keys after ringing the doorbell and waiting several minutes for someone to answer the door. He must have lived alone, or his partner was out. Either case the house looked empty. It sounded empty too. No TV blaring in the background. No voices but ours.

The house had a lingering smell of coffee and something sweet. I walked into the kitchen and touched the coffee pot. It was cool to the touch. He could have made the coffee early this morning before he went fishing. Or it could have been yesterday. Keith wasn't sure about the time of death yet so we couldn't say when the last time he was in his home was.

It was evident that Mr. Davis loved the color green. There were hints of green all throughout the house. The primary bedroom had a dark green vanity in the bathroom. In the kitchen the backsplash was also green subway tile. The front door to the house was green. It was everywhere and yet it wasn't too much. It didn't make it look outdated or overdone. Just enough. He had an eye for detail and a hatred for clutter and dust. There was no dust anywhere. Not on the bookshelves or the ceiling fans. The house was neat. No clutter on any surface. Nothing on the hardwood floors.

There was also no sign that someone else lived with him. I searched his closet and bathroom. There was only enough room for his things. Only his clothes in the closet. Only his toiletries in the bathroom. Two nightstands, but only the one on the right had anything in it. Mr. Davis took care of himself. There was a treadmill in one of the spare bedrooms along with an exercise bike and a weight bench. The treadmill looked like he actually used it to work out and not a place to hang his clothes. There was no dust on the exercise equipment either. In his fridge there were a variety of fruits and vegetables, almond milk, Greek yogurt and fresh salmon. He was the kind of person that ate kale. I never understood the appeal. I'd rather eat spinach. On the counter next to the fridge there were vitamins and supplements. He tried his best to be healthy. He had nothing fattening. No bacon, no processed foods and no sugary sweets.

I commended his dedication, but I couldn't help but feel sad for him. He did all that work to stay healthy and live longer and yet he died alone on the shore of the lake. It was a sad thought.

Zelina and I wandered into his office and searched his desk. I found his business card which had the name of where he worked.

"He was a journalist for the *Pine Brooke Register,*" I announced.

"The newspaper?" Zelina asked. "People still read those?"

"Apparently so."

There were notebooks that we bagged. I couldn't understand the writing, but I figured it was important. "I think he might have written his notes in code," said Zelina. "A way to stop someone from stealing your story. Can't steal what you don't understand."

"I wonder if anyone in his office could understand it."

"That should be our next stop."

I inclined my head slightly. That was my next thought. What did the two journalists have in common? Why would someone kill them?

Our next stop was in fact the newspaper where he worked. When I walked in it was clear that word hadn't gotten around yet. While at his home we searched his address book for any family. There weren't any—at least none that shared his last name. I found that strange, but then I thought maybe his boss or HR would have contact information for his next of kin.

I hoped they did because I didn't want his family hearing about it on the news. That would have made things a lot worse.

A receptionist with short brown hair and big brown eyes smiled brightly the moment we walked in. "Welcome to the *Pine Brooke Register*, officers."

"That obvious?" I asked.

"I know cops when I see them. How can I help you?"

I held up my badge. "We need to speak to whoever's in charge here. And actually, it's detectives."

She froze for a long moment. The word detective meant something. Cops could have been there for many reasons: noise complaint, looking for someone, to arrest someone. But detective meant something serious happened. She stared at me like she was trying to figure out what it was.

"Okay." She stood up and gestured for us to follow her. We headed down a long hallway with several cluttered desks on either side, to the last door before you rounded the corner. She knocked twice on the door, which was emblazoned with the name Kimberly Bates, Publisher.

"Come in!"

A tall, thin blonde woman in an impeccably tailored pantsuit opened the door. "Who do we have here?"

"These are detectives, and they say they need to speak with you." The receptionist hovered by the door, like she hoped we forgot she was there so she could listen in. My mother did that sometimes.

"Okay, Carli. Thank you." She stood up. "Close the door."

Carli looked in the room one last time before she did what she was told. The boss held out her hand. "I'm Kim Bates. What can I do for you?" She shook our hands before gesturing for us to take a seat. Her office was spacious and modern, and her desk neat.

"Does a Mark Davis work for you?"

She leaned back in her chair and clasped her hands in front of her belly. "He does. What is this about? I can't imagine Mark doing anything wrong."

I took a deep breath. "His body was found this morning by the lake."

She gasped, her body immediately straightened. "Seriously? Was it a heart attack?" She opened her mouth to say something but paused. "If it were natural causes, you wouldn't be here. What happened to him?"

"That's what we are trying to figure out. He was fishing by the lake. Did he do that often?" asked Zelina.

She twisted the gold ring on her middle finger as she spoke. "He loved fishing. He said it allowed him to clear his head. I guess because it was so quiet."

"Was he having any problems with anyone?" I asked.

"I don't think so. Mark was a good guy. Even when he was doing a story, he always tried his best to be objective. That's our job, report the news. Don't twist it."

"What about next of kin? We need to contact them before it's in the news." Zelina took out her pad and paper ready to write down what she said.

She shook her head. "There isn't one. He became a loner after his partner died. His parents died a while ago, and his sister died a few years ago of cancer. I don't think he was close to his father's side of the family. Some kind of rift there that his father started, and it only got deeper after he died and left everything to Mark."

I leaned forward. "What was he working on? Could that have had anything to do with his death?"

She sighed and leaned back in her chair. "I doubt it. It's a cold case. Every year the paper runs the story, interviewing whoever is left that had anything to do with the case. It's our hope maybe one day someone will come forward."

"How old is the case?"

"Twenty years."

I could tell by the look on her face that she didn't think it would ever get solved. Cases that old and older have been solved. There was still a chance all be it a slim one.

"He was the one writing the article this year?"

A ghost of a smile kissed her lips. "He writes every year. He worked here when it happened and interviewed the girl's mother and the detectives working the case. It... well it meant a lot to him. So he took it on every year. I know he hoped the killer could be found."

"Did he have any hate mail? Stalkers?" I asked.

She laughed. "Sorry. The idea of that is hilarious." She sat up straight, her elbows resting on her desk. "Nothing like that. He was a good guy and stayed objective in all his work. Never got a piece of hate mail. Never said anyone was following him or that he felt like he was being watched. If he did, he would have said something."

"What was the case?"

CHAPTER TWENTY-TWO

Riley Quinn

KIM GAVE US EVERYTHING SHE HAD ON THE CASE. EVERY ARTICLE written. Every file Mark had gotten from the police. Every interview he had done with her mother and her family and friends. I was surprised by some of the details he had gotten. The file he had from the police made me wonder if they knew he had it. There were crime scene pictures and the coroner's report.

Cases where children were the victims were always the hardest. Every detective or cop I knew had said that to me at some point. It was something that was just known between us. I hated dealing with child cases. They were so gut-wrenching. Rip your heart right out.

I remembered my first child case. It was before Zelina became my partner and I was still a patrol officer. We had gotten a call to a house that I drove by every day on my way to work. Everyone knew the house. As soon as I stepped foot on the property, I knew something was wrong.

The house was dark, and the cars were still in the driveway. I'll never forget the horrible things I saw that night.

"Did he steal these?" Zelina wondered aloud as she flipped through it, interrupting my thoughts.

While she was doing that, I was searching for the police file, but it wasn't in the computer database. "Maybe. Or perhaps the detective working the case gave it to him hoping he could find something they didn't. He took meticulous notes."

"I know. Better notes than me."

"Hey, Baldwin! Can you come here?" Detective Jesse Baldwin was one of the oldest detectives at the station. He had been there for at least forty years and had no plans to retire.

"Whatcha need Quinn?" He strolled over. Jesse had an unmistakable walk. I could have picked it out of a crowd. It was so laid back like he was never in a hurry.

"Case files from twenty years ago, they aren't in the system?"

He laughed. "Back in the olden days, we did everything by hand. Actually, more like CD ROM... and it's probably in storage. Can't use 'em much anymore." He glanced at the folders on Zelina's case. "What case are you looking for?"

"Lizzie Sherman."

He rocked back on his feet and sighed. "I remember that case. Her poor mother."

I picked up a chair and set it in front of my desk. "Please sit and tell us everything you know about it. Did you work the case?"

"Yeah, I did. With my old partner. In fact, I think I still have my notes. I keep all my notes in boxes in the garage. My wife keeps saying I need to throw them out, but I can't. One of them might come in handy one day." He shook his head. "Lizzie Sherman was found by the lake brutally murdered. She had one of her socks shoved down her throat so hard she choked on it. we never knew if that was on purpose or if he was just trying to get her to stop screaming."

"Signs of rape?"

He drew in a loud breath. "We never released that information to the press. Thought it best to hold something back and I didn't want her mother to have to see that in the paper. She was stabbed multiple times."

As he talked about the case I remembered parts of it. My friends and I loved hanging out by the lake, but after the murder happened my parents wouldn't let me go. I tried to tell them all we did was watch the fish and play. But my mother forbade me for a long time. Ruined my plans for the summer.

"I knew her mother through my wife and my youngest. Our kids used to play all the time, so this case cut deep. There was nothing left at the scene. No DNA. No fluids. No murder weapon. It was so strange given the brutality of the murder. I was sure we were going to find something. I never figured out if she was going to meet someone there, or if she just happened to be there at the same time a maniac was walking by."

"Did you have any leads? Any one you thought was good for it, but couldn't prove it?" asked Zelina.

"There were a few. Track coach at the school who girls said was way too friendly. Youth director at the church. He was seen on several occasions touching her in an inappropriate manner. We couldn't link him to her death, but there was something off with him. Come to find out several years later it came out that he had been molesting the young girls at the church. Mark Davis actually broke that story. He was able to get one of the girls to trust him enough to speak to him, and then she told a few of the other girls about him and they told him their stories too."

"Wow! But even with that he wasn't looked at again for her murder?"

He shook his head. "No evidence. And he molested them, he didn't kill them. And the morning Lizzie was found, he was out of town at some retreat."

"Who was your main suspect? Someone you knew did it you just couldn't prove it." I had a few cases like that. Deep down I knew the person was guilty of something, but I couldn't prove it.

"My primary suspect was Robert Crow. We knew he did something to her, we just couldn't prove it. No evidence left behind."

"What made him your primary?" asked Zelina.

"Proximity. He frequented the spot where she was killed. People saw him there just about every day. I always found it odd that her murder was the one day he wasn't there. With that, it was the way he reacted when we brought him in. I showed him the crime scene photos to gauge his reaction. Most people would look away in disgust. He just stared and smiled."

"He smiled?" Zelina looked down at the crime scene pictures on her desk. She flipped them over. They were gruesome. Blood and tissue all over the body. He had cut her so deep and so many times you could see her intestines. How was a person able to do that without leaving any kind of DNA evidence behind?

"It made me sick to my stomach. But we had nothing else to hold him on. No other evidence, so we had to let him go. Damn near killed me when I had to tell her mom." He stood up slowly. "I'll see if I can locate that file and my notes for you."

"Thank you."

As he walked away, I wondered where Robert Crow was and what he was doing now. I searched his name.

"He was arrested soon after the murder for robbery and assault. Spent five years in prison and then was let out and... he still lives in town. You know that trailer compound near the beach, Z?"

"Yeah, the one with the RVs and all that."

"He lives in that area."

Zelina closed the file. "Want to stop by? See how he's doing?"

A smile pulled at my lips. "You mean see if he had the strength to kill two people who might have figured out he was a murderer? I would love to."

The trailer park was just that. It had been a place where RVs could park and rest. Now it was still a place for RVs, but the trailers had taken over. We pulled into the park. There were more trailers than the last time I had been there. There had been a domestic incident and we were called to break it up, but that was years go.

"It's strange how they are arranged. I wonder if that was on purpose."

Zelina looked at me, her brows furrowed.

"It looks like there is one trailer in the middle and then the others kind of branch off. Like a flower or something."

She smiled. "You notice the oddest things."

"I'm taking it as a compliment."

We had no idea where we were going. At first, we wandered around the sea of trailers until we saw someone. A woman with long blonde dreadlocks pulled into a high ponytail. She wore a black flowing skirt and a white top with a happy face on it. She reminded me of those pictures of hippies from the sixties. All she was missing a joint and it would have completed the look.

"Hi there," she drawled with a beaming smile. Her voice was low and soothing. She spoke like she was singing. A soft lullaby.

"Hi, we're looking for a Robert Crow. We were told he lived around here."

She smiled as her head tilted slightly as she looked at us. "He does. Just moved in. Quite nice. I'll take you to him." She turned left and we followed. She didn't walk so much as she glided down the pathway. She swayed when she walked and hummed.

"How long has he stayed here?"

"A few months or so. He was in Chicago before he came back here. Just trying to get back on his feet and we're here to help."

"That's very kind of you all. Very sweet," said Zelina.

The woman smiled. She didn't ask our names, and she didn't offer up hers.

"I know you think we're all strange, detectives, and most of us are. That being said, just because we're a little strange doesn't mean we're bad people."

"Did you know Crow was a suspect in a murder?" I asked as we weaved through the trailers.

"I heard he was just a suspect, and nothing was ever proven. This is America after all, innocent until proven guilty. We can't shun him because you cops have a hunch. And everyone deserves a second chance."

I didn't think everyone deserved a second chance. Some people, yes. Not everyone.

Finally, we stopped in front of a trailer with a sunflower in the window. "Here he is." She knocked softly on his trailer. The opened a moment later.

"Su —"

She waved her hand dismissively. "These detectives want to speak with you." She gestured toward us and Robert looked up. "Do you want me to stay with you?"

He shook his head. "No. I'll be okay. I haven't done anything wrong, so there's nothing to worry about."

She grinned as she walked away. "Nice meeting you detectives," she said as she passed us. There was something about her that I didn't like. Something... I couldn't put my finger on it, but it left a bad taste in my mouth.

"Hello, Mr. Crow." I shoved my hands in my pockets and walked toward him. Zelina stayed where she was surveying the area around us. "We just wanted to ask you a few questions."

"I didn't kill that girl."

I looked back at Zelina for a moment. She was looking at something beyond the trailer next to us. "Which girl?"

He looked at me and stumbled back. "What do you mean what girl? Twenty years ago, you thought I killed that young girl. I didn't."

"Umm... that wasn't me. I was in my teens then."

"Huh." He fumbled with the glasses hanging from his neck. He lifted them to his eyes. "Oh, yeah. Way too young. But it was an officer."

And a man. "A man was killed by the river recently. Stabbed several times. In the exact spot Lizzie was murdered in, and your name came up."

"Huh?" Robert looked behind him. He looked like he had heard something, but I didn't hear it. He was an old man now, and I doubt he had the energy or the strength to kill anyone. "My name came up, huh?"

"It did."

"Well, look at me. I can't see without my glasses, and I barely have the energy to get my ass up the steps of my trailer let alone kill someone."

He was right. He leaned against the trailer. His chest heaved like he was out of breath just from standing. I looked back at Zelina. She was still watching the area around us.

"Okay, Mr. Crow."

He looked behind us like he was listening to something that I couldn't hear. A shiver ran down my spine even though it was hot outside. We needed to get out of there. "Thank you for your time."

"Yeah, whatever."

I walked back to Zelina, and she shook her head. "There is something going on here," she whispered.

It was my turn to look around. In the swarm of trailers there were people that I hadn't seen when we walked up. Their eyes were on us and nothing else. Everyone was staring. I looked at the trailers most had a sunflower sticker in the window. "Yeah, let's get out of here."

I followed Zelina, looking behind us to see if they were following us. They weren't, but they were still watching. And it was still creepy.

Z had memorized the way we took to get to Robert's trailer. I had not. Once we were out of the maze, my pace quickened to the car. I didn't like being there. I didn't remember it ever feeling like that. Now it was heavy and suffocating and creepy.

"That place is strange. What the hell is going on?" asked Zelina, as she put the car in drive. We hurried out of there.

CHAPTER TWENTY-THREE

Logan Elwood

M Y MIND RACED WITH A MILLION THOUGHTS, NONE OF THEM tangible. Not one I could grab hold of and focus on. I was all over the place and had been for days. It became so difficult to focus on other things I had to take a couple of days off work. But Nicole was there, and she could fill in for me. She didn't mind doing so, but she did request that I let her know if I found anything juicy. She was like my brother in that regard, always ready to gossip.

Google was a wealth of information although it didn't have everything I needed. I was missing pictures from the actual scene. I could have used those, but I wasn't sure I really wanted to see them. Before Sac left in the morning one day, he pointed out for the millionth time I didn't need to look into this.

"She will never get custody. It will never happen. Let this go."

In truth it stopped being about Jamie getting custody a long time ago. The more I delved into the fire the more I felt like it was about Marie. It was about the secrets she had been keeping from me.

"Huh." I stared at the screen, intently reading an article written on the school five years after it opened. One of the nuns was interviewed.

Interviewer: Sister Lacey, how does it feel to finally open your doors?

Sister Lacey: I am so proud of what we are able to do here. It took a long time, and for a time we weren't sure that we'd ever be able to open these doors. But God has blessed us. This school is truly needed for the time we're in. So many unwed mothers. So many children becoming delinquents. We want to help this community, by instilling virtue and morals in these girls.

Interviewer: Is that who you're taking in?

Sister Lacey: Yes. Unwed mothers. We will help them find a better home for their babies and get themselves together. Get on the right track. We will do the same for young girls who are out of control and wreaking havoc on their parents' lives. Bring them to us and we will straighten them out.

I stared at the picture of the nun. She looked like she wasn't playing... and meant every word she was saying. I wondered what she did to straighten the girls out. Bianca didn't mention abuse, but that didn't mean it didn't happen. I was so focused on the fire, I didn't even think to ask. I wasn't Catholic, but I heard things about nuns and how strict they were.

"School for unwed mothers and unruly girls." I didn't know they took in pregnant teens. My thoughts rested on my conversation with Bianca. I wondered how many of the dead were pregnant teens.

My phone rang. The sudden noise made me jump out of my skin. "Hello?"

"Hey, Log. You wanted to know more about Marie and Jamie?"

"Hey!" I hadn't heard from her friend in so long I almost didn't recognize Pen's voice. "Yeah, I do. Umm... did Kay tell you about Jamie?"

"She did. I can't believe she wants custody. I didn't even think she liked children."

"Well, she does have children of her own."

There was a slight pause. "Oh, didn't know that. After Marie died, I stopped keeping up with Jamie. To tell you the truth, I stopped keeping up with her long before Marie died. Marie might have mentioned it, but I probably zoned out at the sound of her name."

I chuckled. "Yeah, I did that too sometimes. Kay said you've known her the longest so I just wanted to know if there was anything that you could tell me. Anything about their past that might help me keep her away from Dani."

There was another pause, this time longer than the last. She sighed. "I was her friend for a long time. Forever seems like. She was always in my life. And Jamie was always with her. I'm not sure what you don't know."

"I don't know anything. What can you tell me?" I wanted to record our conversation, but I thought better of asking her. She might have not said anything if she knew I was recording. But I did grab my notebook and a pen to take notes.

"Well Marie had gone to the same school that Jamie did, just years earlier. I don't know particulars, but she was at the school because she was... pregnant."

The pen fell out of my hand. "She was what?"

"I can't believe she never told you about that. Umm... yeah, she was pregnant when she was, I think twelve, or thirteen. She never said how it happened. I wanted to ask, but I got the feeling she didn't want to talk about it. She never wanted to talk about it. I remember when we were in college, one of the few times she got away from her family, I asked her about the baby. I asked if she ever wondered how the kid was doing or who was raising them. She said she never thought about them and that it didn't matter. She said she didn't even know whether it was a boy or a girl. As soon as she had the baby the nuns whisked them away. She didn't even get to hold it."

"Damn, I don't know if that's a good or bad thing."

"Well, she made it clear that she didn't want it. I stopped asking after that. I couldn't imagine having a baby that young and never knowing what happened to it."

"Maybe that's why she and Jamie were so close, and she looked after her like she did. She conflated her love and protective motherly instincts with her feelings about her sister."

There was another long pause. "I guess ... but I don't think that's it. Marie protected her, but she didn't really like Jamie. I think everything she did for her was because she was her sister. It wasn't out of love."

"They seemed so close though. Marie loved her."

"Well..." She sighed. "Marie tolerated her. She knew that if she didn't protect Jamie, her mom would be upset and that would cause a whole other set of problems."

"Hmm... maybe it was the age difference. She was so much older when Jamie was born maybe that was why she protected her. I wondered why there was such an age difference."

"Rumor was her mother got around a lot. Most of the men she dated were married with families. Jamie's father was a married man, and his wife died before she gave birth. Then he married Everly, and he died some years later. He was Jamie's father, but he never took an interest in her. Marie said it was like he never wanted them around, just her mother."

"Did she tell you about the fire?"

Pen took a deep breath. "She said she went there that night because she had a feeling Jamie was going to do something. She wasn't sure what happened, but Jamie was upset. She hated being at the school and didn't understand why she couldn't just come home. She hated the nuns, and she hated the other students. She just wanted to go home. Marie said when she got there the building was on fire. Smoke was everywhere and she saw Jamie outside watching it burn."

"And she didn't say anything?"

She sighed. "Marie protected her blindly. No questions asked. After Everly got married, she was very... insistent, on them behaving and not doing anything to cause rumors to spread. it would make the family look bad. If Jamie had started the fire, it would have made everyone look bad."

"I don't understand why she didn't just walk away. She was in college. She never had to go home if she didn't want to."

"Well... her stepfather was paying her tuition. She had to come home on breaks. But once he died, she cut ties and didn't go home. He died her senior year, and her tuition was all paid up so by then she was no longer obligated to go home."

"Makes sense. Um, how did he die?"

There was a long pause. "I'm not sure. I asked her, but she said she didn't know, and she didn't care. But it happened.. after winter break.... like right after. She had just gotten back to school. We were talking for maybe five minutes and then her phone rang. Her mother told her he was dead. Well, that she found him dead. If she said where and how, Marie didn't repeat it, and she didn't seem that interested. I don't remember her leaving for the funeral."

Hearing that was so surprising. It didn't sound like her. Marie was the kindest and the most caring person I had ever known. It was what I admired most about her.

What secrets had she been keeping from me?

CHAPTER TWENTY-FOUR

Riley Quinn

AFTER OUR STRANGE TALK WITH ROBERT CROW, WE HEADED BACK to the station. There was something about him we both found strange and unusual. When he spoke, he didn't look at me. He refused to look me in my eyes. I wasn't sure if that was a good thing or a bad thing, but it made him look guilty. I understood why he had been a suspect purely based on the way he acted. It was unnerving. Zelina thought it was just the way he was.

"Maybe he's socially awkward or something, and doesn't like looking people in the eyes. Maybe being in prison did that to him."

While she might have been right, I thought he was doing it on purpose. He acted that way to put people off and it worked. It made people anxious and frightened to be around him. He used that to his advantage. I doubted he was as strange as he pretended to be. He knew what he was doing and why. That being said we weren't investigating the cold case. We had two new cases now that needed attention. There was nothing concrete, so far, that proved the three murders were connected. Although one of them happened in the same spot.

We didn't even make it to the station before Keith called us and said he needed to show us something. We turned immediately to the morgue.

Keith pulled the white sheet over the body the second we walked in.

"What did you find?"

"The wounds are very similar. Some are the same depth. The only difference... Olivia struggled so her wounds weren't straight. She struggled against the ropes. But Mark, his wounds are clean. There's no movement at all."

"So people were stabbing him, he wasn't tied up, and he didn't try to fight back?" I moved closer to the doctor and the body. "That doesn't sound right."

"Unless he was already dead."

"They killed him first? That's not like Olivia's murder at all." Olivia was alive for all of her stab wounds. I suspected whoever killed her wanted it that way. They wanted her to feel everything and to die as slowly as possible.

"That's what I was thinking. There's petechia in both eyes and the line around his neck tells me he was strangled with some kind of nylon rope. Found nylon fibers in the wound just like with Olivia. I don't think they planned on killing him first."

"What do you think happened?" Zelina leaned against the wall across the room. She didn't like seeing dead bodies. I told her one day she'd have to get over that, but I covered for her when she couldn't. The more gruesome the murder, the more she couldn't stand seeing the body. This one wasn't as gruesome as some others, but she still didn't want to see it.

"I think someone came up behind him with the rope and proceeded to strangle him. He fell out of his chair and was struggling against the rope. They were trying to immobilize him before they stabbed him. But he was fighting back. There's grass, dirt, and skin under his fingernails. I've already sent it to the lab. Appears they continued strangling him until he stopped moving and he was dead by then. And then they commenced stabbing him. I believe they pulled him into the chair before they started. There was no blood pooled on the ground away from the chair, just under it."

"That's why he didn't struggle."

"Also judging by the wounds his heart wasn't pumping. Also, I believe that the wounds on the back of the head are the same. Maybe he was sitting down, someone hit him on the back of the head, but that didn't take him down, and then they strangled him."

"Mark wanted to live," Zelina said quietly.

"I'll let you know when I get the results."

While I headed back to the car I wondered if their DNA was in the system. It was hard to say. Murders like these usually meant the person or persons had killed before or had committed a crime before. But just because they had been arrested before didn't mean their DNA was in the system.

We went back to the station. I hovered in the doorway waiting to see if my phone rang before I sat down. After a few minutes it didn't, so I walked to my desk and sat down. As soon as my ass hit my chair my phone vibrated in my pocket.

I groaned. Zelina looked up at me. For a split second I thought it might have been Brianna wanting to talk. She had called me several times and left a few messages, but I didn't listen to any of them. I still didn't want to know what she wanted to talk about, and I doubted anything could change my mind.

"Yes? Okay. We'll be there." I hung up and leaned back for a brief moment. "Another journalist has been attacked and is on her way to the hospital."

"What the hell is going on?" Zelina jumped to her feet.

"You go to the hospital and see what the doctors say about her condition. I'll go to her apartment and look at the scene. I'll let you know what I find, and you let me know what she says."

Zelina took her keys out of the drawer. "Okay. Meet you on the other side."

Zelina walked out first while I slipped my keys and my phone into my pocket.

"Riley?"

I recognized the voice instantly. I stopped dead in my tracks. The door closed behind me as I looked up. Brianna stood on the walkway leading to the parking lot.

"I wasn't sure if you were working today."

I stared at her with unblinking eyes. *What was she doing here?* My throat was dry. I swallowed several times before any words could crawl out of my mouth. "Brianna?"

She gave a half shrug that looked remarkably uncomfortable. She didn't look as confident as she used to. It was off-putting.

"It's nice to see you again. I've been meaning to stop by, but I got the feeling you didn't want to see me. To see any of us, so I wasn't sure."

I just stared at her, not sure of what to say. "And you came anyway..."

Her shoulders fell. "I missed you. We all have. Been a little worried since you won't return our calls."

I glanced at the parking lot. Zelina's car was already gone. "Look, I have a crime scene to get to."

Her eyes widened. "Oh, I'm sorry. I don't want to get in the way. I'll be in town for a few more days. Call me so we can catch up. I've got a lot that I need to fill you in on." She wrapped her arms around me for a long moment. The hug felt so familiar. She still smelled like oranges and spices. When she released me, I took a step back and watched her walk back to her car. When she pulled out of the parking lot, only then did I walk to my car. I should have known she was in Pine Brooke. That explained all of the phone calls and texts.

I shoved the thoughts out of my mind and headed to the crime scene. The victim's apartment hummed with activity. Crime scene techs took pictures and collected evidence while officers in the hallway talked to neighbors. A metallic smell hung in the air. Blood coated the floor next to a chair that was also soaked with blood. if all that blood was hers, she probably died on the way to the hospital.

"There's no way someone could lose this much blood and still live," I said to myself.

The tech that was cutting up the chair looked at me. "I don't think so."

"Do you know who found her?"

She pointed to the hallway outside the apartment. "I think one of the officers said a neighbor found her."

"Thanks." I walked into the hallway.

"Detective?" I turned to my left and there was an officer talking to an older woman. "This is Roberta. She lives across the hall. She's the one that found the body."

"Okay, thank you."

Roberta was a short black woman in her mid-fifties to early sixties. I guessed at her age purely because of her name. Roberta was a name that had long fallen out of style. Her face and neck were wrinkle free. She stared at the doorway, her fingers worrying the gold cross hanging around her neck.

"How did you find her?" I kept my voice low and gentle.

Roberta clutched the gold cross around her neck. "We go walking every morning. It's our little ritual. We walk in the park and talk. We meet in the hallway. I waited and she didn't show up. I knocked and then I went outside to see if her car was still there, and it was. I knocked again, but she still didn't answer. I have a key so I used it. And I found her... in that chair."

"The apartment was empty?"

"She lives alone, and I didn't see anyone leave before or after I found her. She didn't really like people in her apartment. It was just her, and if she was meeting friends, she met them outside her apartment. She was always working on something, and she wanted to protect it."

"I see. Did she have a boyfriend or someone close to her?"

Roberta shook her head. "It was just her."

"Thank you." I handed her my card. "If you think of anything or remember something please give me a call."

She bowed her head slightly and then went back into her apartment. I went back into the apartment and sidestepped the techs and wandered around the apartment while slipping on a pair of gloves. I found myself in her office. There were papers strewn all over her desk. I sorted through them. "Hate mail," I muttered leafing through some of them. I had seen worse, but I still slipped those into an evidence bag.

Under a notebook, and a stack of papers, there was a letter. I slipped that into an evidence bag too. There was something about it. There was a sun emblem at the top of the page and the letter itself was a jumble of words. It didn't make sense. It talked about an organization and a list of demands. I couldn't tell who the demands were to.

Something about it was familiar, I just couldn't put my finger on it. "I'll have Zelina take a look at it. It might jog her memory." I continued searching through the papers, but didn't find anything until I was on my way out. A folder on a bookcase caught my eye. I opened it and found three more letters identical to the other one. I slipped those in an evidence bag too Before heading back to the station. Half an hour later Zelina returned. She collapsed in her chair and sighed. "Bad news?" I asked.

"She's in a coma."

"Do they think she's going to make it?"

"Doctor pretty much said there was little to no hope for her to pull through."

"Damn. So you didn't get to talk to her at all?"

"She was in a coma when I got there. Something about a bleed on her brain. That and all the blood she lost before she got to the hospital. They were still trying to stabilize her for surgery when I left. Doctor did not look optimistic she would make it to the OR."

"Damn." I leaned back in my seat. "I was halfway hoping she would pull through and tell us who did this to her. But I saw her apartment. The amount of blood … I kinda knew."

"And what did you find?"

I slid over the evidence bags. "I found these on her desk."

She read through them. "Creepy ass letters. Why would someone send these to her?"

"Someone wanted her attention and was desperate to get it. They sent five letters, and judging by the dates they didn't give her time to answer. And they are handwritten which makes them creepier."

"Yeah, it does. That being said, do you think there is a connection between the letters and her attack?"

She slid the letters back over. I wasn't sure if someone would kill over these letters.

Hello,

We know as a journalist you are busy and while we understand that we still need your attention. This is our second letter to you, and we have not heard back, nor have we seen any coverage of our organization.

Therefore, we are writing you again. Trying again to get your attention and bring attention to our organization. We can assure you that we are legitimate as is our charter.

All we want to do is help people. That is our primary goal. We are helping those who can't help themselves. Those that have been thrown away by society.

We are the givers of second chances. Our belief is that everyone deserves a second chance. No one should be thrown away based on mistakes of their past. It is not fair, and we endeavor to ensure that it never happens.

We know you may believe that you have nothing to do with this and are actively ignoring our letters. We wish you wouldn't. We want you to help get our message out there. To help bring more people to the light and forgiveness.

You could help save so many lives. Or you could destroy them. The choice is yours. We hope you will choose wisely.

"Sure got hella creepy at the end," remarked Zelina.

"Right. Which is probably the reason she wouldn't do the story. They sound like a cult or a really creepy group of people."

Zelina laughed, but only for a moment. Then looked at me, her eyes wide.

"I wonder if any of the other journalists got these letters."

CHAPTER TWENTY-FIVE

Riley Quinn

ZELINA SLID THE LETTERS BACK. I SPENT TWENTY MINUTES STARing at them. Reading each one over and over, looking for inconsistencies between the letters. Each one was written using the same words as the next one.

It didn't look copied. The person who wrote them wrote each one by hand. They were identical.

"This is so weird," I muttered.

I stared at the heading of each letter. It looked so familiar. My fingers drummed against the desk. "You think Olivia or Mark got these letters?"

"It would prove a connection if they did." She sighed. "We need to get back to their homes and see what we can find."

"Now that we know what we're looking for."

I went to Olivia's home and Zelina went to Mark's.

I searched her room and her desk. I searched through stacks of books, envelopes, scraps of paper with notes scribbled on them.

I was just about to walk away when I felt something at the back of the drawer in her desk. A stack of envelopes all the way in the back. I pulled them out.

"There you are," I whispered triumphantly. In the envelopes were the same letters as the latest victim, with the exact same wording and handwriting. I placed the letters in evidence bags and then headed back to the station. A few minutes later Zelina joined me, red-faced and sweaty.

"He had all kinds of hiding places. Found these under a squeaky floorboard underneath his desk."

"I found hers in the very back of her desk."

"Why were they hiding them?" Zelina set the letters next to mine. "They look harmless. I don't understand why they thought they should hide them."

I placed all the letters side by side on the desk. They all had the same emblem and the same wording. "What is the point of these letters? It's like whoever wrote them wants attention and the journalists weren't giving it to them. Maybe that made them angry."

The letters seemed harmless on the surface, but there was something else to them. The specific wording gave me pause. In the beginning, it seemed okay, but toward the end it sounded threatening to me. The letter writer told the recipients to make wise choices. As if not covering the organization was not a wise choice. There wasn't a written threat, but it was implied. Heavily implied.

Rising Sun. That was the name of the organization. It made sense because of the sunburst on the letter. That was their mark. It was a weird name for any organization, but we figured it was a cult. With that name it had to be.

I searched the name, but nothing came up. They must have been a new cult. Or one that wasn't big on advertising on the internet. If they were a cult, one that specialized in threats and murder, they wouldn't want to advertise that.

I had never dealt with a cult before. I never understood them. How could someone be so persuasive that they could talk someone into giving them all of their money, sell their house, cut off their family and follow them?

"Killed them out of revenge, maybe?" Zelina was staring at the pictures. "Revenge for not doing what they wanted?"

I shrugged. "They wanted news coverage and that is exactly what they are going to get now. I mean... I hate to say it, but they are getting exactly what they want. People will be talking about them once all of this gets out. It can't be a coincidence."

She looked at the letters. "Maybe we should hold this back?"

With every case, a detective will hold something about the case back from the press. It wasn't because we wanted to be deceptive or lie to the public. I was once told by the captain why it was always a good idea not to reveal too much to the press.

If we held the letters back, we might be able to draw them out. It wasn't a coincidence that all three victims had gotten the letters. If we didn't give the group what they wanted, then maybe they might do something that would draw our attention. I just prayed it wasn't another body.

"You two!" The harshness of the captain's voice drew my attention immediately. He pointed at us and gestured for us to get in his office. He closed the door behind us.

He sat on the edge of his desk and waited. It was clear he wanted us to fill him in on the case, so I started talking. I told him everything we knew so far and about the letters.

"I talked to a buddy of mine. I couldn't get that marking on the body out of my head."

As soon as he said it, I sat up straight. I suddenly remembered the coroner didn't say anything about a mark being on Mark's body. We also forgot to ask.

"It looked so familiar, so I asked him about it and showed him a picture. He remembered the case immediately because it was one of his few unsolved cases when he worked in Chicago. A woman was killed, stabbed several times, and she had the same sunburst carved into her chest. Her killer was never found., but he said they were only looking for one guy."

I shoved my hands in my pockets. "What was their working theory?"

"He said they never settled on anyone. She lived alone, was quiet. Had no ex or current boyfriends."

"What did the family think?"

"Well, he said they had no proof so they couldn't pursue it and found no evidence in her home. But the family believed she was part of a cult."

"But they could never prove it?" asked Zelina.

"He said they asked her friends and her neighbors. She was behaving differently, but they... she wouldn't talk about it. She wouldn't talk about what she was doing or what she was getting into. Also, when they found her body there was a packed bag next to her foot."

"Hmm, either she was going on a trip, or she was afraid of someone and running away," I said.

He handed me a slip of paper. "I'll see if I can follow up, get any more information."

"Okay. Thanks."

We left the office and walked back to our desk. I sat down and stared at the letters and the number. The letters drew my eye every time I tried not to look at them. "You think the letters have something to do with Robert Crow?"

Zelina stopped shuffling her papers. "Do you?"

"Every time I look at them, I think about him."

"You think about Robert Crow? Why?"

Every time I looked at one of the letters, I thought about the look on his face when we first met him. The more I looked at them the more I wondered if these murders had something to do with his case. There were too many coincidences in this case and I didn't believe in coincidences. Maybe his case was where this all started.

I gathered the letters together and then I noticed a file on my desk. I hadn't left it there. "Did you put this on my desk?"

She glanced up for a brief moment and then shook her head. I opened the file and gasped.

It was Lizzie Sherman's case file. "He found the file."

It was covered in dust. The first items I saw were her autopsy pictures and then the crime scene pictures. I flipped through the file studying every picture and reading ever written or typed word.

"What is that?" I wondered aloud as I looked at one of her autopsy pictures and then read the coroner report. "Look at that mark on her chest." I slid the picture over to Zelina. "Coroner makes no mention of it the report."

"She has multiple stab wounds. Maybe he figured the killer was going to stab her there and then changed their mind. Hesitation marks." She slid it back over.

"Possible. Or maybe someone started to carve a moon in her chest and got distracted. Zelina straightened in her seat. "To me it looks more like a circle or the start of a circle then a hesitation mark."

She pulled the picture back. "Okay I guess I can see that. Part of a circle and then a small line. Part of a sunburst." She looked up and stared at me. "They're connected?"

When I looked at the sunburst, I thought of the letters, and I thought about Robert Crow, and then I thought about the first time we met him in the trailer park. And then... I thought about the sunflower on the window of a trailer. "You know, Robert had a sun on his trailer. On the window. I noticed it because I saw another trailer that had a sunflower in the window."

"You think this is related?"

"Sunburst, suns. Might be something there. It looks like whoever this group is they want some serious attention. Maybe the cult is in the trailer park."

I looked up the meaning behind suns and sunflowers. I learned there have been a lot of meanings and symbolism over the years. Some cultures worshiped the sun as a god. Egypt for starters. The sun can also be the symbol for justice, hope and renewal.

Were they looking for justice because the journalists weren't listing to them? Maybe they felt slighted. Sunflowers could be the symbol of loyalty. My mind immediately went back to the trailers. There was one sun and two sunflowers. Were they loyal to the sun?

It was a hunch, but it felt right. Felt solid. There was something going on at that trailer park. Now we just needed to figure out how to approach things. I didn't want to spook them, so I wasn't sure about bringing backup. But there were so many of them, not bringing backup—just in case—was stupid.

I tapped my pen against my desk. We needed to come up with a game plan before we went out there. Just in case.

CHAPTER TWENTY-SIX

Logan Elwood

IDIDN'T UNDERSTAND WHY IT WAS SO DIFFICULT FOR ME TO FALL asleep. My body wouldn't relax. My brain wouldn't shut up long enough to allow my body to relax enough to fall asleep. It was a bitter cycle and by two in the morning, I was exhausted, but apparently not enough to actually go to sleep.

I sat up in bed and scrolled through my phone for what felt like an hour, it was only ten minutes. The house was silent. Everyone else was asleep in their beds. I crawled out of mine and got dressed. I needed to get some air. The beach had always been one of my favorite places to think. The sounds of the waves crashing against the sand was like white noise to me, calming. I needed a sense of calm at the moment. Everly still hadn't returned my calls and there answers only she could give me.

I drove to the beach and found a spot in the sand. I loved the feeling of sand between my toes. It was a pain in the ass to clean up, but it felt amazing in the moment. It was cool to the touch. I closed my eyes and relished the feeling. A car door slammed behind me. I checked my watch it wasn't even three yet.

"We have to stop meeting like this."

The sound of Riley's voice brought a smile to my lips. This was the second time we met, unintentionally, at the beach early in the morning. It seemed we both had a challenging time sleeping. She kicked her shoes off before sitting next to me.

"It wasn't planned."

She laughed. "Of course not. I've been tossing and turning for the last few hours, so I decided to get up and get dressed. I was going to go to the station and start working on the case, but changed my mind before I reached it. What's your excuse?"

I told her everything that I had learned about Jamie and Marie and how I felt about it. She nodded as she listened and when I was done talking, she sighed. "I understand how upset this must have made you. But it doesn't matter now. Marie is dead, her involvement in the fire or whatever you think happened is immaterial. It doesn't matter. And yeah, now you feel like you never really knew her, but digging all this up is not going to change that. She's not coming back to explain herself. Might be time to let it go."

She was right. In my heart I knew she was right. Digging into Marie's past would not change my present. And yet I just couldn't let it go. I felt like a dog with a bone. Now that the thought was in my mind it was there. It felt like I couldn't rest until I knew everything. Until I learned if Marie was really the person I thought she was, or if she was more like Jamie than I cared to admit. Even as she gave me her advice, I knew I wasn't going to take it. Instead, I changed the subject.

"Okay, what's really bothering you? Is it the case or are you still thinking about your friend?"

Riley's shoulders deflated. "My friend Brianna is in town. She came to talk to me."

"Okay. That's good, isn't it?"

She didn't share my enthusiasm. "I haven't spoken to her since I left LA. That was by design. I don't have anything to say now."

"If you didn't have anything to say, I don't think you would be as upset as you are. It's bothering you for a reason. Maybe it's not that you don't have something to say, but that you are afraid of what she's going to say. She clearly has something she wants to say to you. She came all this way. Where is the harm in hearing her out?"

She shrugged. "I already know what she's going to say. I know where this conversation is going to go, and I don't feel like hearing it."

I exhaled slowly, my eyes fixed on the waves. "You know, or you think you know? It's not the same thing." Riley looked at me for a long moment before I continued. "You think you know what she's going to say because you have built this up in your head for a long time. You feel responsible so everyone else must believe that you are too. People always see you differently from how you see yourself. Just because you believe it doesn't make it true, and you'll never know if it's true or not until you listen to them."

She exhaled loudly. Silence filled the space around us. "Have you heard from your mother-in-law?"

The sudden change in the subject confused me for a moment. "Umm... no. I've been calling her, but I haven't heard back. I figured she was tired of dealing with all of this and needed a break. I know I could use one. Why?"

"We got a call at the station. Someone is looking for her. A boyfriend or something. She never made it home and isn't returning calls."

"Maybe she decided she needed a break and drove off. I hope she didn't get in an accident or anything."

"We have people looking into that. I just figured you might have heard something."

I shook my head. The news soured my stomach. I thought Everly was just ignoring me after the mediation. I couldn't blame her. But now this sounded a little suspicious. I immediately thought of Jamie, but I shook the thought loose. Jamie was a lot of things, but I didn't think she'd kill her own mother.

We sat in a comfortable silence for a few hours. Making comments here and there about the weather or on how beautiful the sunrise looked over the water. The sky was painted purple and a soft orange. It was gorgeous. I wished I had taken out my phone and took a picture, but I didn't need to. I wanted to be in the moment.

Shortly after the sun rose people started appearing on the beach. Some people were walking, while others were out for a run. I looked at Riley who was already pulling herself to her feet.

"Want to get some coffee before work?" I asked. She was dressed for work, but I still needed to get ready.

"Sure. I'll drive to the station then meet you by your office."

I hurried home to get dressed and make sure Dani got off to school okay.

"And where were you this early in the morning?" Isaac stood in the doorway of the kitchen eating a piece of French toast.

I rolled my eyes. "I couldn't sleep so I went to the beach."

He straightened. "You still do that?"

Something about the water has always calmed my mind. When I was a kid, and my mother and brother were getting on my nerves, I would take the bus to the beach and stay there for as long as I could. It was the best place to think, at least for me. "I needed to think some things through. And now I need to get ready for lunch." I patted Dani on the head while I passed her on the stairs.

"Good morning papa."

"Morning, Dani." In my room I changed my clothes and got myself together. When I emerged downstairs, Dani was on her way out the door with Bonnie. I gave her a hug and a kiss. "Have a good day."

"You too."

I closed the door behind them before going into the kitchen.

"I made some French toast and some Canadian bacon and cheesy scrambled eggs. You could make a breakfast sandwich."

That was exactly what I did, while Isaac went back upstairs to bed. He didn't have to get to work until the afternoon, so he had time to kill. I wrapped my sandwich in foil and headed out the door. Riley was right where she said she'd be, outside my office.

"Thought you forgot there for a second."

I smiled. "Nope. Just had to make sure Dani got to school and all that."

Riley nodded slowly. "Right."

We walked into the coffee shop and ordered our drinks. Riley got an extra pump of espresso and caramel apple syrup. I looked at her while I paid for the coffees.

"What?" She grinned. "It's not that much sugar. The extra shot of espresso counteracts the extra pump of syrup."

"Is that what it does?"

Her mother, who stood behind the counter eying us, laughed. "That's what she always says, but it's still extra sugar."

"Umm... excuse me ma'am, you should not make your customers feel bad about their drink of choice."

April threw her hands up. "Not making you feel bad, just pointing out your logic is flawed, as the doctor can attest." She handed Riley and me our drinks and then waved us off so the customer behind us could get their order.

"You and your mom are funny," I said as soon as I stepped outside.

Riley laughed. "She's like that with all of us. You should see her and my dad together. They're hilarious."

"Can I walk you to the station?"

Her head tilted slightly before she shrugged. "Sure. I take it you don't feel like going into work right now."

"Or maybe I'm just enjoying your company." I took a sip of coffee.

"Don't try to smooth talk me, Doctor Elwood."

I spit out my coffee as a laugh bubbled up my throat nearly choking me. Riley laughed.

"I'm not that smooth."

"Sure..."

"So what's on your mind?" she asked as we crossed the street.

There were a million things on my mind, but none of them wanted to come out of my mouth. If I never said them then they were just thoughts, but once I said the words out loud, they became real. Tangible.

It was silent for a moment. "Do you think that Marie knew Jamie was going to do something stupid, and that's why she went there that night? Maybe she thought she could talk her out of it."

"It's possible."

"Maybe she was crying because Marie caught her in the act, and she didn't know what Marie was going to do."

I inhaled sharply. "That might have been it. I can't believe she didn't turn her in."

"I would have turned my sister in, in a heartbeat. But then again, I have a strong sense of morality when it comes to mass murder."

"So one or two murders are okay?" A smile tugged at my lips.

"Uh... depends on the reasoning behind said murders. But I draw the line at mass scale murders and hurting children."

"Glad to know where you draw the line."

The way she said it... there was a slight playfulness on the edge of her voice. I couldn't tell whether she was serious or playing around. I didn't want to ask either. We stopped in front of the police station.

"I seriously think after you solve this case, because we both know you will, you need to call your friend and go out for drinks and hear what she has to say. Put that to bed so you can move forward. Until you do, you'll be in a constant state of guilt for the rest of your life."

Riley smiled. "Why do you always know what to say to make me feel better?"

I shrugged. "Dunno. Guess I'm just that good."

She laughed and swatted my arm. "Don't push it, Doc."

CHAPTER TWENTY-SEVEN

Jamie Washington

J AMIE SPENT MOST OF HER DAYS FOLLOWING LOGAN AND HIS FAM-
ily around. Once she understood their schedules, she knew where
they would be, and when, without thinking about it. She knew Isaac
went to his NA meetings most nights before going home. Logan went to
work, to the diner for lunch, and then back to work before going home.

Their schedules were quite boring. They did nothing interesting or
out of the ordinary. They had singular pursuits, work and staying clean.
When she was sure Logan was settled in at work, she went to the coffee
shop and waited. This time she had her computer with her so she could
do some research. April was there and the first person she saw when she
walked in. She was always there.

"I usually work front of the house, and my husband is in the kitchen.
We realized early on it was better that way."

"How?"

April laughed as she sat down across from her.

"He is the sweetest man you will ever meet, but he is not good with the customers. It doesn't take him a long time to get annoyed and some customers can push your buttons. Well, his buttons. He blew up at someone who couldn't make up their mind on what they wanted. They were in line for ten minutes going back and forth. He didn't find her indecisiveness endearing. Especially since she always got the same thing every time she came in."

Jamie laughed. "I get it. That would have bothered me too."

Up until now, April and Jamie had spent many days talking. April talked about her family and Jamie learned so much about the cop named Riley who kept following Logan around.

She was smart and kind, allegedly. But Jamie still didn't like the look of her. She couldn't stand seeing her around Logan or knowing that she met Dani. She knew what was going on. She knew what Logan and Riley were doing. They wanted to replace Marie.

"But enough about that. How have you been, dear?"

"I've been okay. What about you?"

"Pretty good." She sat in the seat across from Jamie. "Everything hurts most days, but I still get up in the morning so I can't complain. Well, I can, but I won't." She looked back at the register. "Let me know if you need anything."

Jamie smiled before going back to her research. The coffee was good, and the pastries were better. Her phone vibrated in her pocket. She was already annoyed when she fished it out of her pocket. She was fairly certain it was her husband before she answered. She had no interest in talking to him. Not at that moment, anyway.

"Yes?"

"Is this Jamie Washington?"

Jamie paused. The voice wasn't familiar. "Who is this?"

"This is Dwight Moore. I'm your mother's boyfriend."

Her heart seized in her chest. Her mother had no boyfriend. Who was this playing a trick on her? "I'm sorry, but my mother doesn't have a boyfriend. You must have me confused."

"Aren't you Everly's daughter?"

"Yes." Jamie leaned back in her chair. "Why are you calling me? I didn't know she had a boyfriend."

"You two weren't that close, so I understand that. But have you seen her?"

Jamie couldn't wrap her mind around it. Who would date her mother? Who would love her enough to look for her? "Umm... not since the mediation. Why?"

"I've been trying to call her, but she's not answering. She said she would be back by now, but no one here has seen her."

"Well, I don't know what to tell you. I haven't seen her since the mediation. Things didn't end well. I haven't heard from her since that day. I haven't seen her. I just assumed she was going home."

"No. It's been a few days now. It's not like her."

Jamie rolled her eyes. It was like her. It was just like her. She always left them and never said a word about when she would be back or if she would be back. She left them by themselves for weeks. She never even called... they had to fend for themselves. Who the hell was he? He didn't know her. Not who she truly was. It was all a facade. Her mother was great at wearing masks. Showing people what she wanted them to see.

"She wouldn't tell me where she was going even if I saw her. We don't have that kind of relationship."

"I know. I just thought I'd ask."

Jamie winced. He said 'I know.' How did he know? Her mother talked about her, or maybe she didn't talk about her. Only enough for him to know she had a daughter. It was like a knife in the gut. She knew they never got along and that Everly didn't really like her, but his words sealed it. She wondered for a brief moment what else her mother had said. Did she talk about Marie too? Did she say only nice things to him and her friends? Did she make Marie the good one and her the evil one, when really, they were two sides of the same coin? Marie was just as evil as Jamie, she just did a better job hiding it.

"Hope you find her." Jamie hung up before he could say anything else. She had kept her voice steady, but her heartbeat was a drum in her chest. She never thought anyone would come looking for Everly. Who liked her and why? If someone loved her mother something must have been wrong with them. There was no love in her. No gentleness. Nothing.

But now she had another problem. If he came looking for her that would be bad. Jamie thought about her plan for Dani. It wasn't ready yet, but she needed to do something before anyone figured out her mother was in the flowerbed. She didn't want to still be in town when that happened.

Jamie stared at her coffee. She knew she would be the first suspect. Rightfully so. She did kill her. If this boyfriend came to town he would come straight to her. If that happened, Jamie knew she'd have to pretend to care. Throw him off her scent by worrying about Everly's safety and whatnot. She was sure she could fake it or at least try to make it believable. He didn't know her, so it might work.

Her fingers drummed against the table. She had to work on her plan and get everything finished. The call caught her off guard, but she hoped her voice didn't have the slight tremble she thought she heard. She wasn't prepared for someone asking about her mother's whereabouts. It never dawned on her that someone would care that much. She sure as hell didn't. She worried her mind over a thought. She wondered if it came across how little she cared for her mother, and if that would make him worry about her a little more.

It was no secret that she and Everly didn't have the best relationship. He made it clear that he knew that. He couldn't have been surprised by her attitude. She worried about Everly about as much as Everly worried about her. And technically she knew where Everly was, she just didn't want anyone else to find out.

Jamie went home early that day. The call had frayed her nerves, and she couldn't concentrate. She was worried her facial expressions and inability to follow a conversation would make April worry about her and start to ask questions. It was best she left right away.

She bought a smoked salmon croissant to take home and another latte to go. She wasn't too concerned about Logan's whereabouts after work. He did the same thing every day. She knew where he was going without having to see it firsthand.

Jamie went home. She set her food and coffee on the kitchen counter, before pacing the length of the hallway from the front door to the kitchen. Her mind moved about as quickly as her feet.

"Nothing will come from this," she told herself over and over, trying to make herself believe it. There was no way he would come to Pine Brooke in search of her mother.

The days seemed to blend together. She did the same thing every day. Followed Logan and Isaac and checked on Dani. Dani was the carefree child she wished she had been at that age. If she had a mother who cared more about her children than herself.

It made her heart smile watching her play in the playground at school. Not a care in the world. Jamie wanted to give her that freedom as well. She would try her best. Jamie stood in front of the breakfast nook staring at her computer. Her plan was coming together. She had the funds, the new birth certificates and social security numbers. They both had new identities. She obtained the new papers from a friend she met at school when she was a teen. They kept in touch over the years. While Jamie tried her best to live free from trouble, her friend made no such effort.

She flipped through articles touting the best places to live if you wanted anonymity. Most of the towns she had never heard of. This made them good candidates for her needs. The doorbell rang. Jamie froze in front of her computer. She hadn't ordered anything, and people practically never knocked, least of all rang the doorbell. She inched toward the door and looked out the peephole. There was a man with a thick dark brown beard with slivers of gray and dark rimmed glasses. He didn't look familiar. Nor did he have a package in his hands.

She took a deep breath and a glance around the room before opening the door. She was sure she had removed all traces her mother had ever been there.

"Yes?"

"Hi, you're Jamie, right? You look just like your sister, Marie."

The comment shook her to her core. After Everly told her who her real mother was, everything made sense. She did look like Marie, more so than Everly. She hadn't noticed it before, maybe her brain didn't want to admit it.

"Who are you?"

"Oh, um... I'm Dwight. Everly's boyfriend." He held out his hand and she shook it slowly. Her heart stuttered in her chest. She couldn't believe it. He actually came to find her mother. She never imagined he cared that much.

"Right. You called. I take it you didn't find her."

"No. I've called everyone I know that knows her. I've stopped by her usual haunts. No trace of her anywhere. Well, except for here."

Jamie froze. *What was that supposed to mean?* She looked back in the house trying to figure out if he saw something she might have missed. "I'm sorry, what are you talking about?"

He held up his phone. I traced her phone to this address."

Jamie's stomach soured as her mouth filled with saliva. She wanted to vomit right there on his feet. "I can't see how. I haven't heard it ringing and she's not here."

"Was she at some point?"

The best lies were the ones tinged with the truth. "She did stop by. She walked here from wherever she was staying. She didn't tell me where. It was after the mediation. She tried to talk me into going back with her. She sat on the sofa; we talked for a bit... umm... she wanted a tour of the house. She liked it. And then she told me to take care of myself and keep my temper in check. Then she left. I assumed she went back home. I haven't seen her since. Are you sure her phone led you here?"

He held the phone up again, this time in her face. "Pretty sure."

"Unless it fell out of her pocket while we walked around—but again, I haven't heard it ringing or anything. And I feel like she would have come back for that."

"She would have. Do you know where she was staying?"

Jamie shook her head. "But it's a small town, there aren't that many places she could stay. Do you know the car she was driving?"

Dwight nodded and shoved his hands in his pockets.

"You could drive around town until you see it. It should be a short ride."

He stared at her for a long time before thanking her for her time and walking back to his car. She closed the front door slowly. Her heart was a drum in her chest, the rhythm became more frantic as she walked away from the door and collapsed onto the sofa. She didn't need this to happen now. Why was he here? Jamie couldn't wrap her head around the fact that he actually showed up looking for her. In a million years she never would have seen that coming. And now what was she supposed to do? And where was her mother's phone?

Jamie couldn't remember checking her mother's pockets before she buried her. She should have, but she wanted to get it over with, the least amount of steps the better. She jumped to her feet; a thought slowly took shape, and she had to test it. She grabbed her cell phone and stepped outside in the backyard, close to the flowerbed. She called her mother and to see if she could hear her phone ring.

Bell chimes, soft and muffled rose up from the flowers. Her heart sank into her stomach. Her phone was with her. She stood there for a long moment eyeing the flowers and mentally running through her options. She thought about digging her mother up and getting rid of the phone. But that would have been extremely suspicious. If he tried to trace her mother's cell again, and it showed up as being somewhere else, that would have made her a prime suspect. The phone just so happened to move the day after she was asked about her mother's whereabouts and told the phone traced back to her home. It made her look guilty.

She was, but it was best not to appear so until she was on her way out of town with Dani.

Digging her up again would also raise suspicions with her neighbors. The couple always seemed to be outside when she was, watching her and asking her questions. She didn't want to run the risk of them seeing something they shouldn't. They had been nice to her, and she didn't want to have to kill them. She would, but she didn't want to if she didn't have to.

As she walked back into the house, Jamie realized she only had one option. She needed to move up the timeline of her plan before someone came looking around.

She had no problem with anyone finding her mother, she just didn't want to be there when they did.

CHAPTER TWENTY-EIGHT

Logan Elwood

I WISHED I COULD THINK OF SOMETHING ELSE. ANYTHING ELSE. BUT the fire consumed my every thought, so I took another day off to do research. After having a few more conversations with Marie's friends, I learned that Marie was always covering for Jamie. Even when it was clear that Jamie was in the wrong. It never mattered. Marie and Everly would cover it up. Once Everly's husband died, she had enough money to pay people off.

"Jamie hurt someone real bad. And the next thing I knew it wasn't in the news even though it should have been. She wasn't arrested and the family didn't press charges. I knew Everly had something to do with it. When I asked Marie about it, she said that it was handled. I knew what that meant. All I could do was shake my head. If Jamie was never

held responsible for her actions, then she would continue on with
no consequences."

I understood what Kay was saying. It was why she acted the way
she did. She had gotten away with so many things. She thought she was
untouchable. Marie and Everly cleaned up her messes. But Marie was
dead and Everly seemed like she was sick of her bullshit. I had tried
calling Everly several times, but she never answered. Maybe she was sick
of my shit too.

There was a soft knock at the door. I wasn't expecting anyone.
Bonnie was spending the day out of the house and Isaac was at work.
I opened the door. Riley smiled at me with a thick folder in her hand.

"Heard you were trying to investigate a couple of murders."

"Sixty-five to be exact."

Riley nearly dropped the folder. "What?"

I ushered her into the house. She sat on the floor of the living room
surrounded by papers I had printed out. I poured her a glass of Isaac's
mango and raspberry lemonade.

"That looks pretty."

"Yeah. Sac made it. He told us to put the mashed raspberries in first
so the glass will have both yellow and purple until you mix it yourself."

"He's so fancy."

I laughed. He was getting pretty fancy. "So what brings you by?"

"Well, I heard you were still working on the case. While I was waiting to hear back on some test results I decided to look into things and
see if I could help you. Not sure what you are looking for though."

I explained that I knew Jamie was not getting custody of Dani, but
since I learned about the fire, I couldn't stop thinking about it. It amazed
me that no one ever talked about it. A horrible event like that and everyone seemed to sweep it under the rug. I understood that it was a difficult
thing to talk about, but still… Marie never mentioned it. Jamie never
said anything, and neither did Everly.

Riley slowly lowered her head as if she was trying to think of the
right answer. "I understand that, kind of. Once I get a case in my head I
can't stop thinking about it. Not until I figure it out. Like I have to know
everything. Every detail so I can put the pieces together. It's annoying,
but it is what makes me good at my job. And I love my job."

"I've noticed."

"Shut up. Now where have you gotten so far.?"

I explained everything I found and who I spoke to. I told her about
Bianca and what she said.

"Well, here is what I learned. Jamie went to the school, but so did Marie. She went fourteen years earlier."

"Marie was twelve when she went to the school," I said.

Riley's fingers tapped on the papers. "I know."

"You think she was pregnant?"

Riley looked up at me for a long moment, her eyes glassy. I knew the answer before she said it. Once I realized it, it all made so much sense. Why Marie was so protective of her. Why they always came to her defense even though she was wrong.

Riley took a breath, but held my gaze.

"I couldn't find Jamie's birth records, which I find extremely strange. I mean they should be there, but they were either burned up in the school or somehow destroyed. That being said, I can't say definitively that Jamie was her daughter, but the math adds up." Riley flipped through the folder.

"I did however find the police report from that night. And it's interesting. Jamie was questioned extensively. Several times. This shows me that you aren't the only one who believed she had something to do with it. While it was arson, they couldn't prove she had something to do with it. The accelerant was not found on her. They tested her clothes and her hands. Nothing."

"So how did she start the fire and not get anything on her?" I asked.

"How did she start the fire and not get any soot on her nightgown? Her nightgown was clean and fresh. No burn marks, which would have been present if she was close to the fire."

"Which she would have been if she started it."

"Exactly. Now it's a stretch, but maybe she had a spare nightgown outside and changed once she got outside and the fire had started. But then again, no accelerant was on her hands. Her fingernails weren't charred. There was no evidence that she started the fire."

"Damn... maybe she didn't do it."

"No one believed that though. Even after they cleared her, people still thought she did it."

"I get that. I still think she had something to do with it."

"More to the point, another reason they thought it was her was because the fire started in a place she was known to hang out when she couldn't sleep. The library."

My conversation with Bianca flashed in my mind. Bianca said Jamie wasn't in her room when she warned everyone about the fire. "She liked going to the library?"

"That's what one of the witnesses said. She was often found there in the morning. Curled up between the stacks. It started there."

"Maybe we're thinking about this all wrong," I said. "Maybe she was the target."

Riley's eyes snapped to me. "You think someone tried to kill her?"

"I don't know. I understand what could get them there. Not saying it's right, but it's a feeling we all know too well."

Riley shook her head. "I put in a request to get the crime scene pictures. They weren't in the file and I'm still waiting to hear back."

"Did they interview Marie?"

She closed the folder and handed it to me. "Why would they?"

"She was there."

Riley stared at me. "I looked through the files before I brought them here and Marie is not mentioned. If she was still there when they started interviews, she would have been in the file."

"Maybe she snuck out before they saw her because she wasn't supposed to be there."

"She went there to see Jamie?"

"Yeah, Jamie didn't want to be there anymore. She hated being at the school and wanted to leave. She wanted to go home. I think she went there to calm her down, but the school was on fire."

"Maybe she hated it enough to burn it down."

"I don't know."

Riley's phone dinged and she looked at the screen. "And I have to go. The test results are in. I gotta go." She jumped to her feet. "If I get the pictures, I'll send them to you. Don't do anything stupid without me or your brother."

"Nothing I do is stupid," I called after her as she walked toward the door.

"The jury is still out on that." I heard the door open and close. I went to lock it. If Jamie was Marie's daughter, what did that mean? Did Jamie know? Was that why she was so clingy?

I tried calling Everly for the millionth time, but she didn't answer. I sighed back onto the sofa.

Riley did eventually send the pictures. I was thankful for them. Instead of looking at them on my computer, I printed them out and spread them on the table. One picture caught my eye. I called Everly immediately. Yet again, she didn't answer.

Marie was in two of the pictures. She was in the back of both pictures, way out of the way. If you weren't looking for her you would have missed her. But she wasn't interviewed. She ducked out before they could get to her or got lost in the chaos.

I needed more answers. I needed to talk to the other survivor.

Riley called me again. "Oh, I had one more thing."

"What's up?"

"Have you seen your mother-in-law?"

I sat up straight in my chair. "Not since mediation. She was angry at Jamie so I figured she might have left. Gone home and didn't want to deal with us. I've been trying to call, but nothing... why?"

"Everly's boyfriend is in town looking for her. He says that she never returned home, and he's been calling her, and she doesn't answer. He says it's not like her."

My stomach soured.

"Jamie did something. I have no proof, but I'm telling you she had something to do with it."

"Okay. Noted. I'll call you if I hear anything."

"Thanks, Riley."

I sank back in my seat. Jamie did something to her mother. I hadn't seen her since the mediation either. She hasn't stopped by or called or sent any notes. I half expected her lawyer to send me a letter or something. But it never came.

Jamie didn't give up. She was definitely up to something.

CHAPTER TWENTY-NINE

Riley Quinn

ZELINA AGREED WITH ME, AS DID THE CAPTAIN. WE HAD NO HARD evidence against anyone so we couldn't go there and arrest them. We didn't even have enough for a search warrant. What we had was a hunch, and those didn't fare well in court.

I wanted to go back to the campground, but I still wasn't sure about it. Something told me the answer I was looking for was there. I just didn't know what to look for or where to find it. There were so many trailers there…

"Do you know of any officers that have dealt with any complaints there? They might have seen something that might help us."

Zelina typed on her computer. "Officer Rainwater gets sent out there a lot. More than anyone else."

"I wonder why?"

We tracked down Officer Rainwater at the diner. It had been difficult in the aftermath of his partner being arrested. He was a serial killer and just about everyone in town couldn't understand why he hadn't known about it. But when you trust someone and believe they will have your back you get a little blind. You don't want to see the bad in them, and I thought that was the problem. He didn't complain though.

I spotted him in the back booth, slowly chewing and staring at the wall. I slid into his booth. "Hey."

He stared at me with rheumy eyes. "Hey."

I felt bad for him almost immediately. He wasn't complaining, but everyone turning their back on him was hard to deal with. "It'll get better."

This comment elicited a low chuckle.

"Sure. What do you need?"

"We noticed that you get called to the campground a lot. Curious why?"

"Punishment, I guess."

I rested my elbows on the table. "No one else goes there?"

"Have you been there?"

"Yeah, that's why I'm asking. We went there and it was... I don't think weird is a strong enough word for what it was."

Zelina slid into the booth next to me. "There's something going on there, but we couldn't place it. Serious creepy vibes."

His head bobbed slowly. "Yeah, that's why I get stuck going. No one else wants to go out there. Those people... at first it was okay, but within the last year or so, the people have gotten weirder and weirder. When I and—my ex-partner—used to get called out there we noticed it. Before it felt light and fun, and people were just hanging out with each other. Sharing campfires. Sharing food. Mostly all we got were noise complaints."

"When did it change?"

His shoulders rose and fell faintly. "Not sure, exactly. But last year we got called out for a domestic thing. There were a lot more trailers in the area than before. The atmosphere was heavy, and the people were watching us. I mean the whole time it gave me the creeps. When I tried to talk to the woman involved in the call, she wouldn't talk to me. She would look at this other woman before she would utter a word. It was crazy. She didn't want to press charges, and we got the hell out of there."

"What did the woman look like?" Zelina took out her notepad and pen. "The one she kept looking at."

"Slim frame, big eyes, blonde dreadlocks."

Zelina stopped writing and we both stared at him.

"What's wrong?" His eyes narrowed.

"We met that woman," I said. "We met her the other day. She seemed really nice, on the surface… but there was a—her sweetness seemed fake. Not forced, but not genuine either. She walked us to the trailer we were looking for."

"I wouldn't trust that woman. She's up to something."

"Thanks for talking to us."

Zelina headed toward the door. I stopped mid-step and turned around. "If we need backup, I think we might, will you be there?"

"Of course."

"In that case can you keep an eye on the campground? We're not ready to go there just yet. Still need to figure some things out."

"You can count on me."

"Thank you." I met Zelina in the car. "I just asked him to keep an eye on the campground."

"You feel sorry for him?"

"I do. It's not his fault Blaese was a serial killer, and yeah, he made some mistakes, but… in the end, he told us what we needed to know."

"One rotten apple spoils the whole bunch, and Rainwater was the closest apple to *him*," she blurted out as she got in the car.

She had a point, but I still trusted Rainwater. He was a great cop before he was partnered with *him*. If he had known for certain what he was doing, I did believe that he would have said something. I believed in him until he proved me wrong.

We drove back to the station in silence. I didn't know what Z was thinking, but I couldn't get Olivia's body out of my head. All of the multiple stab wounds. I walked into the building with Zelina in tow. I sat down at my desk, a thought nagging at me. "Could be a cult that did the murders."

Zelina looked up from her computer. "You think?"

"I'm just thinking about the multiple stab wounds and how the other victim's family believed she was involved with a cult. Maybe they moved down here and laid low."

"What made them want notoriety now?"

I shrugged. "I don't know. How can we find out?"

I leaned back in my chair and scanned over the papers on my desk. There had to be a way that we could find out what cult she might have been involved with. The captain emerged from his office and walked to our desk.

"What did you learn about the campsite?"

I told him what Rainwater said. "I told him to watch the camp-ground and let me know if anyone leaves. I don't think they know we are looking at them for these murders, but... I'm not sure. There's something... I can't explain it, so I won't even try."

"I understand that. Sometimes you just have to trust your gut."

"Mine is screaming at me."

"You think all of them are a part of it?" asked Zelina. She stretched at her desk before resuming reading through a file.

I didn't know how many people were involved. It was difficult to say, but they all lived there. They had to know, right? "I can't see anyone there not knowing what's going on." But what was going on? Was it a cult? Or was it just a group of people helping each other out?

"Do you think I could talk to her mother? The victim from Chicago. I want to ask someone who knew her a few questions about her behavior. Maybe they know who she hung out with."

"Give me a minute." He disappeared into his office for a few minutes. When he returned, he had a slip of paper. "This is her mother's number. She is always eager to talk about her daughter, so this might be a long conversation."

I sat back at my desk and readied myself for this conversation.

"Hello?"

"Hi—"

"Are you the detective from California? They said you'd call. I don't know why, my daughter never went to California."

"I understand that. I wanted to talk to you because I was told you thought your daughter was part of a cult. Do you still believe that?"

"I do."

"Can you tell me what makes you think that? Was there any evidence that she was involved with a cult?"

She sighed. "The detectives said there wasn't, but I know my daughter, and she was behaving strangely before she was killed."

"Can you be more specific?"

"She was a quiet girl and lived a quiet life, then all of a sudden, she started going out and hanging with a group of people that she wouldn't let us meet. I knew all her friends, and none of them knew the people she was hanging out with. She seemed happier, though. I thought she had gotten a boyfriend or something."

"No one met the friends?"

"No. I think her friend Corinne saw her with a blonde woman that wouldn't introduce herself, but that was it."

"Can I speak to Corinne? Do you know how I can get in touch with her?" I held my breath hoping for a yes, but preparing myself for a no.

"I do. Give me a moment." I heard her set the phone on the table. A few minutes later she returned. "I still have her number. I'm sure she'd be okay with speaking to you."

I wrote down the number she gave me. "Thank you so much for speaking with me. If I learn anything about your daughter's death, I will let you know."

"I appreciate that. They took everything. Her savings, her car, everything in her home that had any value to it."

"You said they took her car?" My blood froze in my veins. There were a lot of cars at the campground. "Do you remember what kind of car?"

It was quiet for a long moment. "I can't remember the year. I was never good at identifying cars. It was my husband's. An old Mustang, that I remember. It was red with a black stripe down the middle. She loved that car. She took better care of it than she did herself. She never would have sold it. Not the last piece she had of her father. It was far too precious. She wouldn't just give it away either."

"Okay. I'll keep an eye out." I hung up the phone and immediately started dialing the number I was given. After several rings, a woman answered the phone. "Hello, I'm Detective Riley Quinn with the Pine Brooke, California PD. I'm looking for Corinne —"

"What's wrong?"

The panic in her voice surprised me at first. But of course, she was surprised. The police calling her out of the blue immediately meant something was wrong. "Nothing. I just want to speak with you about your friend Carol."

"Really?"

"Her mother said you saw her with a woman once, that would not introduce herself."

"Yeah. I knew who she was. She changed a little, but it was still her."
"Who?"

"Bella Harlow. Bella is short for Belladonna if you can believe it. I recognized her immediately and called her by her name, but she wouldn't answer me. She wouldn't even look at me. Carol looked confused, but when Bella told her they should go, she left with her. Didn't ask any questions. Just left."

"Were you two friends?"

"Not really. Bella was two years older than me and hung out some-times with my older brother. I think they dated once, but he said she was too weird."

"Did he say what the weird things were?"

"No, he never wanted to talk about her. I think in the beginning he felt sorry for her because she came from a broken home and her father wasn't a good one. But after they broke up, she came over to me once, and talked to me when my friends and I were hanging outside. Before she could even get a word out, my brother whooshed past her, grabbed my arm, and yanked me away from her. He told me never to talk to her and that she was dangerous."

"Do you know the new name she was using?"

"Uh... it was something stupid... Sun... Sunflower. That's it. She still had her blonde hair, it was just in dreadlocks now. They looked really messy like she wasn't taking care of them or something."

"Is your brother still around?"

"I'll—why do you need to speak with him? I thought Carol's case was cold."

"It is. But we think her case is connected to three of my current cases."

"You think Sunflower killed someone? Wouldn't put it past her. Give me a minute, I'll get his number."

CHAPTER THIRTY

Riley Quinn

LTHOUGH WE HAD NO CONCRETE PROOF THAT THIS SUNFLOWER and Bella were one and the same, I had a feeling it was. When I got the number for Corey, who had supposedly dated her, he answered on the second ring.

"Is this the detective?"

"Umm..."

"My sister just sent me a text that you would be calling me."

"I just hung up with her."

He chuckled. "C is fast, and texting is her usual method of communication. What can I help you with?"

I glanced at the clock on my computer. "I'm sorry to call you so late. I just need to ask a few questions."

"Don't worry about it. I'm always up this late. I'm an animator and working when the world is sleeping is less distracting."

"I get that. I wanted to talk to you about Bella Harlow."

Corey coughed several times. It sounded like he swallowed something and maybe it went down wrong. "Are you okay?"

After several more coughs, he answered. "Yeah, I'm okay. Sorry about that. You want to talk about Bella? What did she do?"

"What makes you think she did something?"

"You calling me and asking about her... Bella was always up to something."

"In what way?" He was silent. "Corrine said that you broke up with her and never wanted your sister to talk to her. There had to be a reason for that."

He inhaled sharply. "I put all of that behind me. I put her behind me. I never thought about her after I graduated and moved away. I was told she moved soon after, but I didn't want to hear it."

"What did she do to you?"

He took a long slow breath. "I don't know, and that's what bothers me. We went on a date one night. This is when we were still in school. And then we sat in the parking lot and talked. She had gotten some Schnapps from her father and so we started drinking. I don't know what happened, but I woke up, alone in my car, half-naked with a sunburst carved into my shoulder. There was blood. My pants were down. I don't know what happened, but she was nowhere in sight. I got myself together and went home and acted like nothing was wrong. I knew that was our last date."

"What did she say when you saw her at school?"

"I walked up to her locker and her eyes were as big as saucers. She was surprised to see me. And then she whispered, 'You're still alive?' I told her to stay away from me."

"She was surprised to see you alive. She was trying to kill you that night?"

"I don't know. I think so. That's why it surprised her seeing me walk around."

"Do you still have the sunburst?"

"I covered it up as soon as I could. I wanted no memory of that night on my body. Sometimes, when it's cold or raining, my shoulder still hurts. It's like an ache that won't go away."

"Why a sunburst?"

"She used to talk about the sun a lot. She admired the ancient Egyptians who worshiped the sun god. She was obsessed with the sun, and I think she wanted someone to worship her. She tried to manipulate me to do whatever she wanted. She wanted to control every part of my day and who I talked to. She was a control freak and wanted people to think she's special. She's not, though. She's just like every other child with daddy issues."

"Thank you for speaking with me. I really appreciate it."

"Whatever you think she did, you're right. Her father thought so. When we broke up, and I was avoiding her, he cornered me on my walk home. He was drunk of course, but he asked what she did to me. I didn't answer, I just kept walking, but he knew. He knew she had done something."

"I'm going to try to find him, and talk to him about her too. He probably knows her better than anyone."

"That's a good place to start."

I hung up and leaned back. It had to be the same person. Had to be. I searched Belladonna Harlow and so much popped up it made my head spin. She had an extensive police record. I looked up her last case and found the arresting officer. After a few more searches I found his number.

"Yes?"

"Hi, Officer McNeil. This is Detective Riley Quinn from the Pine Brooke police department. I have a few questions for you about Bella Harlow."

He laughed. "What kind of trouble is she in now?"

"You were the last person from Chicago that had any dealings with her. You also arrested her quite a few times. I was wondering what you can tell me about her?"

"How much time do you have?"

"As long as you need."

"I see. She must have done something pretty bad to warrant this call. And you must be lacking evidence to tie her to anything... Okay, I'll tell you what I know, but most of it I can't prove. She is a persuasive psychopath. She loves talking about herself, nothing makes her happier, and she is manipulative and a smooth talker. I'm tellin' you, she could talk the panties off a nun. She's smooth too—you almost don't notice what she's doing unless you're looking for it. I wouldn't be surprised if one day she created her own cult."

A shiver rippled through my body. "Yeah... a cult, you say?"

"Yeah. I think she was starting one here in Chicago, but I didn't have any proof. She kept it very quiet, but she had a small group that followed her around the city. Can't remember any of their names, but she always had an entourage."

"What do you mean you have no proof if you knew people were following her?"

He sighed. "I mean I had no complaining victim. The families complained, but it wasn't their house, or their money, so there was nothing we could do."

"What were the families complaining about?"

"Bella had manipulated their loved ones into selling their house and then giving her the proceeds. Selling their cars, cleaning out their bank accounts. Some mothers and fathers left their kids at a relative's home and never returned. I mean they left their whole families behind and never looked back. She ruined many lives in this city and the people are way too brainwashed to come back."

"Wow, I was—and wasn't—expecting that."

"One thing is for sure, that girl is full of surprises so stay on your guard. You got a pen handy? You should talk to her father. He is always willing and able to talk about his daughter. He can't stand her and wants her to get caught."

"I do." I wrote down the number and said goodbye. He told me if I needed anything else, to call him. I looked at the clock. It would have been polite to wait and call him in the morning. But the answers I needed were so close. If I went home right now, I wouldn't be able to sleep until I knew more about Sunflower. I dialed the number and waited. It rang three times before someone answered.

"Who is this?" he asked, his voice heavy with sleep.

"Detective Riley Quinn with the Pine Brooke, California Police Department. I'm looking for Jack Harlow."

"I've never been to California." There was less sleep in his voice this time.

"I need to talk to you about your daughter."

There was a heavy sigh on the other end of the line. "Give me a minute to get myself together. You woke me up out of a dead sleep. I thought someone had died."

Several minutes later, Jack sounded like he had had some coffee or something to drink and was sitting upright. His voice was clear. "What has my daughter done now?"

"I'm not sure. I need you to tell me as much about your daughter as possible. Do you have any pictures you can send me?"

"I think I kept one or two. Don't really want any trace of her in this house, but... anyway. She was a disappointment from birth. I named her

Belladonna because she poisoned her mother from the inside out. My Annie was never sick for a day in her life and then she gets pregnant and all of sudden she's sick constantly. Then she had liver failure. And then they discovered a tumor. Once she had the girl, she never recovered. She died before Bella was a month old. Never even got to hold her." He recounted all the things his daughter had done. Killing animals, hurting herself to get attention. Hurting others to get attention.

"If you ever get the chance to shoot her, you should. You would put the world out of its misery." He hung up before I could say anything. I couldn't tell if Bella was always this way or had her early years with her father molded her into the woman she became? He sounded like a harsh man who blamed her for his wife's death. He might have taken it out on her.

But that still didn't excuse her behavior. I rocked back in my chair as I stared at my screen for several minutes. I needed to know for sure that she was the one we were looking for. My phone dinged. Mr. Harlow had sent one of the only pictures he still had of his daughter.

Bella looked to be in her early twenties. Her hair was just starting to lock up. I held up my phone to get Zelina's attention. She gasped.

"That's her. Definitely her. How did you get that?"

"Her father sent it to me."

I recounted all of my conversations to her and then to the captain, who was leaving for the night.

"It looks exactly like her."

"Okay. What are you two going to do now?" he asked us.

"Think of a way to get her to drop her guard. Officer McNeil said she loves talking about herself. It's her favorite thing to do. I think there might be a way we can use that to our advantage."

"Good idea. But get some sleep first. You both look exhausted."

"Well, thanks," said Zelina. She was ready to go home and so was I. The drive home felt longer than it should have. I was thankful I made it into my driveway without falling asleep. Luna ran around chasing something I couldn't see. It might have been a bug or her imagination. I whistled and she spun around.

Luna dismissed what she had been doing earlier and came running. Before I could get my key into the door she jumped on me. I pulled my fingers through her soft fur and kissed her on the top of her head before going inside. She padded behind me as I closed and locked the door.

There was a note on the counter from my sister letting me know that she did feed Luna and what time she did it. I looked in the fridge and decided to make something to eat. Nothing fancy. I took two croissants and split them open, then I fried up some bacon and two over easy eggs. I put some avocado spread on both croissants then added Muenster cheese, the bacon and then the egg before folding the croissant. They weren't the healthiest of sandwiches, but they would do the trick so early in the morning. I had to put something on my stomach. All I had yesterday was coffee and chips. Several bags of chips and several cups of coffee. I wouldn't mention it the next time I saw Logan.

A smile bloomed on my lips. I wanted to call him and ask if he was staying out of trouble, but it was too late—or rather too early to call anyone in town. I ate my two sandwiches in bed and then rolled over and went right to sleep. I felt Luna breathing next to me. I wrapped my arm around her and dozed.

Later that morning I woke up. Luna was gone. She had disappeared from my side. I missed her warmth almost immediately. I rolled over and stared at the ceiling for a little while. I still hadn't thought of a way to make Sunflower speak with us. I had a feeling as soon as we started asking her questions about the murders she would clam up and call for a lawyer and we'd never get a chance to speak to her. We needed something that would make her want to speak...

I rolled over and fell asleep again. This time it was more of a cat nap than anything else. I woke with a start, my body bolting upright before my eyes opened. And an idea sprang to mind. I jumped out of bed and headed to the bathroom. After a long shower I felt human again. After feeding Luna and grabbing my things I hurried out the door. I called Z on my way to the station. She was also on her way and about to call me. We met by the front door.

"You think of something?" she asked.

"I think I did. What if we just gave her what she wanted?"

Zelina stared at me for a long moment before she answered. "You mean give her the news coverage she's been wanting all this time?"

I nodded. "She likes talking about herself. I say we play to her ego. I don't think she'd be able to pass it up. Give her what she wants and hopefully she'll end up telling on herself."

Zelina sighed. "But how do we do that? You don't think she'll see right through it? That she'll know we are on to her and want her to confess."

I had thought about that on the way over. Sunflower or Bella liked being the center of attention. She liked all attention, good or bad. She might jump at the fact of talking about what she's created. Or she might recoil. I thought it was a good gamble either way.

Zelina and I went inside and spoke to the captain. I explained my plan and he seemed intrigued.

"So, you want to give her the attention she's been looking for hoping that she might slip up and say something incriminating."

"Hopefully. Officer McNeil said that she loves talking about herself. She loves attention, and after speaking to Corey I doubt she believes she did anything wrong."

He cocked his head. "What do you mean?"

I explained my conversation with Corey in more detail. "After what she did to him, when he saw her the next day, she was surprised that he was still alive. But she never apologized or even acknowledged it. I don't think she saw what she did as wrong. She was still trying to talk to him and his sister afterwards."

"She has no conscience?" asked Zelina.

"Or maybe she just doesn't care. I mean she's been doing this shit since she was in high school. She also used to kill animals as a child, and she's never been held accountable for any of it. Maybe she doesn't care because she thinks she can always get away with it. Especially if it's not her doing the killing."

"Or maybe a group of them including her are doing it together. So, if any of them try to tell on her they too will go down," said the captain.

"That's a good point. I truly believe playing to her ego will get us the answers we need."

The captain stared at his desk for a long moment. His hands rested on his stomach, his fingers twitching. He always did that when he was thinking about something. "I think you might be right, and it's an angle that we can try, but you two need to be careful. If she is a psychopath, then everyone that deals with her is one too. Take backup."

I glanced at Zelina.

"I know. She'll definitely be suspicious, but you will need backup. There are too many people at that compound for you to take on alone."

I nodded. "I understand."

"See if the station will let you borrow a camera crew and then change out some of those guys for ours. Backup should stay out of sight until you give the signal. But I want them close enough that if something goes sideways it won't take them long to get there."

"We'll make sure of it, sir." I followed Zelina out of the office and back to our desk. We still needed to create a game plan and see if the news station would play along. I hoped they would. Bella would recognize local news anchors and that would lend more validity to our plan.

But local anchors might get in the way. But then again, they would know the right questions to ask which would come in handy.

I tapped my finger against the desk. It would make more sense to use a real news anchor, but the police presence could be there for protection.

That might work.

CHAPTER THIRTY-ONE

Riley Quinn

WE SPOKE TO DONNA AND HER BOSS WHO WERE BOTH EAGER TO help.

"You think it's a cult?" asked Donna. "All they want is attention?"

"They've been writing to journalists trying to garner attention to their group and what they're doing. Thus far it hasn't worked and that has made them angry. If we show interest in them, that might get her to lower her guard."

"Okay. How can I help? Do you want me to write down the kind of questions you should ask?"

I glanced at Zelina, who stared at Donna. "Actually, we were hoping you would come with us. We would switch out your camera guy for one of our officers and we would be there the entire time to protect you."

Donna stared at her boss, speechless.

"I don't like it," said Mr. Wilt, the senior producer at the station. "But it's your choice, Donna. Detectives, can you ensure her safety?"

I held up a hand. "I know it sounds daunting, but you will be safe, I promise. It's just easier for us to take you than for you to teach us how to act like a journalist in search of a story."

"I —I understand that." Donna's fingers played with her lips like she was trying to peel the skin off. "Alright. Let me get my things."

Before we left, her cameraman Gary taught Officer Strauss how to use the camera and what buttons to press. Officer Strauss was one of our tech guys, so he knew what he was doing and yet he still stood there and listened and asked questions to make Gary feel more at ease.

"Please don't break her." He glanced at Donna. "Either of them, but especially Betsy."

"Betsy?"

Donna pointed to the camera. I smiled. He named his camera, an interesting man. Our next stop was the campground. My pulse thudded in my throat. My neck felt tight as I tried to swallow. I wondered as I looked over the crowd which ones helped Sunflower kill those people. As soon as we entered the campground the people swarmed us. Whispers rippled through the crowd too low to make any sense out of the words.

Sunflower stood next to her RV, the one with the sun in the window. I glanced around at the others, and they all had suns in their windows. She was the sun, and they were her sunflowers.

She smiled sweetly when we walked over.

"Detectives, what can we do for you?"

I swallowed hard. "This is Donna—"

"I know who she is. I watch on Channel 7." She grinned at Donna. Surprisingly Donna did not recoil like I thought she would. She must have been used to interviewing bad people and knew how to handle herself. She smiled at Sunflower. "It's nice to meet you."

"She would like to know more about your organization." I glanced behind me. "We are just here for backup."

"We aren't violent. You have nothing to fear from us, I can assure you. We just wanted to get the word out about what we have to offer the lost of the world. The ones trapped in darkness."

"Only light can drive out the darkness," I replied.

The corner of her mouth twitched into a half smile. "Exactly, and what is brighter than the sun?" She held her hands out as if she was the only answer to that question.

"Was it worth killing those people? Just to get your point across?" Her smile dissipated. "It worked, didn't it? You're here."

I looked at Donna for a second. "Can we speak inside your RV?"

Bella grinned. "Why, of course."

I followed behind Donna as we entered the RV. Sunflower closed the door behind us. She gestured for us to sit down in the small seating area. It reeked of weed in her RV, but I overlooked it. I sat next to Donna while the cameraman stood next to Sunflower. She looked at the camera for a long moment.

"Have you turned that thing on yet?" she asked as she glided to the seat across from us.

"No ma'am. Give me one moment." Officer Strauss placed the camera on his shoulder. A few seconds later, once he was in the right position to capture all of us in the frame, which was difficult to do in such a small room, the light clicked on. Sunflower smiled. She sat up straighter. Looked poised.

"Ask your questions."

I gave a curt nod at Donna and then leaned back. I wanted to make myself small so Sunflower would forget I was there. If I asked her a bunch of questions, she could ask for her lawyer and then the interview would be over. But Donna interviewing her for a segment on the news might garner us a little leeway. I was just there for her protection. If a judge asked why Donna needed protection, I would just show him the picture of the dead bodies her group was responsible for.

"Okay, Sunflower. Please tell me about yourself and what led you to create this organization. Start with your name and then the name of your group."

Sunflower beamed as she looked at the camera. "My name is Sunflower. I started this organization because I saw so many lost souls looking for guidance, but unable to find any. People who wanted hope. Community. That's hard to find these days with everyone on their cell phones or computers. I wanted to give people like me what I always wanted, but never had ... a place to belong."

"That was something you were missing as a child?"

Sunflower raised her chin while glancing at the camera. "Yes. I always felt out of place. At home and at school. Didn't really have friends. No one to talk to. When you are different, especially in school, children can be cruel and that leaves a mark, well into adulthood."

"I understand that. And so, you wanted to create a place where people from all walks of life could feel safe and have a sense of belonging. That is admirable. How did you get started?"

While Sunflower spoke, Donna took notes like she would with any other interview. Sunflower smiled at that and the camera. She liked the idea of finally being heard. "Well, after high school, I went to college for a little while, but I just never thought it was for me. I never liked the confinements of school. It was stifling. My grades were okay, but I was so bored. I didn't see the point of it. By then I had amassed a small following. Other students that felt ostracized and were looking for a sense of community."

"And where was this?"

"Chicago. I wanted to get as far away from my father as possible, but I couldn't afford to go away for college, so I had to stay in the city. It was really just a group of people looking to make friends. We hung out a lot and I dropped out and got a job, and so did a few others. We became nomads for a bit, but then settled back in Chicago because it still felt like home. It will always feel like home."

"When you returned to Chicago did you add any more members to your group?"

She grinned. "We did. Quite a few. More than I expected. I didn't think we would the second time around, but we did. Some of those members are still with us. Sadly, some are not."

"Did they choose to leave? Was there a reason behind it?"

"I guess. Some wanted to stay with her family, or some found the nomadic lifestyle was not for them. Which, at the time, was understandable. Asking people to pick up and move, to put their lives behind them, is a big ask. I understand why some people can't do it."

"Was that the only reason people left? They couldn't let go of their old lives? I don't think I would have been able to. I would miss my family too much."

"That's understandable. My father was horrible, so I never had that problem. But mostly yes, that was the primary reason people left. Although one woman was killed."

Donna's eyes went wide. "What? What happened?"

"She was killed in her home. I think the police thought it was a robbery or something like that. I was a suspect for some time."

"Why would you be a suspect if you were just trying to help people?"

"She truly believed in the cause. She was willing to give up everything to follow us. Her family was upset that she was willing to do that. She sold her house, her belongings, and her car so she could have the money to follow us. Her family didn't believe she would do those things, but she did. She sold everything because she said she wasn't going to need them anymore. She gave the money to me to hold for her while she said goodbye. She went home that night, and we never heard from her again."

"Maybe her family was a little too angry that she was willing to sell everything and walk away from them? Maybe it started a fight."

"I have always thought that might have been possible. Maybe they were looking for her money that night since she sold everything. Or maybe they just didn't want to let her go. She told me she never felt like she belonged with her family. She always felt like an outsider, and so leaving was not a big deal for her. Apparently, it was a big deal for them."

"That's tragic. But you were able to use the money to further your goals for the group."

"Exactly. She left us a great gift and we thank her for it every day. I wish she was still here."

"I understand it. It must have been difficult for your group to work through in the beginning. Everyone must have been so upset."

"Yes. She had become family to us. To me. She was so sweet and always willing to lift a hand to help anyone. Her loss was felt throughout the group. The way her murder was... it was horrible what she went through. All those stab wounds... I often wondered who hated her so much. She was such a pure soul."

"So after her murder, was that when you moved here, or did you go other places first?"

"We moved throughout the country. We went East, then through the South. Some states in the Midwest. We stayed in Arizona for a while, but the heat was unbearable. I never understood how people could live there and be happy about it. Phoenix was beautiful and surprisingly the police were nice. We stayed for a week, maybe two before finally coming here to Pine Brooke. One of our members used to live here and he suggested it. Said it was a beautiful place, with some of the nicest people he had ever met in his life. He was right."

"Yeah, our town is filled with some really nice people. And more serial killers than one would expect for such a small town," said Donna.

A smile tugged at Sunflower's lips. "I'm sorry, what?"

Donna recounted my last two cases in more detail than I remembered. Sunflower looked surprised. "I guess we must have missed that. Strange little town. But at least you caught them."

"It has been quite the year for us. People we thought were good guys and were well-loved by the community turned out to be monsters."

Sunflower smiled. "Aren't we all monsters? Aren't we all capable of monstrous things if pushed past a certain point? It doesn't sound that interesting. Those men just gave in to that temptation."

"I guess. I don't think I can be pushed to do horrific things. You didn't see all of this in the news?"

"I don't follow the news too closely. The world is a horrid place, and I don't want all of that negativity in my head throughout the day." She leaned forward. "Can you tell me more about these cases?'

Donna glanced at me, and I shrugged. They were old cases and could still be found in the news so telling her about it wasn't going to make a difference. I doubted Donna knew anything we didn't so might as well.

"Well, the first case someone we all knew and loved turned out to have murdered several young girls and his wife. He buried them all over. Buried his wife under his front step."

"Oh, that must have made you all very busy trying to dig them all up."

"Yes," I said. "It was a busy time. But he told us everything we needed to know about the bodies and when he buried them. Once he started talking, he refused to stop."

"And what about the second serial killer?" There was a sparkle in her eyes. She was interested in the serial killers, but that didn't surprise me since she was one herself.

"Well... he was a cop, and was killing women that looked like his ex-wife."

"How did you get him to confess?"

I swallowed hard. I remembered the confession like it was yesterday. How angry he was. "I brought his ex-wife into the room, and he was so pissed at her it all just came out. We had to stop him from attacking her."

"To hate someone that much... that's a powerful kind of hate. I don't think I've ever hated someone that much. Not even my father."

"He hated her because she was strong enough to finally leave him. I don't think he thought she ever would. She was his punching bag for so long that he thought he owned her and when she finally walked away..."

She stared at me for a moment. "Why didn't he just kill her?"

"He would have been a suspect."

"Ah, right. It's always the husband."

"Right."

"I understand why she left him. My mother did the same to my father."

I blinked. Her father said her mother died when she was a month old. "Your mother's alive? I thought she was dead."

"Who told you that? My father?"

I raised my shoulders in a slight shrug. She already knew the answer to that question.

"He blamed me because once I was born my mother left him. She realized he was a horrible husband, I guess. She realized she hated him and couldn't stand being around him any longer. So she left him."

"And she left you there in that house?" asked Donna. "What kind of mother does that?"

"She was so sick and tired of him, and she wanted to be free of him and I had to pay the price for it. He never forgave her or me for that matter."

"Did you ever see her again?" I asked.

"I did when I was older, in my twenties. She was happy. With two children, a loving husband and a dog. In Rhode Island. I believe they are still there. They looked so happy. I haven't seen her since. I don't really want to see her again. She didn't think of me the whole time she was gone. So I don't think about her."

"Okay. Let's get back to your organization. Right! So now I want to talk about the particulars of your group."

CHAPTER THIRTY-TWO

Riley Quinn

"W HY OF COURSE. WHAT DO YOU WANT TO KNOW?"

"Well..." Donna paused for a moment and stared at the window behind Sunflower. "Sorry, I was just mentally going through all of the questions that I have for you. There's a lot. I mean... some people would say that your group is a cult. What would you say to those people?"

Sunflower rolled her eyes. "People always speak negatively about things they don't understand. We are not a cult; we are a family."

"So was the Manson Family. I think that is the reason people see a large group of people coming together and forsaking their past lives, family, and possessions and immediately think *cult*. If you're not a cult, what is the one thing that is separating you from that classification?"

Donna was asking good questions. The kind that made Sunflower pause and think. Questions that surprised her… and that was exactly what we needed.

"To start with, our members can leave whenever they want. We aren't holding them hostage here. They want to be here with us. Also, no one is forced to do anything that they don't want to do. We don't harm or force children into things."

"That's great to hear. Is this a religious organization?"

Sunflower leaned back in her seat and crossed her ankles in front of her. "I never thought of it like that. The sun has many meanings, one of which is new beginnings, and that was what everyone who has ever come to us needed. A fresh start. A place they would not be judged. A place they could call home. I wouldn't say we're religious though."

"So if you're the sun, they are your what, sunflowers?" Donna asked. She smiled.

"I saw the sun image on your window and the sunflowers in the other windows around the compound," Donna added.

"I appreciate you understanding that. Yes. I am the sun, and they are my sunflowers. I will protect them and help them grow strong into the most beautiful flowers."

"You will always protect them?" asked Donna.

Sunflower smiled as she played with the bracelet around her wrist. "Of course. I treat them like they are my children. I never had any. I would guard them with my life. They mean more to me than everything. Than anyone. So yes, I would protect them."

Donna nodded. "Okay let's start with the particulars so our viewers know what you're about. What is the name of your organization and what are your goals?"

The interview was going well. I craned my neck to look out the window to see how Zelina was doing. She was still outside with two officers watching the crowd. The crowd moved closer to the officers. I saw their mouths moving, but I couldn't hear what they were saying.

"The Rising Sun is our name. It took a while to finally rest on this name. We went through so many, but none of them really felt right. But this one does. Our main goal is to amass as many people as possible. I want to be a voice for the voiceless. I want to teach people how to be themselves. How to trust their instincts and that it is okay if you are not normal, or rather what society sees as normal. You can still find a place to belong."

"That's admirable. So many people out there feel alone and have no one to look to. So that is your mission statement?"

"Essentially."

Donna wrote it down. "How far would you go to protect the group? If someone was threatening them and everything that you built here."

I glanced around the room. She hadn't really built anything. The RV was old and beat up. It was obvious no one was caring for it and hadn't in a long time. If they were giving her all their money, where was it going? It wasn't going into her RV. Maybe a bank account. Why wasn't she using the money? And if she was… on what?

Sunflower sighed. "I would go to any lengths to protect us from those trying to dismantle us."

"Who is trying?"

"The police for starters." Sunflower cut her eyes at me. "They know that the people are stronger when we are together, so they keep trying to keep us apart."

"What lengths?"

Her head snapped back. She stared at Donna and then glanced at the camera. "What?"

"What lengths would you go to? I think it's important for any viewer who might want to join you to know how far you are willing to make sure they are okay. They might be more susceptible to joining you. Personally, I would."

Sunflower's shoulder relaxed for a moment as a smile crept across her lips. "If you are asking me if I would kill to protect them, then yes I would."

"Is that why you all killed those news anchors? The police found your letters at each crime scene. The anchors never responded. I know that because we never did a story on you. How did their dismissal make you feel?"

Sunflower leaned back. "There was no *you* all, just me. And yes. I had a message to get out and they refused to help. I sent them warning after warning and nothing worked. Who were they to deny my sunflowers' requests? We could have helped so many people if they had just listened to me."

My head was spinning. Was it really that easy to get her to admit to murder? She didn't even have to think about it. She confessed to murder on camera and didn't bat an eye. Officer McNeil said she was smart. Was this all part of her plan? Was she up to something? I tried to look at it from every angle and I couldn't see where this worked out in her favor.

"You freely admit that on camera?" asked Donna. Judging by the look on her face she was just as shocked as I was.

"Of course. I did nothing wrong. They were in our way of getting you here." She gestured to Donna. "They had to be removed. Like I said, had they just done what I asked it wouldn't have been a problem. They created their fate by ignoring me. Not even a phone call or a letter. Just silence."

"I see. It was just you? Because the coroner says that the bodies were stabbed multiple times by different people."

She grinned. "Maybe I used different knives. Maybe I was playing around."

Donna leaned forward, her elbows resting on her thigh. "This is what I don't understand, why admit to this so freely?"

Sunflower leaned forward, mimicking her posture. "Why keep it a secret? Seriously, what good does that do? I want potential followers to know that I would go to any lengths to make sure they are heard and seen. I would kill and or die for my sunflowers. I am not ashamed of what I've done. Would it have been better not to get caught? Of course. But it changes nothing. My sunflowers will always turn toward the sun, no matter where *it* is."

She stared at me when she said the last part. A shiver tore through me. She was a creepy woman. I was right. She hadn't thought she had done anything wrong. If someone wasn't ashamed of what they had done they'd have no problem confessing to it.

"You know I'll have to arrest you now." It was the first time I had in nearly an hour. My throat was dry, and the words came out hoarse.

"Of course. I suspect that is what you came to do." She stood up. Sunflower was annoying and a murderer and manipulative, but she had an elegance to her that was... in a way beautiful. The way she stood up ready to accept her fate. The way she glided across the floor like her feet never touched it. Part of me wanted to know where she learned. She had to have learned it somewhere.

She placed her hands behind her back and I cuffed her. The cameraman turned off the camera and lowered it before backing up and opening the door.

When he did, all of the noises were an assault on my ears. It was so loud out there. Yelling, barking orders. I pushed her outside quickly so I could see what all the commotion was about.

The shouting stopped immediately. As soon as Sunflower set her foot on the grass the loud voices quieted. The hush that fell over the crowd was so immediate and dense that the officers who were shouting at her followers stopped and spun around to see what had captivated their attention. Zelina was sweating profusely. Her face was red as she mouthed the words 'thank you'. They looked like they were being over-run by followers.

"What are you doing with her?" A man's booming voice sliced through the silence. Donna jumped next to me. "You're not taking her anywhere."

"Now, now."

He froze at the sound of Sunflower's voice.

"She's just doing her job. And we were just doing ours. Something great will come from this. Trust me."

"We can't leave without you!"

"You can't leave us!"

They were creepy before, but now they were downright frightening. How did she have this much power over them?

"You all need to make room so we can take her into custody."

The group tightened around us like a boa constrictor ready to enjoy its meal.

"No! You are not taking her!" People started shoving us. Pushing the officers out of the way. I kept my hands on her cuffs, so I didn't lose her in the commotion. Just then the sound of sirens descended on the campground. But the noise did not stop people from pushing and throwing punches. I yanked Sunflower behind me to get her out of the way. "You need to stop it now or you will all be arrested!" My heart hammered against my ribs, the beat fast and panicked.

I glanced over at Zelina who was pushing people away from her. Trying to get some space between them. A glint of silver caught my eye behind her. I raised my gun. A man with a shaped knife lunged at her.

I squeezed the trigger. The sound rippled through the crowd. Everything stopped as he crumpled to the ground. Zelina spun around, gun drawn, only to see the man on the ground behind her. She stared back at me and smiled. A shriek tore through the silence.

Sunflower ran through the crowd to the man on the ground, hands still tied behind her back. She screamed. "What have you done!"

An officer pulled her to her feet.

"You will pay for this!" She screamed the words over and over again as she was led to a police car. The crowd stopped paying attention to us and focused on the man. While they were distracted Zelina ran over to me.

"Thanks."

STRANGERS IN THE PINES

"Anytime," I called for the corner. The second I hung up my phone, it started ringing again. "Hello?" My eyes nearly bulged out of my skull as I stared at Zelina.

"I'm on my way."

CHAPTER THIRTY-THREE

Logan Elwood

I STARED AT THE ADDRESS OF THE NURSE WHO REFUSED TO TALK TO me. I needed to ask her some questions. If she still didn't want to talk to me, so be it, but I needed to try.

I jumped in the truck and headed out of town. I sent a text to Bonnie letting her know I would be a little late.

Nurse Helda lived in an old Victorian house, complete with a turret, a wrap-around porch, and beautiful stained-glass windows. There was a door knocker instead of a doorbell.

I knocked twice. A few minutes later, a young man answered the door. "I'm looking for Helda."

The man in the doorway stared at me blankly. "Who are you?"

"Logan Elwood."

He sucked his teeth. "She doesn't want to speak with you."

"I understand that. Talking about the fire is difficult, but I need answers. I need to know if my sister-in-law was responsible for the murder."

He sighed and backed away from the door. "Follow me to the kitchen."

I stepped inside. The house was hot. Stifling. I followed him to the kitchen which was nice and old-looking, but well kept. I sat at the kitchen table, a small square table with silver chairs. It looked out of place.

"My aunt... it's still traumatic for her to talk about. She doesn't like talking about it. She was never the same. That's what my mom told me. She was a ghost. A shell of her former self. She stopped speaking like she used to, never married, never had children. Now she rarely leaves the house. She might have walked away unscathed on the outside, but something in her died that night."

"She never had children?"

"She thinks children are monsters. She avoided me until I was an adult and could take care of myself."

I found that interesting. After the fire, she believed children were monsters. What made her believe that? "I need to know what happened that night. And she's the only one that can tell me."

He sighed. "You can try. But don't get your hopes up."

"I never do."

Helda sat in the parlor staring out of the large window. Her back was toward us so she didn't see me walk in.

"Who is that with you, Ed?" She kept her eyes on the window, but she knew someone else was there. She wore a long black dress.

"This is Logan Elwood. He needs to speak with you about the fire." Ed picked up a chair and moved it closer to her. He gestured to the chair, and I sat down.

Ed sat on the sofa, far enough to be out of earshot, but close enough in case she needed him.

"Hello, ma'am. Thank you for speaking with me. I really appreciate it."

"What do you want to know about the fire and why?"

"Do you remember a student named Jamie —"

"That little monster."

I didn't even say her last name and she immediately knew who I was talking about. She must have left a hell of an impression. "Her sister was Marie."

Helda waved a hand dismissively. She knew who Marie was and didn't need reminding. "Marie was just as bad as her sister."

I straightened in my seat. "She was my wife," I said. There was no way Marie was just as bad as Jamie. Marie was a good person she just...

"I can't believe someone married that girl."

I squeezed my hands into fists. She didn't know Marie. Who the hell was she to make those kinds of remarks?

"It was a mask. It was all a mask. Both of them. All children have this sweet and innocent mask, but underneath there is a monster."

I looked at Ed, and he shrugged.

"You want to know what they were like? Fine, I'll tell you everything. But only for your protection."

Helda

If this man wanted to know the truth, I would give it to him. I closed my eyes, and let the memory wash through me. I would tell all of it. Finally. Maybe it would let me go.

I was a nurse for a long time. I always liked helping people even before I joined the order. Making them feel better was something that always called to me. When I arrived at the school I was excited. Happy to be helping girls straighten out their lives and offer care for them and their babies.

My excitement and enthusiasm were short-lived. I had never known such unruly children. The other nuns had warned me. I was too friendly with them and the girls would take advantage. I didn't believe them, but it turns out they were right. I grew close to one... named Marie. By the time I arrived at the school, Marie's belly was already very present.

We would take walks together. I'd told her getting exercise daily was good for her and the baby. Marie finally relented after a couple of weeks and walked with me. We talked on those walks. And the more we talked and walked, the more I was convinced Marie should never be allowed to have children.

Her words were innocent enough at first, but then things took a turn. She hated the baby growing inside of her and wanted to get rid of her. "I can't want to get her out of me. I don't like it. I don't like feeling her kick. I hate it. I hate her."

I'd tried to soothe her. I tried to tell her that her baby was a gift from God and that it should be loved. "Your baby is a gift," I told her. "Even though you aren't keeping her, she still needs your love to grow."

You know what she said?

She said, "She doesn't have it. She has my disdain and my disgust, but nothing else. If it wouldn't hurt me, I'd throw myself down the stairs."

I was shocked. Marie seemed like such a nice girl. I didn't know what to say to her after that. We still went on our walks. I let Marie say whatever she wanted. I let her vent believing that it was what she needed. I knew how Marie came to be pregnant. I knew she was angry and had no one to tell her feelings to.

One night there was a loud scream that bounced off the walls. I jumped to my feet and rushed out of the room. I ran toward the murmurs and the scream of pain and came to the grand staircase. At the bottom was Marie, doubled over in pain, trying to pull herself up. Blood pooled between her legs onto the floor.

I looked up for a moment. The stairs were empty. It was just Marie at the end of the stairs and the girls who came down after the fact.

"What happened?" I asked her.

"I fell," moaned Marie.

Sister Dolan ran over to the stairs. "She's going into labor."

I felt like I couldn't move. My body felt like a statue glued to the spot. Had Marie fallen or did she do what she said she was going to do? It achieved what she wanted. Now she had to deliver the baby that night.

I never looked at Marie the same. She didn't want to hold Jamie or look at her. It was like she didn't exist. As soon as the doctor pulled Jamie free, Marie wanted nothing to do with her.

The nuns tried to get her to hold the baby. To nurse her. It was what was best for Jamie.

But Marie refused.

Sister Dolan left Marie with the baby hoping that her crying would force Marie to comfort her. But what happened was something entirely evil. Jamie stopped crying and the nuns felt like Marie finally held the baby. Sister Dolan and I went to check on them, both of us smiling. In the room, Marie held Jamie's head in the water basin at the front of the room used for washing the babies.

I remember how I screamed and snatched the baby. Sister Dolan slapped Marie so hard that she fell to the floor. I rubbed Jamie's back and tapped between her shoulders a few times. Jamie started screaming as water bubbled out of her mouth.

"What is wrong with you?" I hissed at her.

Marie stared at me. "I told you I didn't want her. That I didn't want to hold her, but you keep trying to push her on me. That little bastard can go to hell for all I care. Find someone else to feed her!"

A chill ran down my spine, as Jamie wiggled against her looking for comfort. I held her tight and walked out of the room.

"Go to your room!" Sister Dolan pulled Marie to her feet and pushed her out of the room. Marie passed by me and Jamie in the hall, and she spat next to my feet.

I'd never seen such anger. I didn't know it was possible for someone so young. I exchanged a look with Sister Dolan.

"She leaves in the morning," Sister Dolan announced. "I'll call her mother and tell her she has to come get her daughter in the morning. I don't want her here anymore. She can recover at home."

"What about Jamie?" I was the one who named her. I'd always liked the name and loved how it could work for male or female. My older brother was named Jamie.

"I don't know. They didn't specify what they wanted. I think her mother doesn't want to think about it. But I cannot in good conscience send that baby home with Marie. She'll kill her."

"I agree. She seems intent on doing it," I agreed. "I'm going to find her some milk."

"I think Sister Jade has some bottles already made in the fridge, just in case."

Now believe me, I was not an unfeeling woman. I understood Marie's anger. When a man rapes a child so young, and then she is forced to bear his child, anger is understandable. But what I tried to make Marie understand was that it wasn't Jamie's fault. Jamie came into this world blameless. But Marie didn't want to listen. She didn't care. She hated everything and everyone and that kind of rage could not be quelled. Not by us.

"We could beat it out of her," Sister Jade said, while she heated up a bottle.

"I think that will just make it worse." I knew it was hopeless.

The baby was given to Everly, Marie's mother, to be raised as her daughter—as Marie's younger sister. It wasn't what any of us wanted, but in the end, we had no say.

I hoped Marie would never step foot in the school again. And while she didn't, Jamie returned years later. The same age as Marie when she joined us.

Jamie looked just like Marie when she walked in, with the same eyes and face. By then I'd dealt with many children that broke my heart. Perhaps I should have learned a lesson sooner. When I saw Jamie I was worried. The fact that she ended up at that school told me that she was not the sweet little baby she once was.

She had done something that brought her to us, and I wasn't sure I wanted to know.

"Hello, Jamie." I stared at the girl and smiled.

Jamie cut her eyes at her. "I don't want to be here."

"No one usually does. What did you do that got you in trouble?"

Jamie shrugged. "Killed some cats and broke a boy's arm in a few places."

My eyes had gone wide. It all sounded so familiar. She really was just like her mother. I mostly tried to keep my distance from Jamie, but she liked torturing me too much. I went to my room one night after dinner and found my love birds dead in their cages. Dog droppings in my bed. The Bible was desecrated and charred underneath her pillow. There was never any proof that it was Jamie, but I knew it was her. The way Jamie grinned when she saw me. I knew it was her.

The night of the fire, I was outside walking the grounds. I needed some air. I had been cooped up with those girls so long, I needed some space. As I walked around, something caught my eye.

It was Marie. She was older, but it was her. She and Jamie had the same face and almost the same mannerisms. They even walked alike. I ducked behind a tree and watched her. Marie disappeared around the side of the school. I walked slowly to stay out of sight and saw Marie round the corner, then disappear inside the school. I stood still for a long moment. How did she get in?

A minute later she emerged. Flames licked the side of the building in her wake. I was stunned. I couldn't breathe. Marie ran over to a large shrub and watched. She watched as the fire grew taller and taller, engulfing the entire left side of the building.

CHAPTER THIRTY-FOUR

Logan Elwood

RAGE TORE THROUGH MY BODY. I WAS PISSED AT SO MANY PEOPLE I couldn't keep their faces straight. I was mad at Marie, but she was dead and there was nothing I could do with that anger now but feel it. She had lied to me. Every day since I met her had been a lie.

The fact that she started the fire and killed over sixty people was heart-wrenching. Tears stung my eyes every time I thought about it. That wasn't the Marie that I knew. That wasn't my wife. For the briefest moment, I wondered if Jamie knew it was her. If she knew it that night or if she found out later.

I found it hard to believe that she started the fire. It made more sense if Jamie started it. Helda was certain. Even after all these years, she knew what she saw, and no one could tell her different.

"I saw Marie start that fire with my own eyes," she said.

"Why would she do that?" I asked. I couldn't wrap my mind around it.

"Weren't you listening to my story? She wanted to kill that girl once and for all." My heart dropped into my stomach. She wanted to kill her daughter, so she killed over sixty people. What kind of sense did that make?

I couldn't believe it. She hated Jamie that much. She never told me she was raped or that she had a child before Dani. The more I thought about it the more I felt like I didn't know her. I never knew her.

What would she have done to Dani? I didn't rape her, but what if she decided she didn't like Dani? That she would be better off without children. Tears streamed down my cheeks. I really didn't know her.

It kind of made sense why Jamie was so strange. No one in her life, not in her younger formative years ever loved her. No one truly cared about her since she was a baby. She might not have known that Marie was her mother, but I was willing to bet she knew something was wrong with their family dynamic. I squeezed the steering wheel. What did Everly do?

I couldn't help but wonder if Jamie knew. Or when she found out.

Marie probably never told her about it. She was trying to kill Jamie after all. That was the whole reason for the fire.. and yet Jamie survived.

I picked up my phone and dialed the home number. Dani should have been home from school by now and Isaac home from work. The phone rang and rang. I called Bonnie's cell, but she never answered.

The hairs on the back of my neck stood straight up. Something was wrong. I felt like I couldn't breathe. My whole body went hot. Something was wrong. I felt it deep in my bones. I tossed my phone in the passenger seat and pressed on the gas. My phone rang. I picked it up and looked at the screen. It was the house.

"Where were you guys? I called twice." There was a heavy sigh on the other end.

"Logan, this is Riley. Are you on your way home?"

"You staying for dinner?"

"No. There's been an incident. You need to get back to your house now."

"What's wrong?"

"I'm not going to tell you while you're on the road. Just get home as fast as you can."

CHAPTER THIRTY-FIVE

Jamie Washington

J AMIE SPENT THE MORNING PACKING HER THINGS AND GETTING
ready to leave town. While she was upstairs, she heard the doorbell
ring. Her heart sank. Nothing good happened when someone rang
her doorbell. She walked downstairs and peered through the keyhole.
It was that man again.

She opened the door and sighed. "Did you find her?"

"No. Have you found the phone?"

"No. I looked under the sofa, under the bed. Anywhere I thought it
could have fallen out of her pocket. She wasn't here long."

Dwight smiled tightly. Jamie knew that look, and knew it well. He
didn't believe her.

"I see. Can I take a look around?" He inched closer to the door.

Jamie weighed her options. If she said no, it would look suspicious,
like she had something to hide which she did. If he looked around and

found something she'd have to kill him too. She didn't want to add any more bodies until she was on her way out of town.

She had cleaned the house several times; there was no evidence in the house, and unless he called Everly while he was outside in the backyard then everything would be okay. Jamie stepped back, allowing him to enter. "Sure. Maybe you'll find it. I have to say I haven't heard it ring or anything and I tried calling her myself."

"Hmm..."

Jamie watched him as he moved through the house downstairs. When he went upstairs, she stayed downstairs. Her hovering might have been an indicator she didn't want him to find anything. She waited on the sofa for him to come back downstairs.

"This is a nice place."

"Yeah. Neighbors are nice too. They keep inviting me over to dinner. Tammy's a great cook."

"I can't think of where she might have gone."

"She was pretty upset after the mediation. She might have needed a break. That was her way when I was younger. Instead of talking things out she would go for a drive for days and then come back like nothing happened."

"She's not like that anymore," he spat. Jamie wasn't sure what her mother had said about her, but she could tell he believed every word. "Okay. Thanks for letting me look... are you leaving?"

Jamie stared at him while he pointed to the ceiling.

"Saw the bags on your bed."

"Going to visit my children. I haven't seen them in a while and my husband says they keep asking for me. Might stay for the weekend."

Dwight regarded her, scrutinizing her expression. She felt it. His gaze picking at her, looking for what she was hiding. When he found nothing, he left without a goodbye.

"They are perfect for each other. Rude." Jamie went back to packing and getting her stuff together. Shortly after five her doorbell rang again. She groaned as she stalked toward the door.

"Yes?" Jamie stared at the woman on the other side of the door. It was the cop Logan kept spending time with. She blinked. "What are you doing here?"

"Well, hello to you too." She smiled. The sight made Jamie's skin crawl. "I take it you are Jamie Washington?"

She eyed Riley with pointed eyes. Riley just smiled at her.

"Can I come in?"

Jamie stared at her for a long moment before stepping aside. She wasn't sure at first why the detective was on her doorstep, but then her mind flicked to her mother's boyfriend. He walked around the house and then left. *He must have gone to the police when he couldn't find Everly.* She rolled her eyes internally. She should have killed him before he could leave. Then she wouldn't have this problem now.

"What do you want?"

"Well, we got a report that your mother was missing. Her boyfriend came to us, and we were—well, I was just wondering why you didn't file the report first."

Jamie shrugged before she folded her arms across her chest. "We aren't that close."

"So I've heard. You don't care that she's missing?"

Jamie noted how Riley's eyes darted around every time she asked a question. She was interrogating her while looking for clues. She almost respected her ability to multi-task even though it did annoy her.

"Not really. She never... I never felt like she loved me or cared about me. And she never said or did anything to change my mind. Once I was old enough to get out on my own I did. She doesn't go out of her way to call me, and I don't go out of my way to call her. That's the kind of family we are."

"Hmm..." She looked down the hallway toward the kitchen. "Do you mind if I take a look around? He said he didn't see anything out of order, and I want to confirm that. Once I do, I'll be out of your hair.

Jamie knew she didn't have too many options here. She was a detective, and she could leave and get a warrant, come back and do a thorough search. Her best bet was to be as amenable as possible, in the hopes that she would leave her alone once she couldn't find anything.

"Sure. Look away." She sat on the sofa while the detective started in the kitchen and worked her way through the downstairs and then upstairs. Her search took a lot longer than Dwight's. Jamie heard her moving around upstairs, pulling out drawers, searching the bathroom.

When she looked through the downstairs bathroom, Jamie's heart skipped several beats. Her mother's body spent quite a few days in the tub. But she scrubbed that bathroom until the grout was white and sparkling. Once she left that bathroom and she hadn't found anything, Jamie relaxed. Her mother was never upstairs so there was nothing to find.

Riley stomped down the stairs. "Just as I thought, nothing." She stared out the sliding glass door that opened up to the backyard. "One more thing. Just going to take a look at your yard."

She walked out before Jamie could protest. She jumped to her feet and slowly followed her outside. If she moved too fast, Riley would have thought she was trying to hide something. Trying to stop her from getting to something first.

"Lovely yard. Love the flowers in the flowerbed. They're so vibrant. Does the owner take care of them or do you?"

"They cut the grass and trim up, but I like to deal with the flowers. I planted more a little while ago. I'm hoping they don't die."

"Why would they?"

"Sometimes when you transplant flowers out of their posts they might not take. So far these are doing well. Hope they keep it up. I tried planting basil and that didn't last."

"What do you mean?"

"They died early on. They were doing so well at the store. When I brought them home the leaves were bright green and full. After a week or two the leaves were dried up and limp. Nothing I did brought them back."

"I've thought about growing a garden, but I'm afraid I don't have the attention span for that." She turned around, looking every which way. "Well, it looks good. Sorry to bother you. If we do find your mother, I will be sure to let you know." Instead of going through the house, Riley walked out of the back gate and around the house to her car.

Jamie collapsed onto the sofa in her wake. There was something about Riley when she left. She knew something. She stared out the back door. Riley saw something. Noticed something. And while she didn't have probable cause at the moment to search her home, she was probably on her way to get it. She had another night in this house at the most and then she had to leave first thing in the morning. She wasn't going to take Dani in the morning, she'd have to wait until it got dark. But she needed to be out of the house.

She spent the rest of the day listening for the police and packing up. She decided what she would take with her. She didn't need anything. She could buy new clothes and shoes. She did, however, buy some hair dye. She had been a brunette her whole life. Now it was time for a change. A muted ginger was the perfect color, which she also applied to her eyebrows so it looked more natural. After she washed it out and placed her bags by the front door she went to bed. Her body and mind were exhausted. She just wanted to sleep.

But no matter how hard she tried, sleep eluded her. She tossed and turned and flipped over her pillow, again and again. Kicked the blanket off and then covered herself again. She would go to sleep, wake up again and go back to sleep. Not for longer than twenty minutes

Every time she fell back into a deep sleep she slipped back into the same dream. She was running out of the school because she thought she saw Marie. Jamie thought her sister had finally come to get her. It was no secret Jamie did not want to be there any longer. She hated that school and the people in it. She ran outside looking for Marie. When she found her, Marie was just leaving the through the side door to the library.

Jamie spent many nights in the library. She liked books more than people. She thought Marie was looking for her. A billow of smoke followed Marie through the door. She looked in one of the many windows in the library and saw the fire.

Confusion took hold of her. She didn't know what to do. Part of her wanted to warn those inside, but she wasn't sure what was happening. She couldn't wrap her brain around Marie starting a fire in the school.

Jamie believed that everyone would get out in time. The smoke was thick and surely someone must have seen it. Felt the heat through the floorboards. When Marie saw her, her eyes went wide.

"What are you doing out here?" Marie shook her shoulders. "I thought you were still inside."

"I saw you through the window. Did you come to take me?"

Marie frowned. She looked back at the school before nodding her head. "I figured if the school no longer existed, mother couldn't send either of us back."

Jamie believed her. Mostly because she wanted to. She believed Marie when she asked about the people inside and Marie told her they had more than enough time to get out.

"It was a small fire." She pulled Jamie close and wrapped her arms around her. Jamie started to cry. She didn't know why she was crying. She didn't like anyone in the school, but deep down she knew, everyone would not get out alive. Instead of trying to help them, she allowed Marie to hug her close. It was the one thing she had wanted for so long, for someone to exhibit an ounce of affection toward her. She couldn't let it go.

Jamie woke again drenched in sweat. It felt like the room was on fire. She remembered the night differently every time, but only a few things stayed the same. She saw Marie start the fire and she felt bad for not helping the people inside.

The fire had followed Jamie through most of her life. No matter the evidence, people still believed she had something to do with it. The police interrogated her for hours and had to release her because she hadn't done anything wrong.

Even with all of that, Marie never spoke up in her defense. Not once. She never even acknowledged her presence at the scene. Not even when Jamie was finally allowed to go home and their mother started beating her because she believed Jamie started the fire.

Everly beat her so badly Jamie couldn't leave the house for two weeks. Marie never said anything. They never talked about it.

As she laid in bed, her mind settled on her mother's last words. Marie hated her because she reminded her of the man that had raped her. Jamie was a constant reminder that Marie hated her existence.

She had always known this, but never admitted it to herself out loud. It was just something in the back of her mind that refused to go away. Whenever it bubbled up to the surface she struggled to push it back down.

Marie went to the school that night to kill her. She set the fire in the library, a place Jamie was known to fall asleep, because she wanted to get rid of her.

She shuddered as she pulled the blanket back over her body. It seemed to Jamie that she was more like her mother than she thought.

Jamie sat in her car across from Logan's house. His truck wasn't there. But Isaac's was. Logan wasn't at work, and he wasn't at the diner. Jamie had traveled through town looking for his car, but it was nowhere to be seen. He wasn't in town. Now was the perfect time to take Dani, when he wasn't there to stop her.

She waited for three hours. Finally, Isaac pulled out of the driveway and went left. Jamie waited a few minutes to make sure he wasn't coming straight back. After five minutes she got out of the car and rushed up to the house. Picking the lock was easy after she watched several tutorials on YouTube.

She heard the lock click. Her fingers wrapped around the knob and twisted. The door opened slowly. There was no one in the foyer. She couldn't see all of the living room, but she saw the TV was on. Someone was probably sitting on the sofa. Unless Isaac left and left the TV on.

Silently, she walked through the kitchen. Before she could round the corner to the opposite end of the kitchen the nanny appeared. Jamie was startled.

"Isaa—" Her eyes went wide while Jamie's scanned the kitchen. She spotted a butcher knife on the counter next to chopped onions. Isaac was coming back soon.

She grabbed the knife.

"You're not supposed to be here."

Before she could reach for her phone, Jamie took the butcher knife and when Bonnie turned to run back into the living room, Jamie came up behind her, held her chin, and slid the knife across her neck. Blood sprayed into the air away from Jamie.

She let her body drop to the ground, dropped the knife, and jumped back before any blood could get on her. She wiped her hands on the inside of her jacket before going upstairs. Dani met her on the landing.

"Aunt Jamie!" Dani wrapped her arms around her waist and squeezed. "What are you doing here? Did you and Papa make up?"

Jamie smiled and knelt in front of her. "Kind of. But he did say I could take you for a ride before dinner. I might even be able to stay for dinner."

"Good. I don't like when you guys fight."

Jamie shook her head. "I know, I don't like it either. Get your jacket and we'll go for a ride."

Dani beamed at her. It had been so long since they had been able to hang out together. Jamie had missed her. She had missed seeing Marie in her face, staring up at her.

Dani grabbed her jacket and bounced down the steps. She was about to turn toward the living room, but Jamie grabbed her shoulder and turned her toward the front door.

"Shouldn't we tell Miss Bonnie?"

Jamie guided her out of the door. "She knows. She's going to help Isaac with dinner."

"They like cooking together."

"They do?"

Dani nodded. "Uncle Sac is a great cook. Miss Bonnie helps him with prep. Like chopping vegetables and other stuff. Sometimes I get to help too, but not with knives."

They crossed the street. Jamie guided her into the back seat and strapped in her seatbelt. She got on the driver's side and immediately locked the doors.

"This is going to be fun!" Jamie looked at Dani through the rearview mirror. She smiled at her and Jamie instantly saw Marie.

"Were we going, Aunt Jamie?"

Jamie smiled. "Anywhere you want."

AUTHOR'S NOTE

My dear reader,

Thank you so much for picking up *Strangers in the Pines* and continuing this journey with me and Riley! One of my favorite things about writing this book was dreaming up the setting. I have such a soft spot for those sleepy little towns tucked into nature—specifically the kind with towering pines, winding brooks, and this almost magical stillness. It's the kind of place where you'd want to sit on a porch with a cup of coffee and just breathe it all in. But also… maybe don't wander too far into the woods? There's something about that mix of cozy charm and quiet unease that I can't resist. Creating this town let me take that vibe and turn it up a notch, and I hope you're finding it just as irresistible as I do.

Your support truly means the world to me. Seriously, as an indie author, getting to live my dream of crafting these tales is all thanks to wonderful readers like you cheering me on. If you enjoyed this latest mystery, I would be incredibly grateful if you could share your thoughts in a review or tell your friends who love these types of stories. Word of mouth and your feedback are my lifelines, helping me continue Riley's journey and reach even more readers. Even just a few lines about what you enjoyed can make a huge difference!

If you're looking for your next read, let me introduce you to *The Girl and the Garden of Bones,* the latest installment in my Emma Griffin series. This one takes Emma to an old mansion with ties to a shadowy criminal entity—and into a garden hiding secrets that were meant to stay buried. It's Emma's most gut-wrenching and twist-filled case yet, with danger lurking behind every clue she uncovers. If you love stories with dark mysteries, shocking revelations, and a touch of the unexpected, I think this one will keep you up reading late into the night!

With endless gratitude and excitement for all the adventures still to come, I'm so glad to have you along for the ride. See you in the next book!

Yours,
A.J. Rivers

P.S. If for some reason you didn't like this book or found typos or other errors, please let me know personally. I do my best to read and respond to every email at mailto:aj@ riversthrillers.com

P.P.S. If you would like to stay up-to-date with me and my latest releases I invite you to visit my Linktree page at *www.linktr.ee/a.j.rivers* to subscribe to my newsletter and receive a free copy of my book, Edge of the Woods. You can also follow me on my social media accounts for behind-the-scenes glimpses and sneak peeks of my upcoming projects, or even sign up for text notifications. I can't wait to connect with you!

ALSO BY
A.J. RIVERS

Emma Griffin FBI Mysteries

Season One

Book One—*The Girl in Cabin 13**
Book Two—*The Girl Who Vanished**
Book Three—*The Girl in the Manor**
Book Four—*The Girl Next Door**
Book Five—*The Girl and the Deadly Express**
Book Six—*The Girl and the Hunt**
Book Seven—*The Girl and the Deadly End**

Season Two

Book Eight—*The Girl in Dangerous Waters**
Book Nine—*The Girl and Secret Society**
Book Ten—*The Girl and the Field of Bones**
Book Eleven—*The Girl and the Black Christmas**
Book Twelve—*The Girl and the Cursed Lake**
Book Thirteen—*The Girl and The Unlucky 13**
Book Fourteen—*The Girl and the Dragon's Island**

Season Three

Book Fifteen—*The Girl in the Woods**
Book Sixteen —*The Girl and the Midnight Murder**
Book Seventeen— *The Girl and the Silent Night**
Book Eighteen — *The Girl and the Last Sleepover**
Book Nineteen — *The Girl and the 7 Deadly Sins**
Book Twenty — *The Girl in Apartment 9**
Book Twenty-One — *The Girl and the Twisted End**

Emma Griffin FBI Mysteries Retro - Limited Series
(Read as standalone or before Emma Griffin book 22)

Book One— *The Girl in the Mist**
Book Two— *The Girl on Hallow's Eve**

Book Three— The Girl and the Christmas Past*
Book Four— The Girl and the Winter Bones*
Book Five— The Girl on the Retreat*

Season Four

Book Twenty-Two — The Girl and the Deadly Secrets*
Book Twenty-Three — The Girl on the Road*
Book Twenty-Four — The Girl and the Unexpected Gifts*
Book Twenty-Five — The Girl and the Secret Passage*
Book Twenty-Six — The Girl and the Bride*
Book Twenty-Seven — The Girl in Her Cabin*
Book Twenty-Eight — The Girl Who Remembers*

Season Five

Book Twenty-Nine — The Girl in the Dark*
Book Thirty — The Girl and the Lies*
Book Thirty-One — The Girl and the Inmate*
Book Thirty-Two — The Girl and the Garden of Bones

Ava James FBI Mysteries

Book One—The Woman at the Masked Gala*
Book Two—Ava James and the Forgotten Bones*
Book Three —The Couple Next Door*
Book Four — The Cabin on Willow Lake*
Book Five — The Lake House*
Book Six — The Ghost of Christmas*
Book Seven — The Rescue*
Book Eight — Murder in the Moonlight*
Book Nine — Behind the Mask*
Book Ten — The Invitation*
Book Eleven — The Girl in Hawaii*
Book Twelve — The Woman in the Window*
Book Thirteen — The Good Doctor*
Book Fourteen — The Housewife Killer*
Book Fifteen — The Librarian*
Book Sixteen — The Art of Murder

Dean Steele FBI Mysteries

Book One—The Woman in the Woods*

Book Two — The Last Survivors

Book Three — No Escape

Book Four — The Garden of Secrets

Book Five — The Killer Among Us

Book Six — The Convict

Book Seven — The Last Promise

Book Eight — Death by Midnight

Book Nine — The Woman in the Attic

Book Ten — Playing with Fire

Book Eleven — Murder in Twilight Cove

A Detective Riley Quinn Pine Brooke Mystery

Book One —The Girls in Pine Brooke

Book Two — Murder in the Pines

Book Three — Strangers in the Pines

ALSO BY
A.J. RIVERS & THOMAS YORK

Bella Walker FBI Mystery Series

Book One—The Girl in Paradise*

Book Two—Murder on the Sea*

Book Three—The Last Aloha*

Other Standalone Novels

Gone Woman

* Also available in audio

Made in the USA
Middletown, DE
11 December 2024

66631555R00137